ADVANCE PRAISE FOR *THREAD WAR*

"*The Skids* was special. In the sequel, *Thread War*, Keeling raises the stakes, but don't be fooled. Brilliant imagination? That hold-onto-your-seat action? There's that, yet so much more here. This story and these characters will fill your heart and grab your mind. This isn't just a present-day outstanding adventure. It's a future classic to treasure. True words."

—Julie E. Czerneda, author of the Clan Chronicles

PRAISE FOR *THE SKIDS*

"Like *The Princess Bride*, this book has everything—love, grief, envy, revenge, monsters, heroism, battles, self-sacrifice, sports, and shopping. It does not matter that the characters exist inside a computer game and look like bowling balls on tank treads; the reader's empathy engages immediately, and the story grips to the end. Along the way, we see an imaginative realization of a virtual multiverse from the inside, and an alien culture that is both poignant and credible. *The Skids* is truly a tale for the 21st-century young."

—Sunburst Award Jury

"Wow! Just wow! It's not as it is described on the back cover: "Part *Hunger Games*, part *Ready Player One* . . ." It is something new. It is something fresh and original and it's the kind of fiction that will be used in the future for reference. When you'll read 'Book (insert name here) is *The Skids* meets *The Matrix*,' then you'll know I'm right. It is the kind of story other stories are based on, not the other way around. I don't want to reveal plot or concept; I usually don't like it when others do it. And it's hard to write of *The Skids* without revealing anything and ruining future readers' experience. But what I can still say—it's a superbly conceived new world with its own glossary of terms, unique culture and reality, and yet it's a thrill ride. It's tense and it's fast, and it's complex. You'll love it! Teen or adult, you won't be able to let it go. And then you'll talk about it with your friends and colleagues, and they'll love it. And it will spread like a plague. A benefic one, mind you."

—Costi Gurgu, author of *Recipearium*

"I loved this book. It's been a while since I've found SF that was so fresh, appealing, and original. Well done and highly recommended. Can't wait for the sequel!"

—Julie E. Czerneda, author of the Clan Chronicles

"The main characters—Johnny, Torg, Albert, Bian, Betty Crisp, and Wobble—are interesting and about as well-rounded as they can be, considering they are inhuman simulations in a world of games and information. . . . *The Skids* is definitely an action-driven novel, which is exhilarating. . . ."

—CM: *Canadian Review of Materials*

"Fantastic read! The world came immediately to life, and what a world it was! Each of the places you are taken are so perfectly drawn like pictures coming to life in your head, and the characters! The characters are shaped with the perfect complexity of being absolutely human while not knowing that the human world exists. It deals with fantastic themes of loss, life, purpose, technology, the future, and the immutability of the ever-ticking clock. It's like if *The Matrix* and *The Hunger Games* had a video game baby! So awesome! A really wonderful journey into a world perfectly pictured. I wish I could go back there for the first time all over again. I would highly recommend this book to a friend."

—Amazon Customer 5-star review

"Wonderful ride! Fell in love with the Skids and the Wobble! Was with them in their journey through good and bad. Can't wait to reunite with them when the sequel is published! Soon I hope! This NEEDS to be a movie and Mr. Keeling should be the screenwriter!!"

—Amazon Customer 5-star review

"This is a really creative book, like a cross between *The Hunger Games*, a road trip movie and a pinball game. The author creates this entire world of the 'Skids'—what can only be described as living pinballs with eyes who compete in races and are being watched by something 'out there'—with its own lingo (being 'vaped') and architecture. There are hints about the true nature of the world of the Skids but the author never gives too much away, just enough to keep you wondering. It's an impressive feat for a first novel, expect more from Keeling. I can see it appealing to early teens, pre-teens . . . and probably also their parents (my generation!)."

—Amazon Customer 5-star review

THREAD WAR

FIRST EDITION

Distributed in Canada by
Fitzhenry & Whiteside Limited
195 Allstate Parkway
Markham, Ontario L3R 4T8
Phone: (905) 477-9700
e-mail: bookinfo@fitzhenry.ca

Distributed in the U.S. by
Consortium Book Sales & Distribution
34 Thirteenth Avenue, NE, Suite 101
Minneapolis, MN 55413
Phone: (612) 746-2600
e-mail: sales.orders@cbsd.com

Library and Archives Canada Cataloguing in Publication

Keeling, Ian Donald, author

Thread war / Ian Donald Keeling. -- First edition.

(The skids ; 2)

Issued in print and electronic formats.

ISBN 978-1-77148-432-9 (softcover).--ISBN 978-1-77148-433-6

(ebook)

I. Title.

PS8621.E35T57 2017   jC813'.6   C2017-907115-7

                                             C2017-907116-5

CHITEEN
An imprint of ChiZine Publications
Peterborough, Canada
www.chizinepub.com
info@chizinepub.com

Edited by Samantha Beiko
Proofread by Leigh Teetzel

 Canada Council   Conseil des arts
for the Arts   du Canada

We acknowledge the support of the Canada Council for the Arts which last year invested $20.1 million in writing and publishing throughout Canada.

ONTARIO ARTS COUNCIL
CONSEIL DES ARTS DE L'ONTARIO
an Ontario government agency
un organisme du gouvernement de l'Ontario

Published with the generous assistance of the Ontario Arts Council.

Printed in Canada

IAN DONALD KEELING

THREAD WAR

For my mother, Theresa Keeling, who, for so many reasons, is the reason I'm here.

PROLOGUE

The jungle was a contradiction.

Alive with sound, the trees were filled with hoots and trills and howls, underscored by the *drip, drip, drip* from rain that had fallen an hour before. In the distance, a roll of thunder. And yet nothing moved. The thick heat pounded the jungle into stillness; thick, green trees engulfed by thick, green leaves, dead still in the heat. Even the late afternoon light had a squat, solid quality.

Then one of the leaves moved.

"They're not coming this way." And what had been just another unmoving plant unfolded into a man.

"You're sure?" the woman with him asked, looking back into the valley as she rose to her feet. She cracked her neck and shifted the rifle in her hands.

"Their line ain't straight, but they're definitely heading east."

"What's east?"

The man stretched his arms. "No clue. Might be an ammo dump." He looked around. "Hell of a lot more than there is out here." He shook his head. "What the hell is he doing?"

"Your guess is as good as mine." Shifting the heads-up display on her sunglades, she rubbed at the skin around the socket of her missing eye, then shrugged. "Come on, trail's back here."

For the next hour, the soldiers made their way through the jungle, ignoring the heat. "Those guys might not be travelling in a straight line," the man murmured, "but Chief sure the hell is."

"Yeah," the woman replied, studying the ground. "It's like he didn't care if he was followed."

"He could have just told us where he was going."

"Would have made my day easier. I can't remember him ever—hold up."

Even to the untrained eye, the small clearing had been disturbed. The grass was crushed flat, and there were several visible footprints. "Spent some time here," the man said, scanning the clearing.

"Yeah." The woman stepped forward, slowly and deliberately. Ten minutes later, she looked at her partner in confusion. "There's no exit. Trail stops here."

"Extraction?"

"Not a chance. Look at the treetops, nothing's been near them. It's like he was here for a while, then . . . just disappeared."

The man stared as a drop of water slowly rolled down a broad green leaf. A shiver ran down his spine. "Even Chief can't do that."

"Yeah."

They examined the clearing again, then conducted an outward sweep of the surrounding area. Finally, they came back to the centre of the clearing. "Nothing," the woman sighed. "Let's get the hell out of here. You sure that troop we saw cleared the area?"

"Just because I can't find the Chief, it doesn't mean—"

"Yeah, yeah—relax, I'm just tired." She activated her com. "Ranncon Eight, this is Peck and Templeton, requesting lift at eighty-eight four three."

Twenty minutes later a small craft came sliding over the canopy. Clipping themselves onto droplines, the two soldiers rose into the craft.

"Where the hell have you been?" the officer waiting for them barked as they strapped into a seat and the craft streaked back the way it came.

"Looking for Chief," the woman said, her single eye scanning the treetops.

"Find him?"

"Nope." The woman glanced at her partner.

"Well, don't worry about it, whatever the Chief's doing, I'm sure it's part of his plan."

"Yeah," the woman said, staring at the jungle, unmoving in the heat.

It was still unmoving two hours later, long after the transport had gone, when it began to rain. For an hour the green rattled in the downpour, then the storm passed on, and the jungle went back to its contradiction of noise and stillness.

Two hours after the rain, a spot of black appeared in the centre of the green, and began to grow.

CHAPTER ONE

SLAM!
   "Again."
   SLAM!
   "Again."
   SLAM!

"Again," Johnny Drop said, as he watched the pile of panzers and squids moan their way back onto their treads. They rolled back to the starting line for the crash pads. The safeties were still set, but at least this group was hitting the pads with some authority now. The yellow-beige Level One on the end had a lot of potential. She'd get her second stripe soon.

Johnny let an eye drift, taking in the Combine. Slide Rock filled the massive centre bowl of the training facility, pounding off the walls. Everywhere, Level One and Two skids practiced the skills they needed in the game, desperate to get to the point where they could control their molecules and survive being evaporated. Skids on spin-mats spun, skids on treadmills tread, skids on weave drills weaved.

Next to the crash pads, skids bounced back and forth between pedals designed to bang them around safely. Nothing like what they'd face on Tilt or the Spinners, Johnny thought with a grin, but it was a start. On the pressure pads, two huge blocks not-so-gently squeezed skids between them, getting the panzers ready for the more deadly versions in Tunnel. Skids violently rotated on gyroscopes, while others sat stock-still and tried to track multiple targets in the vision tests. Some panzers worked in empty spaces, absorbing and popping their Hasty-Arms, one of the skills needed to take a skid from Level One to Two.

Dozens of skids worked the row of crash pads, many of them glancing nervously over at the group under Johnny. Despite his willingness to help and their desperation to get better, the majority still wouldn't seek his assistance.

He didn't blame them: it was weird.

"Again," he barked, keeping one eye on his trainees even as he let the other two wander. It was a subtle reminder to any skid watching that they needed to split their vision and focus on multiple things at once. He grinned—there was a Level One trying the gyroscopes for the first time who was still looking at everything with all three of her eyes. She'd be puking sugar before long.

He'd been here, in the Combine, every day since they'd returned from the Thread to find a world reset to the moment they'd left. Except no Albert, Torg, Bian, or any of the others who'd fallen out from the Skidsphere with them to discover a world so much larger and more frightening then they'd ever dreamed. Only Johnny and Shabaz had returned, with Johnny now a Level Ten and Shabaz an Eight.

Although even that was in question. For the first week, Johnny had at least tried to play the games, coming to the Combine only in his off hours. But it had become clear very quickly that Johnny and Shabaz were beyond the games. He remembered vividly the day they destroyed Tag Box: Johnny and Shabaz in the centre of the carnage, every other skid vaped, with half the time left on the timer. They'd looked at each other and left the game. Johnny hadn't been back since. Shabaz had, but not in the same way.

Tag Box had also made Johnny realize he'd moved beyond the games in other ways too: he couldn't vape skids any more. He hated doing it, even with skids over Level Three who he knew would come back. And the first time he vaped a Two after he'd returned, he'd gone out to the woods for a day and broken down, crying the entire time. Since that day, Johnny had been in the Combine continuously, helping any skid who asked.

And the amazing thing was that he wasn't the only one.

"Crisp Betty, Akash," a snarl came from nearby, "stop tickling it and hit the damn thing."

Suppressing a smile, Johnny let one eye drift towards the far side of the crash pads, where a solitary white skid with four red stripes was helping a solitary mint-green skid with two lemon stripes. Although, 'helping,' might have been highly dependent on your point of view.

"I am hitting it, Onna," the squid protested, visibly exhausted. "Give me some credit, the safeties are off."

The senior skid rolled over and bumped the squid's treads, hard. Harder than Johnny would have. "They've been off for two hours. And you've hit it with the same gas the last six attempts. I said: *hit it full.*"

"If I do, I could die."

Onna swung a second eye. Somehow she made it loom over the other skid; Johnny was going to have to learn how she did that. "Or you might never die again." She grinned. "At least 'til you're five."

The squid they'd started calling Akash grimaced. "Easy for you to say," he grumbled. "You've got your name. Mine's just pretend."

Onna's gaze narrowed. Then she sniffed and swung her whole body, rolling away. "Keep hitting the pad that soft and it'll stay pretend." She didn't even bother trailing an eye.

Ouch, Johnny thought, suppressing another smile as a horrified expression spread across the squid's face. It was obvious he had a crush on Onna. It was equally obvious that the squid called Akash was on the verge of Level Three and had potential to do a lot more, otherwise Onna wouldn't have bothered to give him so much time.

Well, maybe that last part's not so obvious, Johnny thought, watching the Two's face. For a second, Johnny thought Onna had gone too far. The poor kid looked crushed.

Then another expression settled into the squid's stripes and he rolled back to the start, slowly but with purpose. He sat there a minute, staring at the pad. An eye flickered in Onna's direction. Then he geared up and tread.

SLAM!!!!

Everyone on the pads turned and looked as the impact echoed through the Combine. The mint body compressed and the two stripes appeared to shatter. Johnny thought it was done; the squid really had hit it too hard.

Then the stripes reformed and the body returned to something resembling round. Almost round. The poor kid looked like he might throw up.

"Crisp Betty," one of the panzers working with Johnny breathed.

"About vaping time," Onna's voice cut through the chatter of the Combine. Johnny was going to have to figure out how she did that too. When a shaky eye swung in her direction, she added, "Nice work, squid." What might have been a smile.

Slowly, the mint green body settled into its three lemon stripes. "I'm not a squid. I'm Akash." He grinned.

Onna sniffed and rolled away. "We'll see, squid." Definitely a smile.

Of the many things that had happened since their return, Onna might have been Johnny's biggest surprise. She was the first skid he'd ever helped; he smiled at the memory of her freaking out when she'd realized who was talking to her in the Combine. He'd been thrilled when she'd made Three, relieved that she would at least survive until her fifth birthday. He'd expected her to do well.

What he had not expected was for her to return to the Combine one week after she'd left.

He'd been helping a group on the pressure blocks when she'd rolled down the ramp, obviously nervous. He'd watched her sit at the bottom of the ramp, staring at the Combine like it was a foreign country. Then her stripes had flared once and she'd rolled over to the grease pads and started barking orders.

She was a lot more tough love and manipulation than Johnny, which wasn't a bad thing—they complimented each other. She got results sometimes when Johnny didn't. And she was only a Level Four, moving up rapidly from Three. She remembered even more than he did what it was like to be a squid.

And she wasn't the only one helping. Shev—the first skid to ever actually *ask* Johnny for assistance—had shown up a week ago, eyes bowed and uncertain until Johnny had pointed him in the right direction. Right now, he was across the centre court, working with the panzers at the tracking station.

Only three of them so far, but they were getting results. Since Johnny had begun training skids, more and more Ones had made it to Two, and more and more Twos had made it to Three. There was a record number of Threes and Fours in the games now; Johnny and Shabaz had been tracking the numbers and there were already seven hundred skids over Three. Given that the numbers had historically been around five hundred, it was an amazing increase.

According to Shabaz, they were doing better in the games too, a significant percentage of the recent Combine grads jumping from Three to Four in less than three months.

Of course, not everything was roses, Johnny thought, catching an image on the hollas of a red-brown Two he recognized getting shredded on a spike-pit in Tunnel. A pain shot through him and he swallowed the grief. That was the worst aspect of helping at the Combine: he cared. Every day he helped dozens, if not hundreds, of Ones and Twos, and every day most of them didn't make it back to the Combine. He hated watching the highlights now; not because he was no longer in them, but because he'd see some panzer or squid he recognized getting vaped. Constantly. Most of the time it was only a vague feeling—like he'd passed them on the ramp—but even that was horrible. It was like every squid and panzer in the Combine had become as important as Shabaz.

At least that one made it, Johnny thought, watching the newest Three make his way out of the Combine. He was Shabaz's to work on now.

That had been Shabaz's solution to their situation: she worked on the skids in the games. It was great, because she took over where Johnny left off, spotting the skids who might have real potential to advance—the future Johnnies and Shabazes—and working on them in the games and the sugarbars and more. Johnny had a feeling she was the reason why Onna and Shev had returned to the Combine.

And maybe there was more help on the way, Johnny thought, as Akash passed a group of skids huddled at the bottom of the ramp, staring into the Combine. There were half a dozen, most of them Level Five or Six from the looks of things, although the yellow-black skid in front was a Seven.

Or maybe not help, Johnny thought, catching the expression on the Seven's face. He did not look happy. Trist—the skid's name was Trist.

The Seven briefly made eye contact with Johnny. Yeah, definitely not pleased. He muttered something to the teal-plum Six beside him, who bobbed an angry eye in agreement. Then the whole group turned and rolled back up the ramp.

Wonder what that's about.

He watched the group leave. Then, with a tilt of his stripe, he turned back to the crash pads.

"Again."

CHAPTER TWO

Shabaz had never liked Tunnel.

Perhaps it was because she'd never been great at racing games; although, until recently, she'd never thought of herself as great at anything. Maybe it was the enclosed nature of the game; other races like the Rainbow Road, Up and Down, or the Slope were open to the sky, whereas Tunnel was an enclosed one hundred kilometres of suffocation.

But mostly it was because Tunnel tried to vape you.

There were other games where the game itself was deadly: Tag Box, Tilt, the Gauntlet. But those games were honest. You knew going in: watch *everything*.

Tunnel was a deathtrap that pretended it was a race. Side tunnels that led nowhere and would close up behind you. Serrated walls, pits of acid, pressure pads that would crush you between them. In some places the floor would just disappear. In others, the ceiling would collapse. The skids trying to kill you were the least of your problems.

Running up the side of a corner, she saw a trailing red-brown Level Two get caught in the spike-pit she'd just dodged. Avoiding the pit was easy if you knew about it. But how were the panzers and squids supposed to remember every trap—there were *hundreds* of them. She felt a brief flash of grief and hoped Johnny hadn't seen it. It would bother him more than it bothered her.

The death did bother her—she cared about the panzers and squids, particularly those Twos that were close but would never make it to Three—but she couldn't grieve for them all. There were so many Level Ones and Twos; she'd never realized how many until she'd come back from the Thread with a whole new perspective on the sphere in which she lived.

Panzers and squids died. Constantly. Another got vaped in front of her, checked into a wall of blades. A minute later, two sped right into a laser mine. She just couldn't weep for them all. Although, Johnny would worry.

It was fine. He probably hadn't seen it.

She turned her attention back to the reason why she was there.

Spotting Tarindu up ahead, she bounced off a clear spot and accelerated. She caught him near a set of pressure pads, got in front, then slowed down. Just enough that if he didn't get out from behind her he'd get caught before he cleared the pads.

His front eye widened and he cut left. She cut with him. He bumped her, but not hard enough. *Come on Tarindu, put a little effort into it*. The pads started to snap shut. . . .

Panicking, he slammed off one of the pads to accelerate and bumped Shabaz hard, much harder than he had before. She let it move her and he jumped forward, but not before the pads closed, catching his back half. For a moment, it looked like he'd still get vaped, panic flaring again across his face. Then the panic was replaced by anger and, screaming, the black-orange Level Six snapped free. He rammed her again, balled a glare that was half triumph, half confused rage—why was she hounding him?—and then sped ahead for the finish line, not far away.

He still had no idea she was helping.

Tarindu was one of half a dozen skids she'd spent the last few days hounding in various events. She couldn't help another skid win an event; that was a line that she'd decided early on she would never cross. But she could help skids get better, especially those with some potential. She'd never seen Tarindu try the bounce-off-the-paddles trick—a trick most skids never even thought of doing. By pushing him, the Six got better without even realizing how.

Shabaz crossed the finish line, coming in twenty-sixth, respectable but nowhere near the top. That still got a few stares, skids struggling to understand why one of the best skids in the sphere never played to win anymore.

It was her way of keeping sane.

The first few weeks back had been bad. Nothing about the world she lived in for her whole life—the world she thought she'd understood—made sense anymore. Johnny had dropped out of the games fairly early, rediscovering the Combine. Shabaz had needed to do *something*. So she'd continued to play the games, trying to go back to something like a normal life, only to discover that normal was gone.

Upon returning from the Thread, Shabaz had been shocked to discover she was a Level Eight. And that was *insane*. Johnny had been made Ten, but at least he'd had a brief window of time at Nine. When they'd fallen into the Thread, Shabaz had been a Six. Now, she would never be a Seven.

And if that wasn't enough, it became very clear once she started playing again that she wasn't really an Eight, either.

She won seven of those first ten games back, and the only reason she didn't win the other three is because, on a whim, *she'd stopped trying*. She hadn't been vaped once. In fact, she was pretty sure she couldn't get vaped in a game anymore unless she tried to make it happen. And Level Eights couldn't do that; hole, she wasn't sure if Level Tens could do that. Whatever she and Johnny were now, it had nothing to do with Levels.

She'd tried helping Johnny in the Combine as a way of dealing with the stress, but that had been a bad idea.

Given what they had gone through—were still going through—it was inevitable that they'd hook up. But spending all day together in the confines of the Combine was not a solution.

Plus, he was still Johnny. Johnny Drop. He was still that guy. The guy who'd smashed Betty Crisp's record; the guy who'd done the Drop. Still the only skid with two names, still the only Level Ten.

Still the guy who, along with Albert, had saved her life.

So yeah, she needed to create a space for herself. Because she cared about Johnny—it was frightening to think how much—but she had no interest in living in his shadow.

So she'd gone back to the games, but with a different focus this time.

At first she'd wanted to help anyone who'd made it past Two, but even though the vast number of skids were panzers and squids, there were still hundreds of skids at

Level Three or higher, a number that got bigger every day. She couldn't help them all. Maybe one day, but for now, she had to prioritize.

So she picked the ones with potential to be . . . more. Especially the ones like her.

Checking the boards, she noted who had finished where, saw that there were four skids who'd jumped a level. Then she checked out the 'lights, ignoring her own to scan for anything that popped. She spotted a peach-blue Level Five nearby and tread over.

"Congratulations, Bufoni," she said, smiling inwardly as she saw the other skid flinch in surprise. "Fifth is a great score. You'll be hitting the podium soon."

"Oh," the surprised skid said. "Uh . . . thanks."

If she was honest with herself, Shabaz was appalled by the way she'd acted before the Thread. All her life living in—what? Self-loathing? Fear? Jealous of so many other skids, living in awe of skids like Johnny or Albert, watching her own highlights in shame. She'd never been great at anything, but she'd wanted to be, yearning with something huge and empty inside.

Some skids you could tell had it, right away. Onna was like that, attacking the games like she was going to break them—snakes, she was going to end up as cocky as Johnny in her own way. But in some, like Bufoni, you could only see it if you bothered to look.

"Keep it up," Shabaz said, smiling as she rolled away.

"Okay, I . . . I will," Bufoni replied, looking confused. But there was a hint of pride behind the confusion.

It was amazing what a little encouragement could do. And sad that it was so rare that it would confuse any skid who received it.

It wasn't the only way skids ignored each other.

On a whim, she poked her head into the Tunnel sugarbar and spotted a tomato red skid with flat red stripes sitting quietly in a corner, watching highlights. Shabaz tread over. "Hey, we still on?"

Once skids made Level Three, they no longer died in the games. Getting vaped sucked, but skids couldn't die in a game.

But they still died. All of them. At five years old.

Seven stripes flinched as a guilty eye swung Shabaz's way. "Oh, hey. Uh, listen, we don't have to . . . to . . . if you don't want . . ."

"Hey," she said gently, popping a Hasty-Arm. She placed it on the tomato red skin, ignoring the flinch as she did. "It's okay, Makaha. I don't mind. If you still want me to be there, I will."

The skid sat still for a time, one eye on the hollas. After a moment, he asked, "Did you let Tarindu get by you?"

She smiled. Skids almost never watched other skid's highlights, but she discovered that a skid nearing their fifth birthday began acting a little different. "He did most of the work."

Makaha continued to stare at the highlights, then said in a quiet voice, "If you want to come later today . . . I'd like that."

"That's fine. Where would you like to go?"

"I was thinking . . . maybe the woods?"

Shabaz smiled. "That sounds like a fine idea. How about I meet you out by the Spike, later on?"

"Okay," the skid whispered. Giving his stripes a gentle squeeze, she turned to leave.

"Shabaz?"

He was looking at her with two eyes, the other on the hollas. "I don't really understand what you and

Johnny . . . I don't really understand what you guys are doing . . . but I think it's a good thing. Some people don't think so, but I think it is."

She smiled again. "Thank you, Makaha. I'll see you later."

She left Tunnel behind, happy to be out in the sun. She tread over towards the Combine, eager to see Johnny.

A group of seven higher level skids were coming out the main ramp. Several she recognized and knew well from the games. At least three were on her radar, although none had appeared to be interested in her help when she'd approached them individually. Blinking in surprise, she was about to say hello, when the ground began to shake.

It was a minor quake. Most skids ignored them, but most skids didn't know what they indicated. Corpsquakes had nothing to do with GameCorps. They weren't part of the Skidsphere; they were part of the Thread, a symptom of it breaking down. And they were happening more frequently. A chill went along Shabaz's stripes.

The group didn't even slow down, although the yellow-black Seven out front glared at her. Changing direction slightly, he tread up to her and snarled, "It ain't right." Then he spun on his treads and rolled back to the group.

Shabaz stared after them. She'd never really talked to Trist, but she had approached Kesi, the teal-plum Six who was with him. Now she was glaring at Shabaz as they rolled away.

"I bet that's a good sign," she murmured. She rolled down the ramp and into the Combine. Catching sight of Johnny by the crash pads, she felt her skin flush.

Until falling into the Thread, Shabaz had never loved anything. Not the games, certainly not other skids. Sure, she'd had her share of snugs in the woods, but she'd been too self-absorbed to really care about anything else except her own fears and inner demons.

The way she felt about Johnny terrified and exhilarated her. She was certain that when they'd first gotten together it was half survival mechanism, the only two skids who shared a past that no one else remembered, with skills that no one else could comprehend. But, very quickly—at least for Shabaz—it had become something more, something *much* more. She thought about him constantly. She was pretty sure he felt the same, but sometimes she would have fits of terror at the thought of a life without him. He drove her crazy sometimes, but she cared for him more than she'd ever cared for anything.

He caught her gaze and smiled and her stripes flushed again. *Snakes*, she thought, *settle down, you're acting like a squid.*

She rubbed up against his treads as they kissed. Then she pulled back and said, "Happy birthday."

CHAPTER THREE

The quake was barely there. A second or two at most, then gone.

Johnny waited, hyperaware of the ground beneath his treads. Could just be a rumble, but it was the second time today, maybe the third. Around him, panzers and squids continued to train as if nothing had happened.

"They're getting used to it," Johnny muttered, unable to relax.

Rumbles used to happen maybe once a month. Big quakes, like the one that had destroyed a sugarbar on the night Johnny had gotten his second name, were very rare. But about a month after returning from the Thread, Johnny had noticed the quakes becoming more frequent. Most were still harmless, like the rumble they'd just experienced, but just last week, a quake had rocked the Combine, taking out an entire wall and killing dozens of panzers and squids. It had even vaped Onna.

Of course, the Combine had been rebuilt by the next day. And when Johnny had tried to arrange some kind of emergency procedures in case a severe shock happened again, all the panzers and squids—even the ones he was coaching—had looked at him like he was nuts. He might get some to let him help them individually, but to get them to work together, even if it saved lives . . .

Give it time. That's what Shabaz had said. Bit by bit, they were coming around, small changes were getting made, skid by skid. First an Onna, then a Shev, then maybe a group. Given enough time, they'd get better.

Provided they had time. Because the rumbles weren't just a part of the game. The Thread was breaking and if the rumbles were coming more often, then it was breaking faster.

Johnny's eye wandered to the sky, even though he could have picked any direction. He wished he knew where Albert and the others were, if Betty had survived. Something was happening out in the Thread; it felt like something new had happened a month ago and he had no idea what it was. Neither he nor Shabaz had heard anything since they'd come back. Johnny hadn't expected to, but if things had changed, or something had gone wrong . . . maybe the reason why they hadn't heard anything was there was no one to send the message.

His eye-stalks twitched. No use in negative thoughts; the Thread hadn't fallen yet and if Betty was right, it had lasted for thousands of years. It wasn't going to fall apart today, or probably in his life.

And, anyway, he thought as he saw a familiar grey-aqua skid roll down the ramp, not all new things are bad.

He smiled and gave Shabaz a kiss. "Happy birthday," she said, and watched his expression change.

Normally, birthdays didn't mean much to a skid. It was the Levels that mattered, birthdays were just an excuse to get particularly vaped in the pits, maybe con someone into a little birthday snug. Even fourth birthdays, theoretically the last a skid could have while still having something to look forward to, tended to be just another sugar-fest. Skids were still living too fast to care.

Johnny had a whole year left. That was a crazy amount of time.

But it no longer felt like it.

Betty had had fifty-five years, most of them in the Thread. Where, despite losing decades to madness and just trying to survive, she'd done things, things that mattered. She'd explored the Thread, collected data, learned new skills to the point where she could put the sphere into stasis; hole, *she'd survived beyond her fifth birthday.*

But she hadn't figured out how to help other skids do the same.

If they were going to change anything, they were going to need *decades*, not years. Johnny had accomplished a lot in three months inside the Combine, but it was a drop in a wave pool of the change he could make if he just . . . had . . . more . . . *time.* Certainly more than a year.

"Hey," Shabaz said, nudging him. "It's a beautiful day. Let it go for now."

They'd been seeing each other less than three months, but already she had a way of seeing right into his heart, deeper than any skid had before. Even with Peg, it hadn't been like this. It terrified and exhilarated him at the same time. Trying to hide that wave of emotion, he said, "Thanks, sweetlips."

The grey-aqua skid rolled all three of her eyes. "I told you: stop ripping off Torg."

Johnny grinned. "He called Betty 'sugar-lips.' This is completely different." The grin faded when he saw her stripes narrow and her expression flatten. "Uh, okay . . . so you were serious about that, then?"

"Do you want me thinking about Torg every time we're together?"

"Right." He sighed. "Got it, lesson learned."

She leaned in and gave him a peck on the cheek. "The thought is nice. Just see if you can find something a little more original." She looked around. "Ready to go?"

"Just a sec. Okay, everyone, good work, keep at it." He checked the boards to see what was coming up. Tag Box, ouch. "Who's in Tag Box in an hour?" Most of them put up their hands, and Johnny suppressed a shudder. The games needed their fodder. "All right, do your best. Stay off the third floor, you don't need the points. And don't just pick a corner and hide. They get systematically spiked and good players will check them sooner or later. It might be scary, but you have to move. Good luck." He turned and rolled away. If he was lucky, he'd see half of them again.

He waved to Shev and Onna. "Okay," he said to Shabaz. "Good to go. Where do you want to go: sugarbar or woods?"

She hesitated, then said, "Woods. I want to grease the treads." They headed for the ramp. "How'd they do today?" she asked, as panzers and squids passed them, staring. The amazing thing was that some didn't stare, having grown accustomed to the idea of two senior skids coming into the training centre.

"Onna coached Akash up to Three," he said, his trail-eye watching as the white-red skid berated a group on the launch ramps. "Got him to hit the safeties off at full in less than three hours."

"Nice. He still got a crush on her?"

Johnny laughed. "Little bit. I think it might be reciprocated. She's tough on everyone, but she's awfully tough on him." A weird smile crossed Shabaz's stripes. "What?"

She looked like she might say something, then the mysterious smirk faded as her stripes tilted. "We'll see."

He was already beginning to learn when he wasn't going to get anything else out from her. He chuckled and changed the topic. "How about you?"

"A couple of Level Threes made Four today. Both were skids you had in the Combine."

"Nice, two in one day." They emerged from the ramp and headed towards the path leading to the Spike.

"That's not the crazy thing." She paused. "I think Onna might make Five soon."

"What? Didn't she just make Four?"

"Three weeks ago."

"And you think she's going to make Five anytime soon? Four to Five is one of the harder—"

"She asked me about mapping."

"*What?*" Every skid had an internal positioning system, able to plot whatever game they were in and track skids around them. But they took a while to access it; mapping was usually one of the skills that bumped a skid to Level Five.

"She said that she thinks the higher level skids are tracking her at times and they attack the races like they know the turns before they happen."

"Huh. What'd you tell her?"

"I told her it was a great concept." She grinned. "If they're starting to guess something, I leave them to figure it out. They might die a few extra times, but the lesson sinks in more."

It made sense. Once permanent vaping was out of the picture, Shabaz was able to do a few more subtle things than Johnny. Of course, that might have been because Johnny couldn't even spell subtle. "Still," he said, "Level Five would be awfully early. Three levels in three months? How old is she anyway—is she even two years old yet?"

Shabaz gave him an even look. "Johnny . . . she's four months from her second birthday. She'll probably be a Six by then."

"What?! A Six? That's . . . that's . . . even I wasn't a Six before my second birthday," he protested, outraged.

Shabaz giggled. "There's the Johnny I remember."

"Hey, it's not that," he said, although it totally was that. "It's just . . . where did this come from? She's just a skid I picked at random, you know that. Now she's the next me? She's better?"

It shouldn't have bothered him, not after all they'd been through, but it did. He'd spent the entirety of his life wanting to be the best, an attitude that had helped kill his friendship with Albert. Nothing was more important than winning, than doing something that would get him remembered. No matter what happened out in the Thread, he couldn't just turn it off. Which was stupid, because he wasn't even competing anymore. If he really gave a gear about results, he could go into every game and destroy it for the next year, obliterating the records.

It suddenly occurred to him that someone might still catch him in that year. With the way some skids were improving lately, if he competed, would it destroy the system or would the other skids just get better?

Nah, he thought with a grimace. *They can't be getting better that fast.*

Shabaz watched him with amusement, then her stripes tilted. "Well, something's going on with the ones we train. They're not thinking the same old way. Onna more than anyone else—she does crazy things out there. I've seen her deliberately get vaped in two games just to try something no one else had tried. I've seen her place in three games because whatever she tried worked. She doesn't think the same way. Results are second to becoming stronger. Results are important, but they're not the most important thing."

Johnny frowned. "Did you teach her that? 'Cause I don't think I did." He had tried a lot of crazy things in the games, but always with the hope it would help him win. He never did it just to see what might happen.

"I think it's the consequences of what we've done. Want to know something really greased-up? Shev's been following her lead. He did a Drop the other day."

"What? He's a Three, for Crisp's sake!"

"Yeah," she laughed. "He didn't make it halfway down."

"No kidding."

"You're missing the point: he did make it through a third of the race. While it was running."

"Wait . . . he started a Drop at the *beginning* of a Slope?"

"Yep."

"That's . . . that's crazy." But it was also a cool idea. Johnny wondered why he'd never tried it, then immediately had the answer: because it wouldn't have helped him win that race. "I'll be vaped, maybe—"

"It ain't right," a voice said.

Nestled up against the outside of the Combine, a group of eight or nine skids. Trist had come back, with a few extra skids in tow. The yellow-black Seven tread forward, a pair of Sixes flanking his side. "I told her the same thing," he said harshly, eyeing Shabaz and then poking the eye towards the ramp. "What you're doing in there . . ." He shifted on his treads and spat.

Johnny frowned. "It's Trist, right? What's the problem?"

"The problem is you," the skid said, his seven black stripes flaring. He had a blizzard glam along them, which Johnny had to admit was pretty sweet against the black. He pointed at Shabaz. "The both of you." Behind him, the others all bobbed an eye in agreement. "What do you think you're doing in there?"

"Just helping a few squids and panzers find a way to survive," Johnny said, amused. "Doesn't really affect you, Trist."

"Who the hole gives a tread about the panzers and squids?" Trist protested. "That's twisted. And it does affect me. It affects all of us."

"I'm not sure I see how."

"How about the fact that the games are flooded with Threes and Fours now? How about the fact that there's more skids so the rest of us don't play as much?"

Johnny hadn't known that. He glanced at Shabaz. "That true? Skids are playing in fewer games?"

She bobbed an eye. "I think it might be."

"So glad you agree," Trist sneered. "You're worse than he is."

Now she looked amused. "Really?"

The teal-plum Six geared forward. "Yes, really." She had shim around all three of her eye-stalks. "He might be wasting his time with squids and panzers, but you're helping skids in the games when you should be playing. And you're playing favourites."

Shabaz chuckled. "I seem to remember offering to help you, Kesi. If you want, Trist—"

"We don't want your help," Trist snapped. "Skids don't help other skids. What the hole happened to you? Fine, he made Ten, okay, whatever. But you? You're an *Eight*. Why aren't you still playing to win? Don't you want to make Nine? Ten?"

"Maybe my priorities changed," Shabaz said.

"From winning games?" Kesi said in disbelief.

"Seriously, who got vaped and made you GameCorps?" Trist said, rolling forward. The others followed. "What gives you the right to vape the games?"

The amused smile faded from Johnny's face as the Level Seven edged towards Shabaz. He wasn't worried; hole, she could probably take them herself, but Trist was getting closer than he liked. This wasn't funny anymore. "Look, Trist," he said firmly. "We're not hurting anyone. You don't want help, fine. You don't speak for everyone."

Trist's eyes swung and he rolled over to Johnny. Now it was Shabaz's smile that faded, replaced by a hard look. *Thanks babe*, Johnny thought.

"They're all afraid of you," Trist said, and that caught Johnny's attention. "Both of you. You think we're the only ones that feel this way?" He waved a hand at the rest of the group. "Most skids feel this way; they're just too in awe of the great Johnny Drop to say anything. Too in awe of the Level Ten." He glanced at Johnny's single stripe. "Though, I ain't seen you in the games recently, so maybe you aren't a Level anything anymore."

That, Johnny thought, wasn't far off.

"Don't vaping smile," Trist said, and he actually bumped Johnny. Johnny didn't think it was deliberate, but still . . . "Tell me something," Trist continued. "I heard you're calling squids by name before they hit Level Three. That true?"

He could see where this was going. "Yeah," Johnny said. "That's true."

"So you're naming squids," Kesi said, disgusted, splitting her eyes between Johnny and Shabaz. "Too good to play the game properly, if you play them at all. Naming squids. You both think you're GameCorps."

That wasn't it, of course it wasn't. But suddenly Johnny could see how they saw it that way.

"You know what's really messed up?" Trist said. "Any panzer born in the last three months is probably going to think that this is the way things are supposed to be. That you show up at the Combine and there's a bunch of levelled skids there to help you figure grease out." Johnny blinked. He hadn't thought of it that way, but it was a possibility. "No one helped me figure out how not to die. No one's supposed to help me but me." Trist looked at Shabaz, and then back at Johnny. "It ain't right." He backed away, looking at them both. "Not one bit." He turned back to his group. "Let's go."

They rolled off in the direction of Up and Down, Kesi lingering in the back to glare at Johnny and Shabaz before she turned. Sparks trailed in her wake as she caught up to the others; it reminded Johnny of the glam Bian used to sport.

"Bian used to have sparks," Shabaz murmured.

Johnny grinned at her. "I was just thinking the same thing."

"Yeah," Shabaz said quietly. Her gaze remained on Kesi, a subdued expression on her face. "You know, Bian and I never hung out at all before the Thread. I was beneath her; she only hung out with higher level skids."

"Yeah," Johnny said. He remembered Torg once noting something similar.

"So we only were together, what, two days? Three?" Shabaz swallowed, her stripes dimming slightly. "I can't believe how much I miss her."

"Yeah," Johnny said softly. They watched Trist's group fade into the distance, then he bumped her treads and said, "Come on, let's go visit some friends."

CHAPTER FOUR

Shabaz continued to look miserable as they rolled into the path leading to the Spike. "Hey," Johnny said. "You okay?"

"Yeah," she sighed. "Thinking of Bian just put me in a mood. We might run into Makaha out here. It's his birthday too. His fifth." She grimaced. "I'm sorry, I should have told you."

"Hey, it's okay," he said quickly. He knew that she'd started to spend time with the skids who were about to hit their fifth birthday, but it still amazed him. "Really, if you need to take off for a moment, we're cool." He tried to recall the name Makaha, but he couldn't place it. "Didn't you just do Patino a couple of days ago?"

"I did Patino *and* Slen two days ago. And Grid the day before that." She sighed. "Not many days go by without at least one."

Johnny shivered. "I don't how you do it."

"Someone should. Do you know how most of us die, Johnny? We die alone. I asked around; no one who had more than two months left had even thought about it, unless they were a Nine early. But the early Nines and the ones nearing the hard death? Almost all of them said they were either going to go for a walk in the woods, sit in back of the stands of their favourite game, or find a corner of a sugarbar. And then they'd just . . . go." A look of anguish crossed her face.

"Hey," he said, trying to comfort her. "It's okay."

"No, it's not okay," Shabaz snarled. "Not vaping close. We all die alone, mostly because we don't know how else to do it. And why? Because we turn five years old." She made a harsh sound. "Betty was right: the Out There has some things to answer for."

He couldn't argue with that.

They arrived at the clearing surrounding the Spike. The giant tower, twenty-one metres high, served as the heart of the Skidsphere. It was funny: he'd been right inside the thing when they'd dived into the Skidsphere to save it, but Johnny still had no clue what the Spike was supposed to be—a memorial, a remnant from an ancient game, a flagpole, who knew?

A couple of Fives rolled out from one of the alcoves that surrounded the clearing. Johnny smiled. Maybe the Spike really was just a sign to the skids: *Come make out here.* "Hey," he said, nudging Shabaz. "You know what we've never done? We never came out here for a snug."

She gave him a flat look. "We snug lots," she said dryly. "What, sneaking into Tag Box when it wasn't being used wasn't good enough for you?"

He laughed. "It was plenty good. And I know we've gone into the woods, but we never grabbed one of these nooks like everyone else. We should do that. You know, like a date."

Now her look softened. "That's a nice idea. Okay, maybe tomorrow." She hesitated, then her stripes flushed and she nudged him. "If you were wondering, that was good."

"I'll remember." He laughed, although he actually would make an effort to do just that. Whatever this thing was between him and Shabaz, there were all kinds of new rules and behaviours that he was trying to learn. Because he wasn't just thinking about taking her into the woods for a bump and grind and then moving on; for the first time, he was thinking long term. And not just months instead of days—he was thinking *years* instead of days. Which might have been silly given he only had one left, but still . . .

Even with Peg, he hadn't really thought about their future. Sure, there had been an intensity with her that had frightened him, but it wasn't until she was gone that he realized he couldn't let go.

Speaking of which . . .

Out of the corner of his trail-eye, he thought he saw a flash of pink, far back in the trees. It was hard to tell; the day was bright with a breeze flashing the underside of the leaves, dappling everything with light. But he was pretty sure. With a nervous glance at Shabaz, he adjusted the angle on the eye. Nothing.

Shabaz sighed. "Flash of pink?" So much for her not noticing.

The first few times he'd spotted Peg after returning, he'd told Shabaz about it, even telling her about speaking to Peg right before their attack on the Core. As he and Shabaz became an item and their relationship began to deepen, however, he realized that while seeing or hearing flashes of Peg might freak him out a little, it had a rather more significant effect on Shabaz.

"Great," Shabaz muttered. "I can't decide what's worse:

that you might be crazy and it's all about your dead girlfriend, or that your dead girlfriend is actually stalking you. If she is, I wish she'd just show up and announce her intentions." Keeping an eye on the woods, she eyed Johnny with one of the others. "She still there?"

"Uhhh . . ." It really was hard to see in the trees with the changing light. Or at least, that's what he told himself. "I don't think so?"

She kept the stare on both Johnny and the woods, then sighed a harsh sigh. "Come on. Maybe she's sitting on her vaping rock." They rolled to the far side of the clearing as Johnny tried to figure out what he'd actually done wrong. Amazing how he now had a whole new set of ways he could get in trouble.

In one of the alcoves, a little larger than the rest, a rock garden lined the back of the nook, eighteen stones in all. "Nope," Shabaz said shortly, glancing at the stone that centred the garden. "Guess she's got other places to be."

Johnny took a careful breath. "Look, you can have all the time you need, I'm just looking for an estimate: how long am I in treadgrease? An hour? All day?"

She sat there with a look like she might want both Johnny and the stone to explode, then sighed again and said, "Nope. I'm done. It's your birthday and it's a beautiful day and your ex doesn't get to spoil it. Besides, it's not like you want to see her." She held the look.

"Of course it isn't!" Johnny said quickly. He was pretty sure that was at least half true.

Rolling her eyes, she nudged his tread. "You're an idiot." Then she turned to the stones. "Hmm. Eighteen of them. There's so many." She chuckled suddenly.

"What?"

She glanced at him and said, "There's a Level Six, Sangzani—black body, crazy ice-blue stripes—all the girls are in love with him."

"Oh, are they?"

"Stay in the race, Johnny. Anyway, he's one of the skids I've been keeping an eye on—shut up—and he's got potential. He'll make Seven, maybe even before his third birthday. He reminds me . . ." She hesitated and glanced at one of the stones.

Johnny smiled, pretty sure he knew what was coming. "Yes?"

"He . . . he reminds me of Albert."

The smile turned into a grimace, but he nudged her treads. "You know, I can hear his name."

"That's not what the look says."

"The look?"

"The look you get whenever I say his name."

"I do not have a look."

She held his gaze, then very deliberately swung a second eye his way. "All right," he said, laughing, "I have a look. Can't help it, we have a history. Hey, I made him a stone."

Now it was Shabaz who laughed. "You finally made it last week."

He loved her laugh. "I wanted to do it right."

"You made his after Gort."

"I liked Gort." He sobered as a pain went through his heart. "Besides, no one's stone is more important than another's. They all matter. Especially the Gorts. Especially the ones who died."

He wouldn't get them all, and that . . . that hurt. Shabaz was right, eighteen was a lot of stones, but it wasn't nearly enough. He had no idea exactly how many skids had fallen with him through the black that first time; no idea how many he'd pulled through. Forty, maybe fifty. But he did know that most of them died during the first Vie attack, many of them without even being counted by Bian or Torg. Dozens gone, and Johnny couldn't have created a memorial for them even if he tried.

"Hey," Shabaz said gently, grazing his stripe with her own. "It's okay. I'm just teasing; what you're doing at the Spike is amazing. I still have no idea how you create them." She grimaced. "We remember who we can. The best we can."

"Yeah," Johnny said quietly. He took a deep breath, exhaling loudly. "So Sangzani's like Albert, huh?"

"Not exactly," she said, studying his expression. "But he is yappy in the game and quiet out. And you should see him grind the corners in Skates."

"Yeah. Albert always could skate." He chuckled. "No wonder the girls like him."

A skid came around the corner of the nook and stopped. "Oh," he said, the tomato red body flushing. "Sorry, someone said they saw you in here. I'm interrupting . . ." His eyes dipped and he began to turn.

"No, Makaha," Shabaz said, waving him into the alcove. "It's fine, you weren't interrupting."

"Uh . . . all right." The skid rolled into the alcove, one eye on Johnny, wide with awe. "I didn't know he'd . . . I mean . . ."

"Hey," Johnny said gently, giving Shabaz a look. "It's okay, I was just leaving."

"Oh."

"Unless," Shabaz said, "you'd like Johnny to come with us too. I'm sure he wouldn't mind."

"I wouldn't want to . . . I mean, yeah, if you want . . ."

Johnny couldn't believe this guy was five years old; he acted like a squid. He counted the red-on-red stripes. Ahh . . . seven. This guy was tapping out at Level Seven. No wonder Johnny didn't recall the name, he was exactly the kind of skid that Johnny would have never noticed just three months ago. He wondered if Makaha had ever hit a podium in his life. "I can come," he said. "I'd like that, if it's okay with you."

The stripes flushed again. "Yes, that would be nice."

"Is there any particular place you'd like to go?" Shabaz said.

Makaha glanced at the woods. "I've always kind of wondered how far back those go."

Well you're not going to find out, Johnny thought. Given that Betty had rolled for three straight weeks before finally breaking out of the sphere, they weren't going to come close to that in the time Makaha had left.

"That's a lovely idea," Shabaz said. "Shall we?" The dying skid hesitated for a second, then followed her into the woods. Johnny lagged a little behind, not sure how much privacy Makaha wanted.

They didn't have to roll far before the woods surrounded them. Shabaz and Johnny often came for a tread out here, but usually they were the only ones. Oh, some skids might go a little way under the trees out of curiosity at some point, but most turned back the minute they couldn't see the Spike anymore. Which was kind of funny, given that anyone over Level Five could always find their way back by mapping.

As they rolled over the low shrub, Johnny contemplated the tomato red skid. Physically, there didn't seem to be anything wrong with him: his stripes and skin looked healthy, his treads rolled clean. The skids that had been hit by the Vies out in the Thread had looked far worse; hole, Johnny had looked far worse. If he hadn't known, he never would have guessed it was Makaha's last day.

Physically.

Mentally, there was definitely something going on. Johnny knew quiet skids, even shy skids. Often there was a sense of awe when they were around Johnny, even before he'd gone through the Thread. But whatever was going on with Makaha wasn't just awe. Oh, there was a little of that—the Level Seven's trail-eye kept flicking Johnny's way—but more, there was a weight and a sadness that you just didn't see in skids. Truth was, they weren't very deep, but Makaha . . . right now it felt like the red skid had all kinds of things going on between his stripes.

"It's really nice of you to do this," Makaha said to Shabaz. Then he flushed a little and his trail-eye swung onto Johnny properly. "You too. I feel kind of stupid for asking."

"You shouldn't," Shabaz said. "And you didn't ask, I offered. I'm pleased you let me come."

"Oh," Makaha said. "Okay." He hesitated then said, "I heard you were with Kear when he . . . you know."

"Yes," she said. "I was with Kear."

Listening to the calm, gentle tone of her voice, it amazed Johnny that this was the same whiny skid that had fallen with them from the Pipe. The Thread had changed Johnny forever, but it'd completely turned Shabaz around. *I'm lucky to have her,* he thought, surprising himself.

"That was nice," Makaha said. "I liked Kear. We hung out a bit in the last few months; I kinda wish we'd hung out sooner. I wish I'd hung out with a lot more skids sooner. I mean outside the games and the sugarbars."

"Well, we're hanging out now," Shabaz said easily.

"Yeah, I guess so."

They rolled in silence for a while. A slight breeze ruffled the leaves in the trees, causing the light to ripple across the forest floor. It really was quite beautiful. Of course, that was the point. It had all been created that way.

Shabaz and Makaha began talking games. "My last one was earlier today: the Pins." His stripes tilted. "I didn't even come close to the podium. I never could figure out the right angles in that game."

As Johnny listened to them talk, he began to understand why Makaha was tapping out at Seven.

In a way, it wasn't that surprising: Makaha was far more representative of the average skid life than Johnny or even Shabaz. Even true Level Nines were rare, never more than ten or so at a time, maybe one percent of the skids to make Level Three eventually reaching that high. The rest hit their fifth birthdays at Level Eight or Seven or Six. Seven was the most common, with half the skids ending there. Most skids ending at Six were either lazy or played scared, like they never truly believed they'd made it past Three.

The ones that made Seven but not Eight usually had more complex reasons for not getting higher.

Makaha was the kind of skid who would always try to math it out. There were skids like that who succeeded, but they tended to be crazy smart, way smarter than Johnny'd ever been. Most of the skids who were too analytical couldn't let it go: they'd never get the artistry of the Pipe or the Skates; never match the ferocity needed in Tag Box or Tilt; never find the daring needed in the Slope or Tunnel or . . . Johnny shook his stripe. They might do all right in Up and Down. . . .

"I won Up and Down once," Makaha said suddenly, and Johnny had to fight down a laugh. At least the poor panzer had won something. "There's a different way skids cheer when you win," Makaha added, and the way he said it made Johnny stop laughing. "It's . . . it's really nice."

"It is," Shabaz agreed. "When was this?"

"About eight months ago. It's how I got to Seven." His stripes flushed as they all did the math. "I was a Seven for a long time. I was hoping maybe I could make Eight before . . . well, I guess that's not going to happen."

"Hey," Johnny said, because the sadness in the poor guy's voice was just too hard, "you made it five years: most skids who are born never get past one. If you think about it that way, you've actually made it farther than I have."

"Oh," Makaha said. "I never thought about it that way." He started to turn. "Okay, I guess—"

And then he was gone. One second there, then next, he just . . . wasn't.

There had been no warning at all.

At. All.

"Vape me," Johnny breathed as a surge of conflicting emotions washed over him. Tears streaked Shabaz's stripes. "How can . . . how can that just . . . ?"

He'd never seen a skid die on their fifth birthday. He'd seen Ones and Twos get vaped by the thousands, and after they'd been thrown into the Thread he'd had dozens die that he'd known or rescued from the void, some right at his treads. But this was different. Every single One or Two got a chance to fight, to survive to Three. Every one of the skids that had fallen into the Thread had died fighting—either the Vies or the Antis or the broken black breaking them from the inside out—but they'd at least gotten to fight. Even the ones like Aaliyah who'd had almost no chance, at least they'd had *some*.

But Makaha had just been taken away. No final stand, no warning, just a life . . . gone.

"This is treadgrease," he spat, as the emotions resolved into anger. "Are they all like that?" He felt like he'd been vaped.

"Pretty much," Shabaz said bitterly. She looked drained.

"So we all go out like that? In a year, that's us? That's— snakes, that's Torg in—what?—a month? Two?" His whole body was shaking. They'd been talking . . . "Betty was right, this is vaped. *There was nothing wrong with him!*" he screamed into the woods, his voice echoing in the trees.

"I know," Shabaz whispered.

Of course. Of course she knew this; she'd already gone through everything he'd just felt. And then she'd gone back again and again, to be there if there was a skid who wanted some company when they died. "Oh, snakes," he breathed. He nudged up against her tread and put his arms on her stripes. "I can't believe you do this every day."

"I did it twice yesterday," she said ruefully, rubbing tears from her skin. "But it's not every day. There's four, maybe five a week, and about half still want . . . they still want to be alone when they . . ." She took a deep raged breath. "But you know something? Even those ones thank me for the offer. Remember Shank? He was a mean old gearbox for his entire life, but when I offered to be there with him, he looked like I'd just given him the best gift he'd ever thought of. Said it was 'lovely' that I asked. Shank said that. Then . . . I guess he went into the woods."

They were silent a moment, staring at the spot Makaha had vanished. "Something has to be done about this," Johnny said quietly.

"How?" Shabaz tilted her stripes. "We can't do anything from inside the sphere, Johnny. And I'm pretty sure the others are going to do what they can."

Johnny thought of Betty, out in the Thread for almost fifty years. He had no real idea of everything she'd been able to accomplish; yeah, she'd been able to put the sphere into stasis to save it, but she hadn't sounded like she was anywhere close to fixing the dying-in-five-years thing.

Not so long ago, in another sim back in the Thread that was both like the Skidsphere and so very different—both sims built to entertain the Out There—Johnny had been side-by-side with Albert, looking down on a body, wondering why anyone would create a world like this.

He remembered Albert's snarled response: "Because they like watching things die."

Then another conversation with Betty, not long after the one with Albert. Rage coating the legendary skid's voice as she suggested that maybe the reason skids died at five years old was that if they lived longer, they might be able to do something about it.

"Something has to be done," Johnny said again, unable to quantify his own feelings of helplessness and anger.

"And how are we going to do that?" Shabaz said gently, an odd expression in her gaze. "We can't just come and go. What if we try to leave and we break the sphere like Betty did?" She sighed. "We can do what we can here, Johnny. We are making a difference."

"Yeah, I guess," he said. Then he had a sudden thought, an extension of something he'd just said without really realizing it—a little more than a year from now, Shabaz, out here, dying alone. A wave of grief and anger swept over him. He'd already be gone, and she would have to . . .

"Whoa, hey," she said, staring at him. "What the hole just went through your stripe? You okay?"

"Nothing," he said roughly, sniffing hard. "It's . . . it's nothing."

Her stripes quirked to one side. A small smile graced her lips as she reached out a Hasty-Arm and placed it on the side of his body. "Okay," she said, holding her hand there for a minute before taking it away. "Okay."

They sat like that, the breeze feathering the leaves and casting dappled light through the woods. Slowly, the anger and darkness faded and Johnny began to feel normal again. Without realizing it, he and Shabaz had taken each other's hand.

Finally, he shifted on his treads and looked at Shabaz. She looked back with the small quirky smile that he was already beginning to recognize and love. "That was good, what you said to him at the end," she said, squeezing his hand. "It was a good thought to go out on."

"Yeah," he said, his throat full. Snakes, that had been hard. "We should probably head back. Maybe we can—"

The ground bucked once—*hard*.

The force of the quake separated them and threw Johnny into an oak, as a sharp, deep crack echoed through the trees. Reaching for Shabaz, he yelled, "Grab on to something, this could be—" He stopped.

The ground was still. The echo of the quake faded into the day.

"That's it?" he said, stunned. Shabaz had landed seven feet away. He'd never felt anything that strong in a corpsquake; and now . . . nothing. "What the hole was that?"

"I don't know," she said, wincing as she rubbed her side. "Snakes, that hurt."

"You okay?"

"Yeah, I just twisted a tread. It's fine." She straightened up and looked around. "Was that a quake?"

"I don't know," he said, echoing her. Everything looked exactly as it had before the shock: a beautiful sunny day in the woods. "If that was in the Thread, something just broke hard."

"I hate not knowing what's going on," she muttered. He looked at her, bemused. Wasn't she the one telling him that they had to be happy with what they were doing? So much for her equilibrium.

She caught the look. "I never said you were wrong. Shut up." She swept the woods in every direction with all three of her eyes. "Johnny, whatever that was, it wasn't good."

No, it wasn't. Johnny couldn't decide which was worse: that the Out There had designed a Thread with so many sims dying for entertainment, or that they'd abandoned it, leaving their creations a broken, crumbling world. Either way, Betty was right: they had a lot to answer for.

His stripe tilted, feeling helpless. "What are we . . . what are we supposed to do?"

Shabaz stared at the woods for a moment more, then sighed. "Go back and do what we can." She turned on her treads and he fell in beside her. "Do you think if it all falls apart, we'll have any warning?"

The thought came uncomfortably close to what he'd thought after watching Makaha die. "I don't know," he said, watching sunlight dapple the leaves.

They rolled away, through the forest in the direction of the Spike. Despite the fact that both trailed an eye, neither of them noticed a shadow, far back in the woods, dart between the trees and begin to follow.

CHAPTER FIVE

"Didn't you make Three?" Johnny said, frowning.

It was the next morning. Johnny and Shabaz had taken the rest of the day off after returning from the woods, talking long into the night. He'd never thought any death would be as horrible as what he'd seen out in the Thread—he'd been *inside* Brolin when he'd died— but Makaha's death had haunted Johnny in a way he couldn't really define. So he'd spent the night with Shabaz, then returned to the Combine, hoping to work on the living, maybe give someone a chance to live longer. If nothing else, he'd continue to help what skids he could.

He just hadn't expected to continue helping this one.

Akash's three lemon stripes flushed into a deeper yellow. "I . . . uh . . . I did. For sure, I got vaped in the Spinners yesterday." The stripes flushed deeper. "I tried to score. It was the first time I ever did that. It, uh . . . it didn't really work."

A smirk worked its way across Johnny's face. "Yeah, that tends to happen. The goalie hits harder than the others. Still, looks like you survived." That got an embarrassed smile. "Which brings me back to the question: what are you doing back here?"

"I only got to Three cause you guys were helping me out," Akash said. "I figured maybe . . . maybe I should do the same. I don't really know what I can do, but I'd like to help."

The fact that his third eye kept twitching in the direction of a certain white-red skid training a group of panzers on the far side suggested that not all his motives were altruistic. Still, that he'd thought to come back at all, that he wanted to help . . .

Johnny thought about Makaha and for the first time since the day before felt a little better. Things were changing, maybe they could eventually do something about—

"You have got to be joking."

Johnny swung an eye in the direction of the ramp in time to see Trist and his group roll into the Combine. Actually, his group was quite a bit larger than yesterday—there had to be at least twenty of them. "Please tell me I'm not seeing this," Trist said, parting a sea of squids and panzers like they weren't even there.

"Seeing what, Trist?" Johnny said, smiling. He decided he'd try smiling and being patient for as long as possible. Hey, it had always driven him treads-up.

"You're letting more people in here?" Trist looked at Akash with contempt. "When did you get that third stripe, yesterday? Roll away, panzer."

"Akash," Johnny said firmly, letting the smile fade a bit, "you can stay if you want."

The overwhelmed Akash stared as Trist rolled up on Johnny. Trist bumped Johnny, and this time it was definitely deliberate. Apparently, the numbers were making him braver. "What the hole's he gonna teach these idiots? Please tell me what a Three's got to teach anyone?"

Inside his head, Johnny clicked on his com. *Babe? You busy?*

It took a moment before she responded. *Watching Tilt. Why?*

One of the things they'd discovered after getting together was that they could now use their coms without speaking aloud. Johnny had no idea if it was because they were in a deeper relationship than other skids—they couldn't do it with anyone else—or if it was because they'd been forced to do similar things every time they'd fallen through the black. Either way, it was useful. Although, there had been moments when he was afraid that she might be able to read his mind.

I might need a little help here. Trist just showed up and his posse got bigger. Another voice of reason can't hurt.

I swear you're becoming a diplomat, came the amused reply. *Be there soon. Stay patient, try not to vape anyone.*

He keeps bumping me . . . Johnny thought to himself as he shut down the com. Aloud, he said, "I have no idea, Trist. We're sort of figuring it out as we go along. You guys should join in," he added lightly. The looks he got in return were not light. *Okay, not going to see the funny then.*

"This isn't funny," Trist snarled. "I thought I told you to cut this out."

Very slowly, Johnny swung a second eye at Trist. He was legitimately amazed at the size of the Seven's stripes. Johnny couldn't remember the last time a skid had gotten in his face. Probably Albert. Not a comparison likely to help him keep his temper. "Actually," he said, no longer completely controlling the edge in his voice, "you said it upset you. Are you now ordering me to stop?"

For the first time, the group behind him shifted nervously on their treads. They might be pissed, but Johnny was still Johnny. They didn't back down, though. A squid heading for the pressure paddles started to cut through the crowd, realized who they were, took one look and zipped away in terror.

Trist didn't even flinch. "I respect everything you did in the games. You got a second name, we all aspire to that. But this . . ." He waved a Hasty-Arm. "This is treadgrease. There's a way things are. Stop messing with that."

"Trouble, boss?"

Onna had rolled over from the far side of the Combine, Shev in behind her. Shev looked uncomfortable as hole, but Onna had a combative look.

"Get vaped, squid," Trist snapped, barely glancing at her.

Onna studied him, then settled onto her treads. "Yeah," she said. "I don't see that happening."

"It's okay, Onna," Johnny said. "We're just talking."

"There's nothing to talk about," Trist insisted. "This has got to stop."

"What are you hoping to accomplish?" Kesi asked suddenly, staring at Johnny with a combination of curiosity and anger.

Trist flickered an annoyed glance at her direction. Which wasn't that surprising; he wanted to control the conversation. Most skids would. What was more surprising was that the group was letting Trist speak for them at all. Johnny would have expected every one of them to have something to say; after all, if they were in this group, they weren't shy. "Kesi . . ." Trist said, impatiently.

"No, Trist, I told you, I want to know." She stared at Johnny. "You're the greatest skid who ever lived. You could have set a record that would never have been broken on the Slope." The reverence in her tone made it clear it was her favourite game. "Why would you stop playing? What are you hoping to do here?"

Johnny's stripe tilted. "Like I said, we're still trying to figure that out."

"Why would you want to, boz?" a crimson-chocolate Level Six protested. "Why would you need to figure anything out?"

Trist rolled his eyes. "Snakes, Dillac, will you let me—"

But it was too late. A burst of protest came from the group, frustrated and confused and filled with a far deeper rage than Johnny anticipated. He realized he was in a room full of skids who, if they got vaped, were going to stay vaped. If this anger at Johnny turned on the panzers and squids . . .

"All right!" Trist barked in voice loud enough to echo. Around them, the central bowl of the Combine went silent; thousands of Level Ones and Twos suddenly noticing the group of high level skids in their midst. Trist ignored all of them. "I told you we wouldn't get anything done if everyone talks. You told me your problems, I'll get to them." He glared at Kesi and Dillac. "Let me handle this."

Johnny stared at him. *He's trying to help other skids and he doesn't even realize it.* He hoped Shabaz got here soon, this could get ugly fast. They weren't listening to Johnny, maybe they would listen to her. He turned on the com. *Babe?*

Almost there, stay frosty.

He was trying to. Out loud, he said, "Look, guys, if you want to talk about this, we can talk. Why don't we go hit a sugarbar and . . ." His voice trailed off.

There was a creature standing on the ramp.

"What are you looking . . . ?" Trist said, adjusting his trail-eye before his voice fell away as well. Slowly, the whole group followed Johnny's gaze, staring at the ramp.

The creature was wearing a strange, mottled glam, like the woods on a sunlit day, but darker. Two bright blue eyes centred a ridiculously small head, and it stood on legs, not treads. There was a rifle in its hands.

Johnny recognized him.

Apparently, the creature did the same. The rifle came up. "You," the creature said. "I know you." The creature took two quick steps forward—everything about him tight and in control. Except for the eyes. There was panic in the eyes.

He stopped and stared at Johnny. Then in a voice that combined confusion and fear and rage, he asked, *"What is happening to me?"*

"What the hole . . . ?" Trist said.

"Trist, I need you to shut up now," Johnny said sharply.

"Now, just a—"

Johnny swung all three eyes. "Trist. Shut. Up."

No one three-eyed another skid. "Okay," the Seven said, frowning. "We can do that."

Johnny swung two eyes back towards the creature, no, *soldier*—Betty had said they were soldiers. His gaze swept the crowd along the way. He didn't think that rifle could do permanent damage in the Skidsphere to the Level Threes, but it could probably vape the panzers. Fortunately, everyone appeared to be staying back.

Which was good, because none of them knew what they were looking at.

Johnny wasn't even sure he knew what he was looking at. "Okay," he said, spreading his Hasty-Arms wide in what he desperately hoped was a universal gesture for don't vape me. "It's okay, no one here is going hurt you. Let's all just stay calm."

"I am calm," the soldier said, and Johnny had to admit, except for the eyes and the edge in his voice, the guy did seem calm. Except for the eyes. "I'm a lake with no breeze. Now what the fuck is going on? Who are you . . . people?"

"Skids," Johnny said. "We're called skids. And you're . . . Krugar, right?" He was pretty sure that was what Betty had said, desperately trying to remember everything she had told them.

"How do you know that? Who are you working for?"

Johnny frowned. "I'm not working for anyone. No one here is. Listen, can you put the gun down? I don't want anyone getting hurt."

"Then don't do anything stupid," the soldier said, his voice getting calmer, as if this conversation was a familiar one. "Talk first, then I'll decide about the gun." He paused, his eyes darting left and right. It must have been annoying not to have them on stalks. "Getting people to back up will help."

"Okay, everyone roll back a tread," Johnny said.

Trist didn't move, an eye on Johnny, an eye on the soldier, and the third swinging between the two. "What is this? Some kind of stunt?"

Crisp Betty. "Trist, I swear if you don't stay out of this until you know the play, I'll start playing the games again and I'll spend every second vaping you before you even find second gear. You want to talk about the Combine after, fine, we'll talk, but for now . . . *back up*."

Trist glared at him, then without turning, rolled back exactly one tread length. The rest of his group glanced at Trist then did the same.

Johnny eyed the soldier. "All right?"

"It's a start." Although he didn't lower the gun. "But I better start getting answers."

Johnny didn't even know the questions. "How did you get here?"

Krugar jerked his head back towards the ramp. "I walked out of that forest that surrounds this place. Followed you and your girlfriend yesterday."

Johnny hadn't seen anything, but he'd also been a mess after Makaha.

Johnny, I'm by the ramp. Is that Krugar? How the hole . . . ?

No clue, Johnny thought, one eye briefly flickering towards the ramp, *just hold tight until—*

In one smooth motion, Krugar pivoted and pointed the rifle at the ramp—at the exact spot Johnny had looked. As he did, he released one hand from the barrel, pulled a pistol out from a hidden holster, and pointed it back at Johnny. "Whoever's there," he barked, "come out slow and hands up." Angling his head so he could keep the ramp in his sight, he said to Johnny, "Believe me when I say I can take you both."

Okay, Johnny thought, *that was impressive.* Before he could speak, he heard Shabaz say, "Okay, I'm coming down the ramp. Let's all just stay calm."

To Johnny's surprise, the soldier chuckled. There was an edge to it, but for a second, Krugar was amused. "I don't think that's going to happen any time soon." He didn't lower the rifle or the gun, but his grip seemed to relax.

"Probably not," Shabaz said. She rolled down the ramp and stopped at the bottom. "Where do you want me?"

Another chuckle and this time the pistol went away. Keeping the rifle on Shabaz, he said, "Over with the rest. I don't have three eyes."

Shabaz started to join the others, then stopped. A second eye joined the first and squinted at the ground, following something to the base of his feet. "Uh, Krugar, is that always there?"

Immediately, his hands tightened on the rifle. "Nice try. Do I look like an idiot? Now stop—" His voice trailed away as he quickly glanced down and up. Then back down. "What the fuck?"

It took a second for Johnny to see what Shabaz had seen: a faint jagged line, running from Krugar back out the Combine.

Then, as he scoped it, the line widened ever so slightly into a fissure. "Oh snakes," he breathed. The crack didn't just run from Krugar's feet up the ramp—it probably ran all the way back to the Spike and then out into the woods. His eyes came up and he caught Shabaz's expression and realized that she'd figured it out too. "Everyone back away!" he yelled, rolling back from Krugar. The fissure grew a little bigger.

"What's happening?!" Krugar yelled. The panic was back. He tried to step away from the gap, but it followed him, growing wider.

There was a loud, sharp crack that filled the Combine. *Oh no*, Johnny thought, fear and dismay filling his heart. *Not again. Not here.* "EVERYONE GRAB EVERYONE ELSE!" Without thinking, he rolled towards Shabaz, his hands coming up, reaching out towards her. "EVERYONE NEEDS—"

He didn't get to finish. The world roared, the crack split wide open, and the entire Combine fell into the dark.

CHAPTER SIX

This seems familiar, Johnny thought.

As the black began to tear at his stripe, he remembered the sensation after falling through the Pipe: a thousand teeth with a thousand teeth. *Lovely. I've sure the hole missed this.* A familiar anger surged through him and he attacked the black.

Because it wasn't the Pipe; for a lot of reasons. He knew what was coming. He was stronger than he'd been, far stronger. And he wasn't alone. He didn't even need to feel Shabaz nearby, he could see her grey-aqua shape. *Hey, you . . .*

I'm fine, she sent back immediately. *Worry about the others, grab as many as you can. I'll work this side.* He felt her attention start to shift away before briefly flicking back: *But it was sweet of you to ask.*

A surge of affection and pride; he couldn't believe how far she'd come from being the skid who complained all the time just three months ago. Another surge of warmth, then he focused. The black was definitely getting to him, but he could hold for a while. They'd almost certainly break through before—

A white-red smear, bright and strong, to his left. *Onna!* He screamed her name into the centre of the smear, backing the name with her colours.

Ohsnakesohsnakes—her thoughts cleared but stayed frantic—*oh, vape me what the hole is this?!?*

Hold on. Think of your stripes and your name. Grab who you can.

How am I—wait, is that Trist? Without any hesitation, he felt her reach out in the direction of a yellow-black shape.

Johnny could almost feel his stripe tilt. *Ah hole, if you rescued Albert, she can rescue Trist. Although, I didn't rescue Albert. Maybe Trist can fend for himself.* Another flash of colour and Johnny forgot about the angry Seven.

The flash was green, but it was wrong—the green wasn't bright like a skid's colour, if anything, it was deliberately *not* bright. Krugar? He reached out for it and felt his grip slide away. Snakes. He tried again and failed again. He was trying to grab the mem like a skid, but this was different. He could feel Krugar fighting the black, but Johnny couldn't connect to help. Colour did nothing. He tried screaming Krugar's name.

Wha . . . e fu . . . s this . . . The voice was weak and faint, like it was being screamed through a sieve.

Shabaz, get over here, I need help.

I'm kinda busy. . . .

Shabaz, it's Krugar, I can't grab—

Are you thinking the right shape?

He could have slapped himself in the eye. Immediately, the colours grew sharper. He pictured reaching out for hands, smaller than his own, with an extra finger. He screamed Krugar's name again and reached out.

What? He felt the soldier mem grab hold. *What the hell is this?*

No time. Just stay tight to me, I've got others to grab.

He had no idea how many fell into the black this time, but he and Shabaz were able to grab a mass of abandoned skids. They still lost some, but they were going to be okay. The black was bad, but he and Shabaz could handle it, provided they found a way out sometime soon. He saw a smear of light and headed for it. *See? We're fine. Piece of—*

It wasn't until he was about to break through that he realized the light wasn't white.

What?!

The skids plunged into a world of grey and it all went spare. It felt like hitting a wall of mud. They still fell, but not nearly as fast. The grey seeped into everything. *What is this?* The black was a constant stream of teeth and knives, but this . . .

I don't like this at all.

He suddenly realized he'd lost the other skids. The grey had crept between them, wet and slimy and deceased. He reached out to find them again, but it was like reaching through old grease. How was he going to—?

From out of the grey, a voice. *Johnny?*

A shiver down his stripe. *Peg?*

A beat, and then . . . *Snakes, you know how to make a girl feel special.*

Bian?!

From his left, what might have been a smear of red and yellow. *Second place will have to do. You're in trouble, Johnny.*

Bian, what the hole? The grey was seeping into his skin, he could feel it, it was getting hard to think. He felt hungry.

There's no time. We have to get you out of the grey. It's all breaking, Johnny. It's all gone spare. They're coming for the Thread, Johnny. They're coming.

Bian . . . He felt a wave of nausea, then his rage flared and he attacked the grey like he had the black.

Not like that, Johnny. The grey's different. You have to think slower. Her voice became faint and the smear of red faded. *Keep your mind open. It won't end with Betty.* A pause. *I'm sorry about Albert. I miss him too.*

Albert?! Bian, I—

She was gone. If she was ever there at all. But how could that be Bian—unlike Peg, he had seen Bian die. Could she have somehow survived? Could—

Another wave of nausea hit him and he ground his teeth in disgust. It felt like the grey was in his mouth. *Run the race you're in.* Instinctively, he tried to pull his skin back from whatever it was that surrounded him and was surprised to feel it work. *Okay, she said slower.* It wasn't easy; slowing down was not his style. But there were games where that mattered—The Pipe, The Skates, Up and Down—so skids could do it.

Torg could have done it, Johnny thought. Snakes, he missed Torg.

Stabbing didn't work; so instead he tried imagining a wall inside him, surrounding his core, then pushing outwards, slowly. Several times he went too fast and felt the grey seep through. He reset and went slower. Snakes, this was taking—

Skid? The thought emerged from the grey sludge, green and clear. He still had Krugar. Or maybe Krugar still had him. *I don't know what the hell this crap is, but we need out. Which way is up?*

Up? Why would they go . . . ? *I don't think we go up,* he thought at Krugar.

I don't give a rat's ass which direction we pick, let's just get out of this. I've got someone else too. Johnny sensed a crimson smear. He wasn't sure who that was. But if Krugar had grabbed a skid . . .

Trying to keep half his thoughts on the wall pushing out from his core, Johnny reached out into the grey. It was like reaching through the sludge-pits in Tunnel. Slowly—snakes, it was slow—he found other skids. He touched Shabaz, felt a surge of relief that she was okay. Shabaz had Onna, or at least that's what Johnny thought she said; it was hard to tell.

He thought he had Kesi, maybe Shev; it seemed like every time he found one skid, another slipped through his arms. And, all the time, the slow creeping feeling of disgust and decay lapped at him from every side. *Vape me, this is insane!*

Krugar's voice came through the sludge. *What's that?*

What's wha—

The grey disappeared.

No falling, no landing, the grey just . . . disappeared.

"What the?" Johnny said, reflexively tonguing the roof of his mouth. He felt like he'd eaten a pile of treadgrease.

They were in a large clearing in the woods. Not the woods around the Spike—these woods were a mix of those familiar leafy trees and the thorny trees they sometimes used around the Pipe. Like the Pipe, it was snowing. Thick, white flakes drifted down, feathering the air and blanketing the woods in a hush. "Huh," Johnny murmured. Wherever they were, it was pretty.

He heard a cough. Nearby, Krugar bent over, bracing himself against a tree. He hocked up a huge spitball. "Tell me you know what the hell we just went through," the soldier said, retching again.

Johnny's stripe twitched. "I've been in the black before. That last thing . . ." He shivered. "I don't know what the hole that was."

"Well, whatever it was, let's not do that again. Ever." The soldier straightened out and Johnny hissed in surprise.

"Hey, you all right?"

"I feel like shit, why?"

Krugar looked different. There were lines around his eyes and he didn't seem to be standing straight. And his skin looked . . . grey. "Look," Johnny said, "I don't have a lot of reference points on this, but you look . . . worse?"

"How?" Krugar brought his hands up and stopped, studying them intently. He looked at both sides several times, then grunted. "Great. Don't care for that."

"What is it?"

"Don't know. My hands look older. There lines on my face?"

"Uhh, yeah."

Krugar shook his head. "Great." He sighed. "I need meds."

Johnny was going to ask what meds were, but Shabaz came around a tree with Onna, Akash, and an indigo-blue panzer in tow. From the other side of the clearing, Trist and Kesi were treading their way. "You okay?" he asked Shabaz, plowing through the snow to her side. He wasn't certain, but it seemed like there were grey-on-grey spots on her skin. The three skids with her looked terrible.

"I feel like I've OD'd on sugar," she said, nudging his tread. "You?"

"Kinda feel the same."

"Yeah," Shabaz said. "I'm fighting it, but this isn't the same as last time."

Had Shabaz not heard Bian? Had Johnny really even seen her? "Uhh," he said, "try attacking it slow. Like push, not punch."

"What do you . . . oh, wait a minute." Her gaze narrowed in focus, then her skin began to clear, the grey gaining a shine. "Yeah, that works. How did you figure that out?"

So that was a 'no' on hearing the ghost of their dead friend. "Uhh . . . just came to me."

She nudged him again. "Good idea."

Yeah, he thought as he scoped the area. The clearing was much larger than the one by the Spike, with Johnny and Krugar landing about fifty metres from the nearest edge. Trist and Kesi were halfway across, heading their way. Another duo—it looked like Shev and the crimson-chocolate skid from Trist's crew—appeared over a small hummock. Other than that . . .

A nasty feeling began to boil in Johnny's stripe as he looked over the hushed clearing. There was the odd little hummock here and there, but no real cover. And the clearing wasn't that big. "Where is everyone?" he said, his breath misting in the cold air.

"I think this is it," Shabaz said softly.

"What?" He scoped in every direction. Nothing. Just him and Krugar, Shabaz, Onna, Akash and the panzer, Trist and Kesi, Shev and . . . "Ten?" Johnny hissed in disbelief. "We only got *ten*?"

"I think so," Shabaz whispered, her voice heavy with grief.

"*TEN?!*" Johnny plowed through the snow to the top of a small mound ten metres away, as if that would change something. "*How could we only grab ten?*" he yelled, his voice echoing across the snow. "Are you kidding me? We saved—what?—five times that many, maybe ten, off the Pipe? When we didn't know what the hole we were doing? And this time we only—"

"Easy," Krugar said, putting a hand on the top of Johnny's body. "Not in front of the troops."

Johnny glared at him. "I don't know what that means."

"It means don't panic. Get angry on the inside. Don't show it."

Don't show . . . ? "Yeah," he muttered. "Good luck with that." He took a deep breath and looked at Shabaz. "Is that really all we got?"

Her eyes dipped. "That's it," she whispered.

CHAPTER SEVEN

Johnny stared at the clearing: ten drops of colour in an empty field of white. He couldn't believe it.

For the last three months, he and Shabaz had been super-skids, having to quit the games or risk breaking them. They were so much stronger than they'd ever been, and yet all that skill and strength hadn't meant anything.

He caught the look of despair on Shabaz's face and a stab of grief for her surged through his stripe. "Hey," he said, rolling off the mound. "It's okay. I saw you. You grabbed who you could. You had it until . . . whatever that grey was."

"I had hundreds of them," she said, the words dragging through sorrow and self-recrimination.

He blinked. That was more than even he'd managed to grab. "It's okay," he said again. "We got who we could." He thought he heard Krugar grunt in approval. He looked at Onna. "You okay?"

Her eyes bobbed in affirmation. "I think so. I feel . . . odd. What was that?"

"Yeah," Trist said, pulling up with Kesi. "What the hole just happened?"

"Let's wait for Shev to get here," Johnny said, watching the silver-green skid and the Level Six beside him. Still no sign of any others. "Then we'll talk."

"Then we'll talk?" Trist said dismissively. "Why, do you know what happened?"

Johnny let his second eye sit on Trist. He was exhausted and didn't feel like dealing with Trist's grease. "We'll wait for Shev." He looked at the Level One, huddling by Onna. "Are you okay?"

The indigo-blue panzer looked like he might pop a gear. "I feel sick."

His skin did look a little pale, and patches of grey mottled his skin. Johnny tried to put on a brave face and said, "We'll deal with that soon, okay?" He glanced at Shabaz. "Nice work, grabbing him."

She smiled an awkward smile and poked an eye at Onna. "Thank her. Pretty sure she did most of the heavy lifting."

"Really?" Johnny said, staring at the white-red Level Four. "You pull him through?"

"I think so," Onna said. "I just tried to keep him thinking of his colours and stripes. Like you always told me."

Always. Johnny suppressed a smile. It had been less than three months. "Well . . . nice work." He looked back at the Level One. "You need a name."

His gaze widened in surprise. "What?"

"Yeah," Trist said. "What?"

Vape me, I think I hate him more than Albert. "Out here," Johnny said, "you need a name. It's going to be important."

"I don't have a name," the One said, staring at him like he was crazy.

"Of course he doesn't have a name," Trist hissed. "He's a panzer."

"No such thing out here," Johnny said firmly. "You have a name you've been dreaming of?"

"Johnny," Shabaz said, "he's awfully young to have already—"

"Zen," the panzer said, his single blue stripe flaring. "I like that name."

Johnny laughed. "I like it too. Zen it is."

"Are. You. *Kidding?*" Trist looked like he was going to pop a gear. "You can't let a One name himself. That's—"

"*Enough*," Krugar barked. He trod through the snow and stopped in front of Trist. "Until we know the situation, one voice speaks." He pointed at Johnny. "His." He glanced at Shabaz. "And maybe her."

Trist stared up at the soldier, flabbergasted. "And just who the hole are you? Actually . . . what the hole are you?" His third eye swung up and down Krugar's torso.

"Trist," Kesi spoke up. "Hold on." She looked at Johnny, then Krugar, then Shabaz. "You know what's going on?" she asked Shabaz.

"Not everything," Shabaz said evenly. "But yeah, we know a little."

Kesi's eye swung back and forth between Shabaz and Johnny, filled with mistrust. "Fine. Let's wait for Dillac and Shev, Trist. Then we'll hear . . . whatever."

"Thank you," Johnny said, but the teal-plum skid didn't look like she cared for his thanks.

Shev finally crossed the clearing. "Snakes, this is thicker than on the Pipe," he said, wheezing.

"Yeah, this is grease, squi," Dillac announced from behind him. "This some kind of new game? 'Cause if it is, the first part really sucks, rhi."

"Pretty sure it's not a game," Johnny murmured. "How you feeling?" he asked Shev, studying the grey splotches on his stripes.

The white flared as Shev laughed. "Been better." When Johnny's stripe tilted, he added, "I don't know, I feel a little nauseous?"

"Yeah," Johnny said, glancing at Shabaz. "We are going to have to deal with that."

"Deal with what?" Trist said. "Hey, we waited for Shev, the gang's all here. What the hole's going on?"

Johnny had always taken the lead before, but he didn't want to automatically do that with Shabaz around. He looked at her and watched a small smile quirk across her lips. "You fill them in," she said. "I'll keep an eye out."

Krugar hefted his rifle. "I can listen and look at the same time. What are we keeping an eye out for?"

Shabaz peered at the dark shadows splitting the woods and the falling snow. "Well," she sighed, "it'll either be black-on-black or white-on-white." She shivered. "Anything white-on-white, we need as much warning as we can get."

"What's she talking about?" Zen said nervously.

"Bad things," Johnny said grimly. "Listen, I don't even know where to start, but let's try this: we're no longer in the Skidsphere. I know that's hard to believe," he added quickly, as Trist opened his mouth, "but you better. Because the most important thing you need to understand is that there are things out here that want to kill us and, unlike the games, they *can* kill us. You die out here, it's over."

"Crisp Betty," Onna swore.

I'm sure we'll get to her in a minute, Johnny thought, rolling his eyes. How was he going to do this? It was the truth: he had *no* idea where to start. How was he going to explain the Thread? Betty? The danger they were in? He wanted to ask Shabaz what she thought, but if he showed any doubt in front of Trist . . .

As if on cue, the yellow skid said, "This sure looks like the sphere. How do you know this isn't just some new game?"

That we just randomly teleported into through a bunch of grey sludge? That's what you're going to believe? "Look, I don't know how long it'll be before we have to move, and we've got stuff to do if we can first. Believe what you want, but if you're smart, don't let anything you see touch you. Let me and Shabaz handle it."

"Can you?" Shev said. "Handle it?"

Maybe, Johnny thought. "Sure," he said out loud, trying to sound confident as he examined the woods. He had no idea what direction they should go. He looked at Shabaz. "Anything?"

"Not yet. But we had to cause a break, didn't we?"

As if in response, the ground rumbled beneath their treads. Johnny tensed, but it quickly faded.

The last time they'd entered the Thread, they'd fallen out from a huge black scar in the sky. No scar in sight here, no black anywhere. And the Vies had responded rapidly last time; if they were coming, they should have seen them by now. "I don't know. Maybe we have some time. If so . . ." He studied Zen and the grey blotches that covered the panzer's skin. They were going to have to deal with it sometime, why not now?

"Okay," he said, treading over to Zen. "That black we fell through? Shabaz and I have fallen through that before. And we've healed what it does before. I'm going to try that with you, okay?"

"Okay," Zen stammered. "Will it hurt?"

"It might a bit, but you'll feel better. I want you to pay attention, because you're going to help. When you think you know what I'm doing, think of your colours and your name and do the same thing." He readied himself to dive into Zen, placing a hand on one of the grey spots.

"Hey, boz," Dillac said, "you said you fell through the black before. What about that grey thing at the end? 'Cause panzer don't look black, rhi, he looks grey."

Great, Johnny thought. *The idiot's smarter than he sounds.*

"Now would probably be a good time for everybody to shut up," Shabaz said in a flat voice he'd rarely heard from her. Then he caught her wink at him and, suppressing a smile, he dived into Zen.

Immediately, he realized that Shabaz was right—this skid was *young*. Maybe a couple of months old. Johnny was both appalled and amazed that Zen had made it this far. *Keep him alive and maybe he'll be something.*

It didn't take long to hit Zen's bright indigo core. Finding a few specks of black on the way in—not as many as he expected—he dealt with them easily. But the grey . . .

The grey was everywhere, and didn't attack the way the Vies tended to attack. It was definitely attacking, but it moved slow. It was like it coated everything; seeping in, not tearing it apart. Patches of grey, mottled and diseased, crept along Zen's core and stripe. Johnny couldn't remember the black ever appearing on the stripes surrounding a skid's core; with Brolin, his stripes had remained clean until they broke apart.

The thought of Brolin brought a wave of sorrow, which Johnny fought down. *The race you're in*, he thought, trying to get under the grey at the core. After failing repeatedly, he grit his teeth, and then formed a wall and pushed slowly out. Several times, the grey slipped past or even through the wall; after the second time, he felt Zen trying to help. Panzer had heart.

Finally, he got most of it moving towards the surface. His consciousness emerged from Zen in time to see the indigo skin regain most of its shine.

"Betty Crisp, that was sweet," Akash whistled.

"I hope so," Johnny said, studying Zen. "How do you feel?"

"Better!" the panzer said cheerfully, stretching his Hasty-Arms. He hadn't learned how to retract them yet. "Still a little strange."

Johnny cocked an eye at Shabaz. "I couldn't get it all. Whatever this grey stuff is, it's weird."

She smiled back at him. "You did fine, he looks a lot better. Do you want to switch or keep doing the others yourself?"

"Do the others?" Trist said. "You're not touching me."

"Trist," Johnny said, fighting a wave of anger, "we're trying to help."

"Help what? I'm fine. Feel a little nauseous." He laughed. "I feel like that most mornings after the sugarbar. Whatever that was with the panzer, don't do it on me."

Johnny stared at him. He could see a grey splotch on Trist's stripes; there was no way Trist didn't see it too.

He was used to travelling with skids who hated him. No matter how much Trist disliked Johnny, it was nothing compared to how much Johnny and Albert had despised one another. But even though he'd hated Albert and Albert had hated him, they'd trusted each other.

Even went he felt Albert was being a jackhole, Johnny knew Al would take care of things. And he was pretty sure Albert had felt the same. Hole, he'd let Johnny take the lead saving Shabaz—he might not have liked it, but he trusted Johnny to do it.

But Trist . . . Trist had seen what Johnny could do and wanted no part of it.

"Same goes for me," Kesi said. "I'm fine."

"You're not fine," Johnny said, glancing at Dillac to see if he was going to protest too. The crimson-chocolate skid seemed to be distracted by a snowflake. "Look," he said, trying to stay calm, "you don't want me or Shabaz to heal you, fine, your loss. But get this through your treads—out here, if we don't help each other, we die."

"And get this through your treads," Trist said, surging forward, "we don't want your help!"

"Trist—"

"Movement," Krugar said suddenly.

"What?" Johnny said.

"Movement," the soldier said again, pointing into the woods.

"He's right," Shabaz said, scoping. She swung an eye towards Johnny.

"There's something back there."

CHAPTER EIGHT

Shabaz didn't remember many specific details from her earliest moments in the Thread.

She couldn't remember exactly where on the Pipe she'd been when that terrifying surge of black had caught her—maybe Torg had been nearby, but she wasn't sure. She couldn't remember those first frantic moments in that strange, hazy-white world after the black; she couldn't remember seeing her first Vie or Anti.

She just remembered the panic. The wild fear of plunging into some unknown world, out of her depth, desperately trying to survive. She would have died without Torg and Bian coaching her and the others—of that she was sure. But everything else until the house where they met Wobble was just a sense-memory of wild, blinding panic.

So it was strange how little panic there was now.

She was crushed by how many skids she'd lost in the grey. Worried about what the black and grey—what was that, anyway?—had done to the others. Concerned for Johnny. Concerned about where they were. A little afraid, even; no matter how normal these woods looked, this was not the sphere and it was not safe.

But she'd survived the Thread before, even when it had almost killed her. She'd helped save herself, and then she'd helped save the Thread. So when she caught something out of the corner of her peripheral vision—and heard Krugar say, "Movement," at almost the exact same instant—a spike of adrenalin had shot around her stripes. But no panic. And she heard herself say in a remarkably steady voice, "He's right. There's something out there."

"Where?" Johnny said.

"What is it?" Kesi whispered.

"Shhh," Krugar said. "I can't see it, but something's there. Straight back, little to the left."

Johnny glanced at Shabaz. She liked that he did that. He was going to lead, there was no way he wasn't. The Thread might have changed him almost as much as it had changed her, but there was no way Johnny wasn't going to race in, stuck in first gear. But twice now, maybe even three times, he'd thought of her before gearing up, and that was sweet.

She returned his gaze and tilted her stripes in answer to his unsaid question. "We need to know if anyone else got through." It was hard to make out anything with the falling snow and the density of the trees.

"If it's skids, they landed pretty far away," he mused, squinting. "Not like last time."

"Not much of this is like last time," she said ruefully.

"You mean other than being lost and in danger?" He grinned. Raising his voice, he shouted, "HEY! ANYONE OUT THERE! SKIDS?"

"What are you doing?" Krugar hissed.

"We need to know if there are any more survivors," Johnny said. "Trust me, whatever might be out here, making noise probably isn't going to make it worse." He raised his voice again. "HEY SKIDS! CALL IF YOU CAN HEAR MY VOICE!"

Silence. Nothing but the falling snow. But far back in the woods . . .

"I'll check it out," Krugar said, taking a step.

"Hold on," Johnny said, grabbing the soldier's arm as he looked at Shabaz. "What do you think?"

She wanted it to be other skids; there'd been so many in the Combine, there'd been so many in the black. But her gut was telling her otherwise. She sighed. "I think both Vies and Antis would be a pain to spot in this mess. Especially the Antis. If it was a skid, we'd see flashes of colour."

"And they're not making any noise."

"And they're not making any noise." Shabaz eyed the direction opposite the movement, feeling a sense of déjà vu. "I say we get clear. At least of the woods if we can."

"I can find out what it is," Krugar insisted. "I know how to move in the woods unseen."

"Do you know these woods?" Shabaz said, wondering how much the soldier was like Johnny. "Whatever's back there, it's probably not something you've experienced."

"And you have?"

"Maybe." There was definitely something moving back there now. And if she had to pick a colour, it would be grey. "Johnny . . . ?"

"Yeah, I got it. Okay, let's create some space." He looked at Krugar. "I'm asking you to trust us on this. We move until we know more."

Krugar looked at Johnny's hand, still holding his arm. Johnny released him. "Fair enough," the soldier grunted, then to Shabaz's surprise, he smiled. "The second best idea is still usually a good one."

"Thanks," Johnny said, turning to the group. "Okay, we're going to put some distance between us and whatever that might be. See if we can't get out of the woods. Stay close together."

"Where are we going?" Trist protested. "Who put you in charge?"

I sounded like that, Shabaz thought, staring at Trist, unsure if she was annoyed or amused. *That's exactly what I sounded like. Snakes, it's a wonder they didn't leave me to the Antis.* She rocked forward on her treads and whispered to Johnny, "I'm so sorry."

He gave her a funny look, then, remarkably, he got it. "Don't worry about it," he grinned. "Can you?"

"I'll take the rear," she said, smiling warmly.

Immediately, they realized the snow was going to be a problem. It was thick and wet, and deeper than it first appeared. Plus, even though the trees were spread far enough apart to let them through, a thick bramble under the snow tripped up their threads. Compared to the speed they'd moved when they were trying to escape the Vies the first time around, it was a slog. Shabaz and Johnny tried warming up, melting the snow, but that just made them sink up to their stripes. And it did nothing to the bramble beneath their treads.

If the others had stayed directly behind Johnny's lead, maybe they might have had some kind of pace. But Trist and his crew—and even Shev once or twice— kept swinging wide to forge their own path; their instincts making it hard for them to follow anything or anyone. She could see Johnny getting impatient, biting his tongue. They were back in a strange world with an unknown danger, and they were once again stuck with skids who hadn't learned to work together. She wanted to tell him it would be all right, it had taken them time to learn to work as a team. She knew what his response would be: *they might not have time.*

At least Zen was staying in Johnny's trail; although, he was really struggling with the scrub. Shabaz kept having to slow to stay behind him, which meant they all had to slow to keep from spreading out. The good news was the grey didn't seem to be catching up. So whatever it was, it probably wasn't Vies or Antis back there—they would have caught them by now. The Antis especially wouldn't be slowed by the snow; they'd just knife along above it.

But no matter what it was . . .

"Zen," Shabaz said, gently but firmly. "I need you to gear up a little."

"I'm trying," he protested.

"I say we leave the panzer," Trist muttered.

Without warning, Krugar's pistol appeared in his hand, pointed at Trist. "How about we leave you behind?"

Trist stared at the gun. "Go vape yourself. If we're in danger, then the panzer's going to die anyway."

Krugar's gaze narrowed. "Krugar!" Johnny snapped. "Krugar, let me deal with this." The soldier glared at Trist, then slowly lowered the pistol.

"Thank you," Johnny said. "No one gets left, Trist. No one."

Trist sniffed. "You know I'm right."

Snakes, he was going to get himself vaped and it wasn't going to be the Thread that did it. Shabaz watched Johnny's stripe flare and rolled forward. "Do we, Trist?"

she said, sweeping a Hasty-Arm across the woods. "Tell me—do you know what's going on here? Where we are? What the rules are? Because Johnny and I don't. Not completely. But we probably know more than you. Can you accept that?"

"For Crisp's sake, Shabaz," Kesi protested, "he's only got one stripe."

Shabaz sighed. "Sooner or later you might learn that's not a bad thing."

"No one gets left, Trist," Johnny said firmly.

Trist held his gaze, then muttered something to himself and got back in line. Shev tread up beside Shabaz. "I'll try to give Zen a bump."

"Thanks. While you're at it, see if you can heal yourself a bit. You don't necessarily need Johnny or me to do it for you." She pitched her voice so the others could hear her, including Trist. "Try to imagine your core, try to feel where the grey is. Then, slowly, you have to go real slow, see if you can't imagine pushing it out."

"I don't . . ." Shev's gaze grew distant, then widened slightly. "Oh, wait, I got it . . . I think?" He grew silent for a second, his gaze intent and focused. "This is . . ." He groaned, then the silver in his skin regained some of its shine. Not much, but better. "I think I did something," he said, grimacing before he exhaled. "Whew! Maybe not. That's . . . that's really weird."

"You did something," she agreed. "Every little bit helps. Take a second to get your breath back, then try again later. You'll get better at it."

"Okay," Shev said, then tread forward to work on Zen.

Out of the corner of her eye, she saw Trist scowl then turn away. However, a few moments later, his yellow skin brightened.

She suppressed a smile. Johnny was great, but he always wanted to help directly. He didn't realize that sometimes you couldn't help; or, if you could, you had to let others help themselves in their own way. The full throttle approach could be sweet—after all, it showed he cared. But it was also annoying sometimes. And with Trist, unproductive.

"That was smart," Krugar said, dropping back to walk beside her. "I hope he's worth it."

"We'll see," Shabaz said. "Give him a chance, he might surprise you."

"Really?" Krugar said, shaking his head. "Leave the weak behind? Before we know the situation? That's disgusting."

"It is," Shabaz agreed. "But you have to understand, in the world we come from that's the norm. We're born to kill each other. We don't help one another; especially the Ones and Twos."

"That doesn't make any sense. You can be born to kill and still help each other. That's how you survive. Besides, you and your boyfriend get it." Krugar nodded in Shev's direction. "He seems to."

"Johnny and I are different. We . . . we went through an experience the others didn't. We're proof skids can change. Four months ago, I sounded like Trist." Krugar gave her a skeptical look. "Okay," she laughed, "not exactly like him but close. Trist might be a gearbox, but he's much closer to a normal skid than Johnny or me. Give him time and maybe he'll come around."

Krugar considered this. "So don't shoot him yet?"

Shabaz laughed. Apparently, there was a sense of humour in there. "Yeah, that would be a start."

The soldier sighed, shifting his rifle. "I suppose it

can wait." He pursed his lips. His eyes never stopped scanning the woods, including the trees above them, which Shabaz hadn't considered. He might only have two of them, and Shabaz had no idea if they scoped, but she suspected Krugar might be seeing more with his two eyes than the skids could with their three.

"What did he mean," Krugar said, "if you die out here, it's over?" When she scowled, he added, "Your boyfriend—Johnny, right?—he said that if you die out here, it's over. When is dying not over?"

He did notice everything. Now, how was she going to explain this? She thought about it—the soldier giving her the time—then said, "That place where you found us? That's the Skidsphere. We spend our entire lives there, playing games where we kill each other."

As she said it out loud to someone who wasn't a skid, she was abruptly struck by just how horrible that sounded. Ever since the Thread, she'd known there was something very wrong with her world and the rules they'd been forced to live by; but saying it out loud, explaining it so succinctly, made it brutally clear.

This must be how Betty felt, Shabaz thought, her stipes tightening.

"Shabaz?" Krugar said.

She sighed. "Anyway, when we kill each other in the games, most skids don't die permanently. We can control our molecules enough that anyone over Level Three can pull themselves together. Only Level Ones and Twos die permanently."

"But out here?"

"Out here, everything can kill you."

"Right." He frowned. "What do you mean by levels?"

"Every skid has a level. A Level Five is stronger than a

Level Four. A Seven is stronger than a Six. Most skids over Level Three treat the Ones and Twos like treadgrease, that's why I was saying don't judge Trist too harshly."

Krugar's expression suggested that he probably wasn't going to stop judging Trist any time soon. "So what level are you?"

She decided to keep it simple. "I'm a Level Eight. Johnny's a Ten. Ten is the highest level." No point in explaining how Johnny and she differed from the rest of the skids, she barely understood it herself.

Krugar trudged through the snow, nodding to himself as he absorbed what she had said. "So, if you can't die once you reach Level Three . . . are you immortal? I mean, back in your world?"

She laughed, but it was a bitter laugh. "No," she said flatly. "We still all die at five."

"I don't understand. I thought you said you were a Level Eight?"

"Oh, sorry—I meant years there. The skids that get past Level Two have five years to live. We all die at exactly five years old."

"That seems overly complicated." Krugar shook his head, bemused. Then he stopped. "Wait . . . are you telling me you're only five years old?"

"I'm only four. Most of this bunch is under three."

He stared at her. "How do you measure years?"

"What? I don't know: three hundred and fifty days?"

"Close enough," he said, looking out at the entire group. "Infants," Krugar said. "You're all infants."

Shabaz wasn't sure what an infant was, but it sounded like a panzer. "So you're older than five? Five years?"

"I'm forty-two years old." Now it was her turn to stare as, just ahead, Zen got caught in another bramble.

"This is ridiculous," Krugar said. "We need to find you a trail. I'll scout ahead." He looked at Shabaz. "Thanks for explaining a few things. You good here?"

"I think so," she said. "I don't think they're catching up."

"We're not losing them, either," Krugar muttered, bounding forward. He moved much faster than the group.

He was also right about whatever was pursuing them. It wasn't getting closer, but Shabaz could still see hints of movement, back along the trail. Of course, it probably didn't help that they were leaving a huge trail plowed through the snow, but she didn't know what they could do about that.

Krugar returned after a few minutes. "There's some kind of animal path a hundred metres over there. It's not completely clear, but it's better. Less undergrowth."

"All right," Johnny said. "Let's try it."

"You do that," Trist said. "I think we'll find our own way back."

"Trist," Johnny said, rolling his eyes. "There is no back to find."

"Yeah, we'll see. Look, I don't know if this is a new glam from GameCorps or a new game—and I have no idea what the hole he is—" Trist jabbed an eye at Krugar as he, Kesi, and Dillac turned off the trail "—but we're done following Johnny Drop. You have your entourage; count us out."

They couldn't see it, Shabaz thought. They still thought they were in the sphere. It was understandable: they weren't in some bizarre, empty white space; no black scar hovered ominously overhead. Instead, they were surrounded by woods. The trees might be different, but this could be home.

Except it wasn't.

"Trist, listen to me," Johnny said, and Shabaz could hear him trying to stay calm. He wasn't very good at it. "This isn't what it looks like. We have to stay together. If you want . . . I'll follow you. You can pick the direction, you can lead the way. Just . . . we need to stay together."

The Level Seven stared at Johnny as if he'd never expected the offer. "I don't understand you at all," he said, bewildered.

"Trist," Shabaz tried. "What do you think happened before we got here? What do you think happened between here and the Combine?"

He returned her gaze as if he knew she'd saved his life but he didn't want to admit it. "That doesn't mean anything. It's like what happens when you fall off the Rainbow Road."

"Trist," Johnny said. "Please."

Shabaz knew how much it cost him to swallow his pride. Surely, that had to mean something.

Trist pursed his lips, snow dusting his yellow skin. "And if I say ditch the panzer and the freak?"

She watched Johnny's expression change, felt it mirrored in her own stripes. What a piece of grease. "Not a chance," Johnny said coldly.

"Then we're done here." Trist said, as he turned to Kesi and Dillac. "Let's slide." He bumped the tree beside him, flattening his treads into skis as he did. The momentum sent him into another tree, then another, each one adding to his speed. Within a few seconds, he was sliding away, Kesi and Dillac following in his trail.

Faster than expected, they disappeared into the trees.

CHAPTER NINE

Johnny watched the three rogue skids disappear, as the ground rumbled faintly beneath his treads. "Skis," he said, shaking his stripe. He looked at Shabaz. "Please tell me you didn't think of that and were just humouring me."

"Nope," she said, looking as bemused as he felt.

He raised two eyes towards the sky, where he'd always looked to the Out There. "Level Ten," he said derisively.

"Maybe he'll get two names," Shabaz murmured.

"How the hell did they do that?" Krugar demanded. "That trick with their treads, I mean."

"We can all do it," Johnny replied. "We should have been doing it from the beginning."

"Uhh . . . not all of us," Zen said. "I figured out skates, but I haven't done skis yet."

Which was the second surprise in as many minutes. The fact that Zen could even form skates this young was amazing. Maybe there *was* something about the ones that survived. Nevertheless, they couldn't carry him. "Okay," Johnny said. "It's okay, Zen. We've been all right so far, we'll keep going like this. Onna?"

"Yes, boss?"

He sighed. "You gonna keep calling me that?"

"Thinking about it."

Great, he thought, thinking of Torg. Snakes, he missed the magenta skid. "Well, as you're thinking about it, see if you can coach Zen here on flattening his treads. If he can make skates, he gets some of the basic concepts already. Shev?"

"Yes, boss?"

Crisp Betty. "She gets to do it, not you."

"That doesn't seem fair."

He stifled a scream. They didn't get it—none of them did. Everything around them just looked too much like home. "Listen to me," he said, trying to keep calm. "I want you to keep a perimeter around us, using skis. You do not go out of sight—and I don't mean scoping, I mean natural sight. You see anything, you do not take a look. I repeat: *do not take a look*. You come right back here. Got it?"

"Okay," he said, and flattened his treads.

"What about me?" Akash said.

"Stay in the line." When he caught the expression on Akash's face, he added, "I know it sucks, Akash, but until we know more, it's best. Help Zen." It occurred to him that he was going to have to be careful about giving even Onna and Shev jobs. He was thinking of them the way he'd thought of Bian and Torg, but Bian had been a Level Seven and Torg had been a Nine. Onna and Shev were a Four and a Three, respectively; they were more like Torres and Aaliyah.

Johnny scowled in the direction Trist and the others had taken off. "Think they'll send someone back if they find something?" he said to Shabaz.

"We can hope," she murmured, one eye on the woods behind them. "Johnny, we should go."

"Right," he said. "Krugar, let's go check out this trail you found."

They rolled about a hundred metres and then the bramble largely disappeared from beneath their treads. They began making better progress, although they still had to match Zen's best speed. Johnny kept checking on Shev to make sure he wasn't doing anything stupid, but the silver skid stayed about fifty metres out, circling the group.

"He isn't very observant," Krugar said, nodding towards Shev.

"Why?" Johnny asked. He knew almost nothing about the soldier—had no clue what he could do or how much he could be trusted—but the man did exude competence.

"Because I'm pretty sure there's movement off that way too."

"Really?" Johnny scoped in that the direction. Sure enough. "Shabaz, is that something behind us still behind us?"

"I think so."

"Snakes."

"There's a fork coming up," Krugar said. "We can take the right, buy time."

"All right," Johnny said. "Don't be too hard on Shev, he's at a lower level than Shabaz or me. His scoping won't be as good yet." How Krugar had seen it, Johnny had no idea.

"Levels. Right," Krugar grunted. They hit the fork and angled off to the right. It began to snow harder. "Do you have any idea where we are?" Krugar asked.

"Not really," Johnny admitted. "I've never seen this part of the Thread."

"What's the Thread?"

"This is. Everything is part of the Thread. The place we came from, the place you came from." He sighed. "It's complicated. There's a skid who, if she's still alive, can probably explain it better than I can."

"The black one," Krugar said, nodding. "With the pink stripe?"

"Yeah. You remember her?"

Krugar grimaced. "I'm not sure what I remember anymore. It's more like a feeling." He shook his head and then exhaled. "This is not the way I normally operate. I have a memory of the black one, except it's like I have the same memory several times. Does that make sense to you?"

A shiver went through Johnny's stripe. "Yeah."

Something in Johnny's tone drew a look from the soldier. "And *that* is terrifying. That it makes sense to you. Anyway, I remember seeing her—just her—several times, but then, in the same time and place, I remember her and you and your girlfriend and a bunch of others. None of this lot, I don't think."

"Yeah. I remember that too. The black one, Betty, is a lot older than most of us and spent time out here. She's the one who explained everything to us."

"But now she might be dead? In your games?"

"No. Not in the Skidsphere. Out here. In the Thread." Johnny's eyes dipped. "I don't know. There was a big fight. She sacrificed herself so we could do what we had to do. But she might have survived. Some of my . . . friends went to find her, after. If we can't find Betty, hopefully we find them."

"Johnny!" Shev called, from off to their right. "I think there might be something on this side."

It was getting harder to see as the snow intensified. Even as he scoped and spotted what might be something moving in the mass of white snowfall against black tree trunks, he heard Krugar say, "He's right, there's something there."

"Snakes," Johnny swore. "Shev, get back here. Stay tight." He suddenly wished he had a gun. Krugar had at least one and presumably knew how to use it. Johnny would have preferred to keep moving rather than fight, but it was beginning to look like that might not remain an option. He knew it was possible to create a weapon, he'd seen both Betty and Bian do it. He just had no idea how. "Hey babe?" he called.

A snort came in response. "Yes, sugarmouth?"

Okay, so she really wasn't fond of pet names. "When you guys fought off the Vies with Bian, you all created guns, right?"

A moment of silence, then: "Yeah, but don't ask how we did it."

"What?"

"We were all so charged up. Bian did it, so I did the same, without thinking. So did Torres and Torg. But I have no idea how we did it. I've been trying for the last half an hour."

So no guns then. Which meant if they had to fight, they were going to have to rely on Krugar. As if on cue, the soldier said, "This is bad." He scanned left and then right. "It's a funnel. We're being led somewhere."

"Trist and the others went ahead of us, so we can't be surrounded."

"Unless they ran into something."

"Oh snakes," Shabaz said suddenly.

"What?" Johnny said, scoping behind them.

"Not back there. It's the others. I heard you mention them, so I brought them up on the map. Check your scans."

I should have kept that active, he thought, silently cursing himself as he checked his mapping system. Immediately, he found the other signals; they were coming back. A chill went down his stripe. Even if he'd hoped Trist would change his mind, it was way too soon. "That can't be good," he murmured.

"What can't be?" Krugar said, his rifle up.

"They're coming back." Except there were only two signals on his scan.

"Johnny," Shabaz said, "There's only—"

"I see it." Johnny frowned. Kesi and Dillac. Were the hole was Trist?

"There's a clearing coming up," Krugar said. "We might not want to be in the open."

Johnny couldn't see anything in the trees now, the snow was getting so thick. "You think it's worse than this? Whatever's out there, it doesn't have guns."

"Why not? We do."

That was a good point. "All right, they probably don't have guns." He looked at Zen. How long had it taken them to get out of the white space the last time? Did he even know what the door to this place would look like if he found it? "Okay," he said, "listen up. From this moment forward, if Shabaz or I tell you to do something, do it right away." He glanced at Krugar. "Come to think of it, listen to him too. Zen, stay between Onna and Shev. Akash, you too. I know you've got your third stripe, but it's awful new. Guys, keep them safe. If you see something black, run and do not let it touch you. If it's white, run faster."

"What if I can't?" Zen said, his stripe shaking.

"Then we'll carry you," Onna said firmly, eyeing Johnny. "We'll take care of them."

They emerged from the woods into a large clearing roughly one hundred metres wide. "If we're going to clear the trees," Krugar said, "head for that rise." About thirty metres away, the ground rose to a small hill. "What little elevation we can get."

The ground was free from any brambles, only short grass under layers of white. But the snow got deeper—in some places the drifts were higher than Johnny. As Johnny's group struggled up the rise, two skids came out of the woods on the far side of the clearing. Even from seventy metres away, Johnny could see they were terrified.

"Kesi, where's Trist?" Shabaz sent over her com.

"I think he's dead," Kesi shot back, in a tone that barely kept it together.

Dillac wasn't keeping anything together. "What the hole was that?!" he cried, his voice cracking with horror. "They ate him!"

A memory shivered through Johnny's stripe: *It killed Peralta!* He scanned the trees. "What ate him?" he commed, trying to stay calm. It couldn't be Antis or Vies, they would've been attacked by now. Antis would have flown over the snow and cut them to shreds.

"I don't know," Kesi yelled, switching off her com and changing her skis back into treads. "They were grey. And there were skids—"

"Skids?" Johnny and Shabaz said together. The only skids out here should have been Albert's crew or maybe Betty.

"They were all grey," Kesi said, plowing through the last of the snow. "There were other things with them. Trist tried to blast through them like you have to do sometimes on the Gauntlet and they . . . they overwhelmed him. And then . . ." Her voice choked up. "And then he . . . he joined them."

"What?" Johnny said.

"Yeah, squi, what?!" Dillac cried. If his eyes went any wider they were going to pop. "What the hole, squi?"

Johnny didn't have any answers. He didn't know what this was.

"What do you mean there were skids?" Shabaz said.

Kesi tried to regain some control. "It was this pack of things. Some of them looked like skids, but they didn't have stripes. I think I recognized one. Coret. She was in our group, in Trist's . . ." Her composure slipped, her voice breaking. "Betty Crisp, what the hole happened to him? That group swarmed him and then he turned grey and joined them."

"You came back here," Krugar said firmly. "You warned us. That was good." Johnny wasn't sure if warning anyone was their intention—he was pretty sure it wasn't Dillac's—but he'd give them the benefit of the doubt.

"Tell me what to do," Krugar said, looking from Johnny to Shabaz. "How do we fight it?"

Johnny's stripe tilted hard. "I don't know. I have no idea what this is."

"Grey," Shabaz said, her eye-stalks scrunched in thought. "We fell through grey."

"Uh, guys," Akash said, looking back at the woods.

Something emerged from the trees.

CHAPTER TEN

It was a skid.

Its skin was mottled grey, like it was sick. One of its eye-stalks was missing and the eyes looked rotten.

No stripe at all.

Another skid emerged beside it. Then another. With a wave of horror, Johnny realized he recognized the third one. "Oh, Crisp," he whispered. "They're the skids from the Combine."

Skids continued to flow out from the trees, more and more, in depth. All the same shattered grey. They weren't moving fast, but there were dozens of them, then dozens more. Johnny swallowed. How many panzers and squids in the Combine at any given time? Ten thousand? Twenty? If the whole thing had fallen into the black . . .

"Are they yours?" Krugar asked, his rifle up and centred on the foremost skid.

"I . . . I don't . . ." Johnny stammered, recognizing two or three now, slowly rolling through the snow like it wasn't there. If they'd fallen through the grey and survived, could he and Shabaz save them? Get inside and drive the grey out? But they'd attacked Trist, made him one of them. And there were so many, with more and more coming. . . .

"No," he said, feeling ashamed. "I don't think so."

Before Johnny had finished the sentence, Krugar tapped his trigger three times, three shots dead centre on the skid in front, the sound echoing throughout the clearing. The skid kept rolling.

Krugar raised the rifle slightly. Two more shots, this time one to each remaining eye.

The skid kept rolling.

"Any weak spots I should know about?" Krugar said calmly.

"I don't know," Johnny said, backing down the far side of the rise. "Let's get the hole out of here."

"I don't know if we can," Shabaz murmured, pointing at the woods where Kesi and Dillac had emerged. A ghostly line of skids appeared through the trees and began to cross the clearing as Krugar's rifle rang out again. The soldier tried the treads and this time had some success. The tread cracked and ground to a halt. The wounded skid strained forward, but the tread remained broken.

He should be able to repair that, Johnny thought. "Keep doing that."

"I'd love too," the soldier said, pivoting for his next shot. "I'm not sure I have enough ammo."

Johnny scanned the clearing. As he and the others rolled towards the centre, dozens of new skids appeared from every side. "Can you stagger a group? Create a hole?"

Krugar stopped firing. "Maybe. We could use another gun."

"I don't think that's a possibility," Johnny said, seeing the pained look on Shabaz's face.

"Oh, boz," Dillac whined, "this is so bad, this is grease."

That was a great help. Krugar stopped three skids in a row, waited three seconds and stopped three more a few feet beyond them, trying to create a gap. It worked briefly, then the skids behind simply pushed forward or rolled right over or came around.

"I don't think this is working," Johnny murmured.

"Oh, boz," Dillac whined. "This is so bad . . ."

"Dillac," Kesi snapped, "shut up."

"No way, boz. This is game over, squi."

They reached the centre of the clearing, as Krugar's rifle rang out again and again. "Down to half a clip," he said crisply. Johnny didn't know what a clip was, but half of one didn't sound good. He scanned the horde closing in. The direction they'd been going seemed thinnest, although that was the direction that Trist had gone.

But Johnny wasn't Trist. And he had Shabaz with him.

"I don't think subtle is going to cut it." Krugar said, flicking a switch on his rifle. "I'll mow a path, you follow, protect the weak."

"No," Johnny said grimly, looking at Shabaz. "We've survived things you haven't. If anyone can break through, it's us." She moved beside him. "Everyone get behind us. If we get overwhelmed, head in the same direction. No stopping."

He looked at Kesi and Dillac, but one was losing it and he still didn't know if he could trust the other. He turned to Onna and Shev. "Keep Zen and Akash between you two. You stay right behind us. Krugar, do the same, but cover our back and sides if you can." He made eye contact with all of them. "You have to go as fast as you can. Stay right in our wake, you should be able to keep up." Shabaz reached out and took his hand. "You sure you don't know how to create that gun?" he asked as the pack closed in.

"I wish." She squeezed his hand. "That one," she said, poking an eye at the largest skid. Johnny wasn't positive, but he thought he might have trained her the week before. "Hard and fast?"

He had no idea. "Hard and fast," he agreed, returning the squeeze. They geared up.

They had to plow through the snow if Zen had any hope of staying with them. Sheets of white sprayed up from each side as Johnny and Shabaz surged forward. Remarkably, they hit a decent speed. It was the first time they'd both cut loose in weeks.

They hit the lead skid and bowled it to one side. Immediately, there was another behind it. Then another. Then another.

Then another.

They began to slow. Grey seemed to clamour at Johnny from everywhere, hands slapping at him, skin crushing inwards—*did something just bite him?* He heard Krugar's rifle ring out time and time again. Dillac was roaring incoherently; Shabaz had his hand clamped like a vice so nothing could squeeze through.

"Johnny!" Onna screamed. "Shabaz!"

Zen had caught a tread on a root or a rock, slowing momentarily. The grey mass pressed in, squeezing towards the fragile One.

"No," Shev said grimly, forcing his way between the grey pack and Zen. He pushed at the swarm with his Hasty-Arms as Onna grabbed Zen and yanked him back behind Kesi. But then Shev's eyes widened as his arms were pulled forward into the grey. "No!" he said again, but this time there was panic.

"Shev!" Johnny yelled.

Before he could start to turn, Shabaz squeezed his hand, hard. "We keep moving forward or we all die," she snarled.

Johnny didn't even have time to respond before Shev was pulled into the grey mass. Three different skids bit into him before Shev's screams died. Then Johnny—who had seen skids literally fall apart in his arms—saw the most horrible thing he'd ever seen in the Thread.

Shev's eyes clouded over, then went white. His silver skin dulled and his green stripe faded into his body.

He turned grey.

"*Nonononono . . .*" Dillac wailed, pressing into Johnny's back. Behind him, Onna tried to push Zen and Akash forward. Kesi was reaching back from behind Shabaz, Krugar was firing shot after shot. Shabaz's grip began to slip. . . .

A screaming sound filled the sky and missiles exploded into the mottled grey horde. A familiar white shape, like a cross between a bullet and a knife, roared into sight. It held a purple-orange skid against its undercarriage.

"Claw-clacks and falcons from the sun!" Wobble cried, a broken-toothed grin somehow visible even in his souped-up Anti form. "GMO, we-we're back again!"

He released the skid, and the purple ball literally fell like a bomb into the front of the horde, cratering the ground as a shockwave hurled the mass away from Johnny and the others. As smoke from her impact curled around her treads, the skid popped her Hasty-Arms, split her single orange stripe with a ferocious grin, and swung two eyes.

"Hey, Johnny. 'Baz." A beam of light, matching her stripe, appeared in each hand like a sword. "How's tricks?" She turned and attacked the nearest grouping of grey, orange blades flashing like the blades in Tunnel.

"Well, all right then," Johnny growled, a huge grin lighting his own stripe, as fire-saws from Wobble took out another group. "Okay, skids," he yelled. "Let's go!"

He and Shabaz tore into the gap created between Torres and Wobble, with the others right behind. A single grey skid remained in their path; Shabaz plowed through it with ease.

Stopping about thirty metres away, they watched Wobble and Torres decimate the grey skids. Torres in particular was a dervish of movement, tearing through the swarm, her orange blades everywhere.

"Who's that?" Onna murmured.

"That's Torres," Johnny said. He couldn't stop grinning.

"Looks like she learned Betty's light-blade thing," Shabaz said, her eyes alight.

Wobble descended from the sky, transforming from his sleek Anti-like knife look. Four arms emerged, one broken. As he touched down onto treads like a skid— one damaged—his head spun with a mechanical whir. "Actors in togas and hooray-hooray-hooray! All is Teddy Bears. Except the monsters-monsters. Wobble." His head spun again, as Torres dispatched the last of the grey skids behind him. "Hello, friend Johnny, friend-friend Shabaz. I-We are warm and fuzzy."

"You are?" Akash said, stunned.

"Yeah," Johnny said, his heart filling. "Yeah, he is. It's good to see you, Wobble." The machine's head spun with mechanical glee as Torres rolled up.

"So . . ." she said grimly, as the light-swords in her hands continued to glow. "What's new?"

CHAPTER ELEVEN

Snakes, it was good to see Torres, Shabaz thought.

When they'd fallen into the Thread the first time, Johnny and Albert had had their thing. They took turns leading in their own way; they took turns hating each other. Torg had been Torg. And as for Betty . . . maybe Johnny had been able to relate to her, but the black skid had skills and experiences far beyond anything the average skid could comprehend.

Which had left Shabaz with the others: holding on, desperately trying to survive, and then, desperately trying to contribute. Because if there was one thing a skid hated, it was feeling useless. She could have just whined and complained like she had her entire life, like she had when they'd first fallen through. But then skids had started dying. Permanently. And Torres, a panzer, had never complained, not once. She'd latched onto Albert, sure, but mainly she'd geared up and decided no matter what happened, she was going to figure it out. It had shamed Shabaz, but it had helped her realize that if a Level One could do it, maybe she could too.

Plus, Torres was just . . . Torres.

"So," the purple skid said, "whatta we got?" She examined the group. "You two, a couple of Sixes, a talented Four, a barely Three, a One and . . ." One of her eyes settled on Krugar. "Huh," she grunted. "Interesting. Still . . . not much of a group."

"Hey," Johnny snapped. "We lost a few too."

A stab in Shabaz's heart as it hit her: Shev. One of hers.

Torres stopped, her stripe flushing. "Sorry, it's been a rough week. Of course you did. We'll grieve when we get safe." She spat. "Safer. Wobble?"

The machine folded into his battered knife shape and spun. "Rub-rub the bars together and watch out-out for gas giants." His point stopped and he sped off through the trees.

"Let's go," Torres said.

Johnny glanced at Shabaz with a look that asked a thousand questions. She tried to return the gaze with a reassuring smile, tilting her stripes. Johnny held the gaze a moment, then turned to follow Torres. As they caught up with her, Johnny asked, "Where's Al and Torg?"

"Torg's at our safehouse," Torres said curtly. "We'll get caught up there."

And Albert? Shabaz thought, as Johnny glanced at her again. What about Betty—had they found her?

They didn't go far before Wobble pulled up at a tree. "One broke-broken door. Wobble."

"That's how we roll, Wobs," Torres said. "All right: you and you and you and you." She pointed at Kesi, Zen, Dillac, and Akash. "You're in a chain with me, lowest levels on the inside. The rest—"

"Whoa, whoa, whoa, sister-say," Dillac said, popping his Hasty-Arms. "I'm not holding anyone's hands! I roll—"

A hum as one of the orange light-swords popped free. Torres rolled up to Dillac, bumped his treads, and held the sword near his stripes. "Listen to me very closely. I don't give a bucket of grease who you think you are in the sphere—out here, I tell you to hold someone's hand, you hold their hand. I tell you to pop an eyeball and eat it, you do that too. Otherwise, you can go back and hang out with those grey things that vaped your friend."

Dillac stared at her, then swung an eye at Johnny. "Who the hole is this?"

Shabaz tried not to laugh as Torres grinned. "I'm Torres. The machine's Wobble." Wobble waved a rickety arm and smiled a gap-toothed smile. "Now grab a vaping hand."

Dillac managed to hold her glare for a second, then his eye-stalks slumped. He rolled over to Akash and sullenly stuck out his hand.

"It's all right," Akash said blithely. "I washed today."

Torres ran her gaze over Onna. "You pair up with them," she said, pointing at Johnny and Shabaz.

"Oh," Onna said, staring at Torres and flushing. "Sure, no problem."

Torres turned her attention to Krugar. The soldier shrugged and raised his hands. "Wherever you'd like me," he said casually. Torres grunted with what was probably approval. "All right, red stripes with Johnny, you take Shabaz." She grinned. "I take it you'll survive not holding Johnny's hand, Shabaz?"

So they were aware of what had happened back in the sphere. Shabaz rolled her eyes and replied, "Stuff it, squid. Where are we going?"

"Question of the millennium," Torres muttered. "Wobble?"

One of the lenses on the machine's frame whirred and the tree opened to reveal a door of black space. But inside the black . . . familiar golden lines.

"What the hole?" Kesi said.

"Oh, boz, no way, boz," Dillac whined, making a sound like a jammed gear.

We told you this wasn't the Skidsphere. "You can trust Torres," Shabaz said aloud. Kesi didn't look like she felt like trusting anyone, but she kept her grip on Zen as they went through the door with Torres and the rest. "Don't worry," Johnny said to Onna as they approached the door. "It'll be weird, but okay." Although as Shabaz and Krugar approached the dark hole in the tree, she wondered if that was true.

Because one of the lines inside was broken.

She felt a familiar sensation of being stretched and then snapped back into place. But under that, another feeling: like barbed wire scraping along her skin. Then the world snapped back into place and they were in one of the Thread's black hallways, lined with straight golden lines. Round doors of golden light—circles within circles—appeared on the walls, the floor, and the ceiling. Like most of the Thread's hallways, there were blank spots where circle-doors should have been, but had been lost to the Thread's damage.

Unlike the other hallways, some of the golden lines were frayed and torn.

"What the hole was that?" Dillac protested, tearing his hands away from Akash. "It felt like the wire in Up and Down, rhi!"

"Hey!" Torres snapped. She released Zen and Akash and grabbed Dillac. "You do not let go until I tell you to let go."

"Get off'a me!" Dillac said, trying to yank his hand away from Torres. "Don't squeeze my karma—*yeeeeeeeooow!*"

Torres popped a light-sword and brought it against Dillac's stripes, instantly filling the hallway with the smell of burning flesh. "Listen to me, you treadmark," she hissed, bringing one of her eyes right up to one of his own. "I am trying to save your life. But I've had a really crap day to go with a really crap week to go with a vaping fabulous month, so I don't have time for squid treadgrease. So shut up, hold my hand, and then shut up some more." The light-sword hissed and disappeared. "Let's go."

"Whoa, hold on," Johnny said. When Torres glared at him, he held up the hand that was clasped around Onna's. "Still holding hands. But Dillac's not completely wrong—what was that? That door wasn't clean."

"We don't travel clean," Torres spat. "We travel broken. And we have to move."

Shabaz could feel the frustration rolling off his skin as he glanced at her—she felt it too. But it was still Wobble. It was still Torres. It sounded like Torg was waiting for them somewhere. "We don't know the race yet," she said, trying to sound reassuring. "They do."

Where the hole was Albert?

Johnny stared at her as if sharing the same thought, then bobbed an eye.

Torres grunted. "Glad that's settled. Now, gimme a minute." She reached into one of the blank places on the wall and closed her eyes. Slowly, a set of four circles within circles appeared. Three of the four were frayed and the fourth barely glowed at all. The circles retreated into one another to reveal another door.

"Crisp Betty," Shabaz breathed. Every line of glowing light looked damaged.

"Don't say that vaping name," Torres snapped. She sucked on her teeth, making a tsking sound. "All right, this will suck grease. We all hold hands in a line. I go first, Wobble comes last. Johnny, Shabaz, you anchor the middle with the panzer between you."

"My name's Zen," Zen said in a peeved voice, then flinched. "Don't burn me."

The orange stripe flared, then softened in the broken glow of the door. "Zen, huh? Already got a name." Torres glanced at Johnny and Shabaz. "Cool." She took a long ragged breath. "We need to get through this and then one other door like that first one. Then we'll all talk and be polite. Is that okay?" For a moment, the tough exterior slipped away and she looked exactly as young as Shabaz knew her to be.

"All right," Johnny said, slowly. "If you think this is best." They all took hands and went through the circular door.

It did suck. The tearing sensation reminded Shabaz of the time they'd dropped into the Skidsphere; unable to find the core, barely holding on, attacks from all angles eating them alive. She poured colour into Zen's hand, sending the One's name pulsing out like a prayer.

Thankfully, the journey was short. A broken golden line moved towards them through the black and they emerged into a hallway.

"Snakes," Dillac snarled, glaring at Torres. "Can I let go now?"

Smiling, Torres released his hand. "Don't go far. Second I say, back with your partner. Don't touch the frayed lines of light. Might bring trouble. Follow me."

"Torres, wait," Johnny said. "We'll follow you, but where are we going? Why did we just go through a broken door? That's crazy. Where's Albert? Did you guys find anything about Betty?"

"Don't say that name," Torres spat.

"What name? Albert? Betty?"

Wobble let out a deflated metallic sound. Shabaz had never seen him look so sad—and Wobble often looked like he was filled with a profound sorrow.

"We can talk when we get to the yard," Torres said.

"No," Johnny insisted, reaching out and grabbing her Hasty-Arm. "We can talk now." Torres slowly and deliberately eyed the hand on her arm. "Oh," Johnny said, "you going to burn me too?"

Torres held the look, then jerked her arm out of his and started to roll down the hallway. "You want to know why we're travelling through broken doors, Johnny? Because everyone's hero has gone spare. Congratulations: turns out Betty's alive." No sooner than she'd started to move, Torres ground to a halt. "And she's destroying the Thread."

Beneath their treads, the floor rumbled.

CHAPTER
TWELVE

Betty was alive.

Johnny felt his heart soar. If Betty was alive then everything would be all right.

Then the ground rumbled and he caught the second thing Torres said. "Wait, what?"

"Yeah," Torres snarled, jabbing an eye at him and Shabaz like it was their fault. "About two months ago we realized Betty survived the Core."

"That's amazing," Shabaz whispered.

"You'd think. Except she didn't just survive. She did better. Somehow, she latched into it, became part of it—we're not exactly sure what. And then she went to war with SecCore. She's trying to kick him out."

"Out of where?" Johnny said.

Torres stared at him. "The Core."

"She's trying to kick SecCore . . . out of the Core?" Shabaz said in disbelief.

"The cops-the cops-are corrupt-corrupt," Wobble said miserably.

"Vaping right, they are," Torres swore. "Betty's taken control of some of the Antis. SecCore's geared up to get rid of her. Which means there are far more Antis fighting each other and far fewer fighting Vies."

As if on cue, a black sphere of spikes-inside-spikes emerged from between two broken lines near Akash. The mint skid jumped back with a startled squawk, as Krugar's rifle came up. But before the soldier could fire, Torres popped a light-sword and—almost as an afterthought—sliced through the Vie. She stared at the spot, then extinguished her sword as if it were routine.

"What the hole was that?" Kesi protested.

"A Vie," Torres said flatly. "They're supposed to be the bad guys."

Johnny couldn't wrap his mind around it. This world felt crazier than the one they'd fallen into the first time. He didn't know where to start. "If there's more Vies than before, why are we going through broken spaces? There's more Vies here."

"There's more Vies everywhere. And the broken spaces are the hardest places for Betty to scan. We're pretty sure she's looking for us and she's better at it than SecCore. Ever since she captured Albert."

"What?"

"When we realized where Betty was and what was going on, Albert went to try and talk sense to her. We haven't seen him since. But not long after he disappeared, we got a message from Betty to come and speak with her. We would have gone if not for Wobble. He didn't like it."

"The cops-the cops are corrupt-corrupt," Wobble said again, but with a different intonation than before. The machine actually looked more miserable than he usually did.

"Yeah," Torres said softly. "When we didn't go right away, more Antis started showing up. We've been on the run ever since." She sighed, and the exhalation seemed to drain her completely. "Look, we're almost . . . we're almost where we need to go. Can we just please just get there and then we'll talk?"

The need to ask questions was overwhelming. It occurred to Johnny that this was exactly how Trist must have felt when they were in the woods. He glanced at Kesi and Dillac. "Okay," he said. "I guess I can wait."

"Thank you," Torres said. They rolled a bit further, then stopped in front of a ring of circles in the floor. Torres looked at Dillac. "Holding hands again." The skid, who had now been silent for longer than any time Johnny had known him, was staring at the broken lines of light. "Yeah, sure," he murmured, taking Torres's hand.

This time the journey was short and painful. They emerged into a wide black space filled with golden grids of light: embedded in the floor beneath their feet, floating in a sky that seemed to stretch up forever, and even submerged below the floor—layer upon layer descending into the depths. In front of them, a massive black block, the thick golden lines around it bright and complete.

Kesi stared at the open space behind her. "Where the hole is the door we went through?" Her voice was strained, but she was holding it together. They all were, even Dillac, although the change from familiar woods to the weird black-gold glow of the Thread had shocked most of them into silence. Johnny glanced at Krugar; the soldier hadn't spoken recently. He caught Johnny's look, nodded once, then went back to studying the environment.

"We'll talk in here," Torres said, "but it probably won't make your head any less messed up." Raising her voice, she said: "Hey, open up, we're here."

The golden lines moved and formed into a door. They rolled into a room filled with hollas. They lined the walls and ceiling, dozens and dozens of them, flickering with a bright light that filled the room. By a bank on the far side, a familiar shape.

"Torg!" Shabaz cried, gunning forward.

"Nice to be recognized," Torg drawled, spreading his arms wide before bumping treads with her. "You, sweetheart, are a sight for sore stalks."

"Sweetheart," Shabaz beamed. "I like that."

"Great," Johnny said, rolling forward. "I've been looking for a cute nickname for weeks and you come up with one in ten seconds." He stopped in front of Torg. If he'd been forced to quantify the feelings coursing through his stripe at that moment, he doubted he could've done so. "Old panzer," he said simply.

"Dumb squid." Torg held the gaze, then a huge smile split his stripes and he spread his arms. "Speaking of skids I'm glad to see."

"We can get caught up later," Torres said shortly. "How are we doing?"

"No," Kesi said firmly. Two of her eyes wandered over the hollas, wide with amazement. The third was hard and stared at Torres. "We can get caught up now. Reunions can wait."

"Straight snakes, squi," Dillac said. "It's answer time."

Torres looked like she was considering the light-sword again. "Listen—"

"No, you listen," Kesi said. She rolled forward and stabbed a finger at Johnny and Shabaz. "It's great that you all know each other and are going to tell each other stories, but we're not with them. They don't speak for us. You said we'd get answers when we got somewhere—well, this looks like somewhere." She poked an eye at Torg. "He's been here for a while, so it must be safe enough."

Torres gazed at her with a bemused expression, then looked at Johnny. "Doesn't anyone like you?"

"Hey!"

"I don't mind him much," Torg said.

"Me either," Shabaz murmured.

"*Stop it!*" Kesi yelled, popping a Hasty-Arm and slamming it down. "I'm not joking! We want some answers."

Torres looked like she wasn't going to respond, then her stripe tilted. "Okay, fine. What do you know already? I don't want to waste time."

"Not much."

Torres scowled at Johnny. "You couldn't have filled them in while you were fleeing?" She caught sight of Krugar leaning against a wall, scanning the flashing hollas. "By the way, does he talk?"

"I talk fine," Krugar said, continuing to study the hollas. "Right now I'm listening."

Torres grunted. "Him, I like." She turned back to Johnny. "Next time fill them in a bit, maybe?"

And that was just about enough. He'd been patient with an awful lot of things recently, but Torres was beginning to act like Albert. "Like you did on the way here?" he snapped. "No matter what it looks like, Kesi's right—we're not exactly all together. In fact, for a time there, we weren't together at all."

"All right, we get it," Kesi said, rolling her eyes. "Breaking off was a bad idea. Trist is dead—do you think maybe he paid a big enough price for not obeying the great Johnny and Shabaz?"

Torres barked a laugh and looked at Shabaz. "Ha, it used to just be Johnny Drop, but now they hate both of you. You're moving up in the world, sister."

Shabaz held her gaze. "Torres, you're starting to sound a lot like Albert and not in a good way. I don't know what happened in the last three months, but I get that it's not going well. But we're not the reason Betty's doing whatever she's doing."

"Who's Betty?" Kesi demanded.

"Betty Crisp," Torg said wearily.

"Betty Crisp is still alive?" Onna said incredulously.

"Yes," Torg sighed. "Although that has now come to have a number of meanings, depending on the skid."

"And she has Albert?" It was shocking to Johnny how upset he was that Albert wasn't here. The second he'd seen Torres and Wobble he'd expected to find Al behind him, undoubtedly with something critical to say. To his surprise, he'd been hoping for it.

"Maybe," Torg said.

"Not maybe," Torres snarled. "You think he's just gone for a roll, Torg? Your girlfriend's gone berk, deal with it." She turned on Johnny. "And someone better sound like Al. He's the only one who ever kept you in check."

"Torres," Shabaz snapped, her voice rising. "I love you like a sister but—"

"Can you freeze these?" Krugar said suddenly.

"What?" Torres asked.

"These holograms," Krugar said, pointing. "Can you pause them? Before they switch to another scene?"

They all hesitated. Then Torg said, "Sure. Which one?"

Krugar pointed at the ceiling. "That one. Two up from the wall, four over."

Torg went to a bank of controls. The holla in question froze on a jungle scene, a mountain top poking out from the trees.

"What's up?" Johnny said, watching Krugar.

Krugar stared at the scene, the light from the unfrozen hollas dappling his face. Then he grunted. "I know that place. I've been there." His head came down. "Except I've never been there." He took a deep breath, appearing to come to some inner conclusion. "All right. I understand that everyone has questions that need answered. But right now, I need that explained." He pointed at the holla. "Because I'm terrified. I can deal with fear, but I don't understand this at all. I feel like I'm going mad." His eyes swept the room. "What am I looking at?" He glanced at Shabaz. "Are any of these the place you came from?"

"Maybe," she said. "Not right now, but the sphere shows up from time to time."

"So they're real?"

Shabaz winced. "Yes and no."

"Explain that," Krugar snapped.

"It's all information," Johnny said, waving his hands at the hollas. "Everything you see here is part of a massive collection of information and data called the Thread. Everything in it—the Skidsphere, your home, those woods we went through to get here, where we are now—it's all just information." Remembering Betty, he rapped his hand off one of the holla banks. "All of it. Including us. We're all programs inside it."

"How is that possible?" Krugar said, stunned.

Not: *impossible*. Johnny's first thought when Betty had explained the Thread was to disbelieve what he was hearing; he could see that disbelief on the faces of the skids around him who'd never left the Skidsphere. But Krugar was, already, instinctively believing it.

The soldier scowled and looked back at the hillside he'd recognized. "Why would . . . ?" He stopped. "Levels . . ." He paused, sorting it out, then looked at Shabaz and said, "You said your kind played games. That's what you said—*games*. Where you kill each other. Why?"

The intensity rolling off him was astonishing. "Listen . . ." Johnny said, trying to protect Shabaz.

"You don't have to get it perfect," Krugar said, exasperated. "Just what you know." He waved at the hollas again. "These aren't for us, are they?"

The soldier was making leaps faster than Johnny could fathom. "No," he said uncertainly. "They're not. We play them for something we've always called the 'Out There.'" Krugar looked up and Johnny shivered in his stripe. That was exactly where a skid looked when the Out There was mentioned. "We don't know exactly who the Out There are, but a . . ." he glanced at Torres and Torg ". . . a friend of mine was pretty sure they existed and that they were the ones who created the Thread."

Krugar took some time to absorb that, but not as much as Johnny would have expected. "So you're entertainment. Like sports."

He didn't know what sports were but it sounded right. Leaps and bounds. "Sure."

Krugar took another second. "And my world?"

"Uhh . . ."

"Because in my world we have programs. We have games. And some of those games involve soldiers like me killing other soldiers. I know because we play them around the base sometimes."

What?! Johnny thought, stunned. The idea that a part of a game would play the game it was part of was something Johnny could not wrap his stalks around at all. But more importantly, Krugar had just—with very little information—summed up who he was and where he came from.

"That's it, isn't it?" Krugar said. "Please, just tell me what you know."

"Okay, and again, I'm just going off what someone told me but . . . yeah. You're part of a war game where . . . where everyone kills everyone until everyone's dead. Then you all start again." As he said it, it sounded horrible. The concept *was* horrible, even worse than the Skidsphere. Johnny remembered how much it had bothered Albert.

Krugar listened without flinching and then asked, "War or battle?"

"I'm sorry?"

"Is the game the whole war or just a battle?"

Johnny had no idea where Krugar was going with this line of questioning. "I don't know."

"How long does each . . . ?" Krugar frowned, figuring it out, as if he were trying to remember something. "God, it's been a long time since I hung out in the barracks. How long does each session take? From the beginning when we start killing each other, to the part where we're all dead?"

Johnny swallowed. Now he understood. "Two weeks. Roughly. Then . . . then the system resets." Although the soldier was no longer inside the game, Johnny didn't know if Krugar would reset when his game did. Which meant it was possible he only had two weeks to live.

But apparently Johnny hadn't understood why Krugar was asking after all. "Laleh . . ." the soldier said, and he collapsed against one of the banks.

"Whoa," Johnny said, rolling forward, but Krugar stuck out a hand. He held it there for a long moment, as around them hollas flickered from scene to scene, snapshots of a million different places, a million different lives.

Finally, his hand dropped and Krugar raised his head. His eyes were wet, but his face was set and dry. "I can deal with death. I've had men and women under my command die. Friends. I deal with death because . . ." His face flinched. "Doesn't matter. We deal. But I have a wife. Laleh. And she isn't a soldier. She has no part in what I do; she stays as far away from it as she possibly can. With my kids, Aden and . . ." For a second, his whole face spasmed, as if he were going to lose the struggle with what he was trying to keep down. "Huma," he said finally, swallowing hard. "They had no part of the fight I left when I came here. I haven't seen them in two months." He took a deep breath. "So if what you're telling me is true, then my wife and kids . . . then they . . . then they don't exist. They never existed. My past is a lie." He looked at Johnny. "Right?"

The emotion coming off of Krugar—even when it was clear that the soldier was holding the vast majority of it in check—was astounding. Johnny stared at him, appalled. He had never seen anyone care about anything like this. He thought about how he'd felt about Peg. About how he now felt about Shabaz. Even that paled before what he was seeing.

Betty, he thought. Betty had talked about the Skidsphere like this. That first time, when she'd put it in stasis to save it; the intensity at times she'd get that made Johnny wonder if she was truly sane. That's how Krugar looked now, except he was holding it in and it was for only three people. It was awful.

"Listen . . ."

Krugar held up a hand. "No sympathy. Just the truth."

Johnny swallowed. "Like I said, I don't know exactly how your part of the Thread works but, yeah . . . they probably don't exist."

Snakes, he felt like a jackhole.

Krugar stared at him for a minute more, then he did the most amazing thing. He straightened up and it was like he put the whole thing away. "All right," he said. "All right. I'm going to need a moment." He looked at Torres. "Is this place safe? At least for a while?"

"For a while," Torres said, guardedly.

"Fine," Krugar said. "You . . . you all get whatever you need sorted out. I'll just be over here." He walked over to a corner, not far from the image of a hill that had set off this whole conversation.

After a short while, his shoulders began to gently shake.

CHAPTER THIRTEEN

"Snakes," Onna whispered, watching Krugar. "That was awful."

Yeah, Johnny thought. He doubted any of them had any idea of just what the soldier was going through. His own love for Shabaz was beyond anything he'd ever felt before, and even that seemed insignificant in the face of the soldier's loss. Although, as he looked at Shabaz, he had a sudden vision of living without her and a wave of emptiness swept through his skin that threatened to overwhelm him.

She must have seen it, because an awkward smile crossed her face, and she mouthed the words, "I know." Which just made the sensation increase.

"Okay," he said out loud, trying to control himself. "Let's give Krugar some space. In the meantime . . ." He looked at the flickering walls, trying to make sense of what he was seeing. He remembered the bunker where they'd first met Betty, how overwhelming the whole thing had seemed: the Thread, the Out There, the danger to the Skidsphere.

This seemed worse.

"How could Betty go nuts?" he said. "Wobble, have you tried talking to her?"

"Dropped the call and three metres short-short of the line," Wobble whispered in reply, his lens shutters tilting into an angle of pain. "I-We-I have failed-failed. Wobble."

"You didn't fail, Wobble," Torg said immediately. He looked at Johnny. "He didn't go with Al when he was captured. There were too many things going on, Al didn't want to spare anyone else. We were working on the missing Wobbles, the ones SecCore made and then destroyed. Albert thinks there's a way to make more, so we were working on that. At the same time, we were trying to map the Thread to find the damage already done. We were trying to find all of Betty's old camps." He looked around. "That's what this is. This is Betty's biggest stronghold. You remember the one we were going to go to?"

Before the raid on the Core. Before Aaliyah and Brolin had died.

"How can we possibly be safe here?" Shabaz said. "From Betty?"

"She already checked for us. Wobble gave us a little warning and we were able to vacate when she came. Then we came back when she left."

"Wobble's got some kind of tie to Betty," Torres said. "It's sporadic, but sometimes he knows she's coming." Her expression fell. "That's how we knew she took Albert."

At one time, Johnny had thought that Wobble might be in touch with the whole Thread, that he might feel it every time something broke. The machine had been with Betty for so long, it wasn't surprising they had some kind of connection.

"Wobble, you can't contact her now?" he asked. All he got in response was a metallic whine. "Okay, so how do we know what she's doing?"

"We don't," Torres said. "All we know is after the battle she got way deep into the Core and somehow became part of it. She's been trying to kick SecCore out ever since."

SecCore had been a huge pain in their stripes the first time Johnny had fallen into the Thread. On the other hand . . . "Isn't SecCore also fighting the Vies?"

"Do we really want him gone?" Shabaz added.

"Not a chance," Torres said. "He's a megalomaniac and he's horribly misguided, but the minute Betty started trying to wipe him out, he's had to focus far more of his attention on surviving. Here, take a look. Torg?"

Torg merged four hollas into a larger holla. A new image appeared.

"Betty Crisp," Shabaz murmured.

"What is that?" Akash said.

"That's a war," Krugar said, coming out of the corner. He nodded once at Johnny, then turned his attention back to the holla Torg had made.

They were looking down on the Core from a great height, the cylindrical chasm sinking deep into the plain surrounding it. None of them knew how deep the Core went, but even from this distance they could see flashes of black and white, far inside. Johnny had seen it before, a black and white kaleidoscopic battle between the Vies and Antis. But this battle was sped up and ratcheted to insane levels. It was hard to look at; the flashes were so frequent it made his skin buzz. Plus, there was something . . .

"What am I not getting?" He stared at the hypnotic carnage. "This isn't just more intense, something else is different than before."

"Oh, snakes," Shabaz said, looking at Torg. "It's who's attacking who. Is that it?"

Torg bobbed an eye. "The Vies are attacking Antis, the Antis are attacking Vies. That hasn't changed. But now . . . Antis are also attacking Antis."

They were going to tear the Core apart. Johnny could see it, despite the distance. Crisp Betty, he could *feel* it.

"We can't get a closer view," Torres said. "It seems to tip Betty off. That's the crazy thing. Both she and SecCore are still splitting their focus, but they can't do it enough. Some of the Antis have gone rogue, no longer with either SecCore or Betty. They're just roaming through the Thread. Some still hunt Vies, but some are just doing damage. So there are fewer of them hunting Vies."

"Which means more Vies," Shabaz whispered.

"And that's not even counting the damage that the battle itself is doing. Everything is breaking faster." Torres looked disgusted. "Here's the truth: the Thread could last another hundred years, maybe a thousand. Or with the damage that's getting done, it could end tomorrow. If we don't find a way to stop this, it could go bad . . . *fast*."

Johnny couldn't help but keep one eye on the war in the Core. "How the hole do we do that?"

"We have to get SecCore and Betty to work together," Torg said firmly.

Torres barked a laugh. "Yeah, like that's going to happen. She's gone spare, Torg, accept it."

"It doesn't change what we need to do," he said, an edge in his voice Johnny had rarely heard. He looked at Johnny. "We're going to go talk to Betty."

Johnny frowned. "Didn't Albert already try that? Didn't you already turn down an invitation to talk?"

"This time we'll have Wobble and Torg with us," Torres said. "We're hoping that maybe the gearbox will listen to reason from people she likes." Torres made a snorting sound that made it clear exactly what she thought of that. "Who knows, maybe it works. Doesn't matter, that's not why we're going. The whole thing's just a feint."

"For what?" Krugar asked.

"We want to get Wobble close enough to Betty and the Core that he can scan her, find out where Albert is. So we can go rescue him."

Johnny looked at Wobble. "Can you do that?"

One of Wobble's shutters clicked halfway shut. He really did look much worse than he ever had before. "The dice-dice may be flat. I-We are uncertain, but We-I have hope-hope. Wobble."

"Wait," Kesi said. "Didn't you say Betty—who I still can't believe is alive—didn't you say she already captured this squid Albert when he went and talked to her? What's to stop her from doing the same with us?"

"For one thing, we're going in more wary than Al did," Torres said. "Second, we're betting on how much she likes Wobble and Torg." She snorted again and looked at Johnny. "Come to think of it, now we got you as well. She always did like you more than Al."

"Hey," Johnny protested, but before he could defend himself, Shabaz rolled forward. "Kill that gear," she snapped. "That's grease and you know it, Torres. Fighting isn't going to get us anywhere." When Torres opened her mouth to respond, Shabaz added, "And if you say I'm only saying this because I'm with Johnny, then fine—that's part of it. But it's not the whole thing and you know that too." Her voice softened. "You're angry, Torres, I get it. Don't take it out on us."

Torres stared at her, her lips pressed shut. Then her stripe flushed. "What you're doing in the games . . . it's good." Shabaz blinked in surprise. "You too, Johnny, the Combine thing—that's really cool. But working the talented ones in the games, maybe getting them to Ten? That's . . . Albert thought that was interesting. And spending time with the five-year-olds, that's nice."

"Thank you, Torres. That's kind of you to say."

Torres chuckled and the orange stripe regained its colour. "Don't think me too sweet. And you're wrong, I have plenty of reasons to be angry with you and Johnny." She looked around the room. "Six to be exact. It's nice you guys are here, but you brought baggage." She eyed Dillac. "No offence."

To Johnny's surprise, the crimson skid grinned. "Hey, candy-stripes, if you don't like the package, don't take it out of the box."

"What does that even—?" Torres shook her stalks. "Never mind. Anyway, we have to figure out what to do with these guys while we go talk to Betty."

"We come with you," Onna said quickly.

"Yeah, *okay*."

"I'm serious."

"No, you're not. You might not know it, but you're really not. The place we're going is dangerous, so you're going to stay here and—"

"This place is dangerous," Onna said, and the ferocity with which she said it made Torres stop. "You said that, right? On the run, etcetera. This is Betty's old base—you don't think she might come and find it again?"

"We have been expecting that," Torg said evenly, glancing at Torres.

"Right. So we're not safe here. Besides, skids don't sit

out the race." She poked an eye at Krugar. "We already know he can handle himself. You really think he—I'm sorry, what was your name again?"

"Krugar," he replied politely.

"Krugar. You planning on just waiting here and watching all the pretty pictures?"

An amused smile crossed the soldier's face. "Wasn't my first choice, no."

"Didn't think so." She looked back at Torres. "This friend of yours, Albert. He important?"

Torres held her gaze. "Yeah."

"He might help keep us alive?"

"He'll do more than that."

"Fine," Onna said firmly. "Then he's my friend too. I'm coming."

Torres stared at her for a long moment, amusement battling with exasperation. "How old are you?" she said finally.

"What? What does that have to do with anything?" Onna jabbed a finger at her stripes. "I'm a Level Four."

"No, not levels—age. In years."

"Oh," Onna blinked. "Uh . . . I'll be two in a month."

"Huh," Torres grunted. Amusement was winning out. It occurred to Johnny that Onna might be physically older than Torres. It was easy to forget that less than three months ago, Torres had been a panzer. "Kinda young to make Four," the purple skid said.

Onna exhaled, exasperated. "I learn fast."

"I'll bet," Torres murmured. "How about that, older than me."

"Well, she's not older than me," Torg drawled.

"Wait, what?" Onna said.

Torres looked back at white-red skid. "You tend to

learn fast out here. Live a week or two, you'll see." She let the gaze linger.

To Johnny's surprise, Onna flushed and looked away. Then she immediately looked back and held Torres's gaze. "I'll do that. Let's start by going to get your friend." She turned to Akash. "You in?"

Now that's not fair, Johnny thought. *Of course he's in if you're asking.*

"Of course," Akash said immediately.

"Me too," Zen said, although he sounded terrified.

It really wasn't fair. Johnny didn't want to take their decision from them; he'd learned that the hard way when Bian, Shabaz, and Torg had insisted on coming with him and Betty into the Core. Sometimes having friends was a good thing. But by the time they'd made that choice, they'd known what was going on. They'd had some survival experience. Akash and especially Zen were getting thrown right into the ether.

"Are you sure, Zen?" he said gently. "I'm sure we could find a place to hide you."

Zen looked like that was exactly what he wanted to do. "You always told us," he said in a shaky voice, as if he were testing a theory, "that in Tag Box, if we just hide in the corners then sooner or later we'll die. No one makes it past panzer playing that way. If you want to survive, you move from place to place."

"That's good advice," Krugar said.

Zen's eye flickered in his direction, then he seemed to steady. "Then I'll move from place to place with you. Whatever you need, I'll try to help. You and Shabaz already saved me at least once."

"Sure as sugar," Onna said. She sent a challenging glare at Kesi and Dillac. "How about you two?"

"I'm not staying here," Kesi said instantly. Which wasn't quite the same as saying she'd join them, but it was a start.

"True too," Dillac agreed. "Ain't gonna miss the party, boz." For the life of him, Johnny had no idea what made him roll.

"Okay, everyone comes," Torres said, giving in. "Try to stay alive. And when we get where we're going, no one talks but Wobble, Torg, or me." She grunted and poked an eye at Johnny and Shabaz. "Maybe them. Got it?" She gave Dillac a hard look, but the crimson skid was picking at something in his teeth. Torres sighed. "I guess if you're all coming, we need to get you outfitted."

As Torres took the others to the lockers, Johnny rolled away from the group, creating a little space. He could get a weapon later, but for now, he needed the space. Badly.

Betty was alive. Betty had gone insane. Betty was now a threat to the Thread and was hunting them down. He couldn't wrap his mind around it. For the second time, he wished Albert was here.

Amazing, he thought.

His gaze wandered over the hollas, a familiar sense of wonder washing over him. So many different environments, so many unique creatures. The sheer variety. There were highlights of everything, including the skids; every few minutes a holla would flash something from the sphere.

It took him a few moments to realize that, under the awe, he felt a creeping sense of unease. One of the hollas in the top corner went black for a few seconds before moving on to an image of buildings that rose and fell like waves. Then another scene went momentarily black further down. Then another. A chill went through his stripe as he thought of the blank spots in the hallways where there should have been doors—data that had been broken or lost.

He tried to remember if there'd been any broken spots in that hallway of hollas they'd discovered, not long after meeting Wobble for the first time. He didn't remember any. They might have happened—on the wall, another scene went dark—but they certainly hadn't happened with this frequency.

Torg rolled up beside him. "Pretty amazing," he murmured.

"Yeah," Johnny said. "What's with the blackouts?"

"Noticed that, did you? They've been happening more and more. Whatever those hollas where showing, it ain't there no more." He grimaced. "It's breaking, Johnny. And she's making it worse."

Johnny's eyes came down from the hollas and settled on his old friend. "Why didn't you go talk to her? She'd have listened to you. She liked you."

"I don't think that matters anymore." There was a bitterness in his voice Johnny had never heard inside the sphere. "She sent knives after us, Johnny. She's obsessed with SecCore—who knows how many times he tried to kill her over the years? She thinks she's the good guy."

Shabaz rolled over. "Torres says we're ready." She studied them both. "You okay?"

"Sure," Torg said, the bitter still lingering in his tone. "Let's go."

They found Krugar playing with a stick. He pressed a button and the stick emitted a soft hum. With a click the stick extended and sprouted perpendicular bars at the top and the bottom, four feet apart. The bottom bars bobbed off the ground. "Heh," Krugar said with a grin, stepping onto the bottom bars.

"We needed to find him some speed," Torres explained. "We might need it." She looked at Krugar. "Twist the top for velocity, tilt to turn."

"Nice," Krugar said, hitting the red button again and the stick retracted to its original size. He checked his weaponry. The rest of them all held rifles, looking at the guns with everything from fear to confusion. Torres tossed one to Johnny.

"You able to create these?" he asked, examining it.

"You mean like by the Spike?" Torres asked, amused. "Haven't been able to since Bian." She looked at Shabaz. "You?"

Shabaz pressed her lips together in frustration. "No."

"Yeah," Torres said.

"You have the light-swords," Johnny said.

"They're small enough to store. Stole them when we went on an ammo run. But creating one out of thin air, like we did before . . . we haven't been able to do it again." Her stripe tilted. "We put the vaping sphere back in place, but I can't program a simple pistol."

She handed Torg a large gun that looked familiar. "Good to go?"

"As good as we'll get. Wobble, are you sure you're up for this?"

The machine looked miserable but resolute. "Aff-affirmative."

"All right," Torres said, rolling towards the door. "Let's go talk to the queen."

CHAPTER FOURTEEN

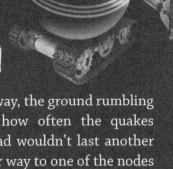

They rolled down a broken hallway, the ground rumbling beneath their treads. Given how often the quakes happened, it felt like the Thread wouldn't last another ten minutes. They were on their way to one of the nodes that would get them into the Core. The plan was to meet Betty further out, on the plains. Johnny had no idea how that was supposed to work, but he figured Torres, Torg, and Wobble were good for it.

Or at least, he hoped they were good for it. When Wobble had first reappeared, Johnny hadn't noticed anything wrong—Wobble had torn through the horde of grey skids as ruthlessly as he'd always dealt with threats. But over the last few hours, Johnny realized there was something deeply wrong with the machine. He'd always looked battered, but he'd always repaired any new damage. Now it was like Wobble had given up. In addition to the hitch in his stride, the one broken lens, and the broken arm he always displayed, one of his treads was loose, and scuffs and scar-marks covered his body.

More troubling was the expression of pain that kept creeping across Wobble's face. Johnny still didn't know how a set of lenses and shutters could be so expressive, but they were. Before, Wobble's default expression seemed to be one of wonder, with the occasional sadness. Now, it was like every few minutes Wobble saw something awful. It was like he was watching the universe die.

Once, Wobble had told Johnny about the Thread breaking, and when Johnny had said he couldn't do anything about it, Wobble had said someone should.

Given the expression on the machine's face, someone better do it soon.

Of course, Wobble wasn't the only one haunted. Johnny had spent the last ten minutes fastidiously ignoring the flash of pink in his trail-eye.

Johnny . . .

It definitely wasn't Bian this time. Johnny flicked a nervous glance towards the middle of the pack, where Shabaz was telling Onna, Akash, Krugar, and Zen about their first time in the Thread. Kesi and Dillac lingered nearby, desperately trying to appear like they weren't listening.

Johnny didn't want to see Peg. He certainly didn't want Shabaz to see him seeing Peg. No matter what he and Peg had—and there was always a pang in his centre when he thought of her—it was nothing like his developing feelings for Shabaz. He didn't want to hurt Shabaz. He certainly didn't want her thinking—

What? he thought, suddenly feeling defensive. He wasn't doing anything. It wasn't his fault there was a pink flash. "Go away," he growled, half to himself, half back down the hall.

The pink flash did not go away.

He dropped back a touch more and swung his second eye. And there she was: Peg, following just behind.

Betty had said she was a ghost, something Johnny had created, but apparently Betty had said lots, and the skid behind him didn't look like a figment of anything. "Stop following me," he hissed. "I'm busy." Which was a stupid thing to say, but what was he supposed to say, anyway?

"You need to show her," Peg said suddenly.

Just great. Betty had said she wouldn't speak, but apparently that wasn't true, either. Johnny sent another guilty glance at Shabaz. "What are you talking about? Show who what?"

"You need to show her the map or she'll never see. And hurry: they're coming."

"Who's coming?" Johnny demanded. "What are you—?"

"Everything okay here?" Shabaz said, rolling up.

Snakes, he'd taken his eye off Shabaz for one second. "What?" he said, glancing at Peg. Gone. He was pretty sure he hadn't taken an eye off her at all. "Yeah . . . I'm fine."

"You sure?" Shabaz said, looking past Johnny. He thought he heard an edge in her voice.

"Yeah," he said, defensive again. "I just needed a moment to myself. You got a problem with that?" He saw her gaze widen and realized that maybe there hadn't been an edge in her voice after all, or, even if there had, his own tone was too much—snakes, why had he said it like that?

"Nope," she said, spinning around. "Take all the private time you need. Although you better hurry, Torres says we're almost there."

Then how am I supposed to take all the time I need? he thought as she rolled away, a wash of emotions spilling through him. He was pretty sure he'd just been a jackhole. He should apologize. Except, there might have been a tone, so she's the one who should—

He rolled his eyes. Yep: jackhole.

"Hey, Johnny, care to join us?" Torres yelled.

"Coming," he muttered, with one final look down the hall. Getting haunted sucked large.

"Okay," Torres said as he rolled up, "some of you know how this works. The rest just hold on. We won't be going far in. Again, no one who doesn't know what's-what speaks. And if things go sideswipe, grab a hand, follow orders and get in between Johnny, Shabaz, Torg, or me."

"Glad we could help," Dillac muttered.

"What was that?" Torres said sweetly.

"You gots a smart plan, mama smart boss woman squi."

Torres grimaced and looked at Kesi. "I swear he got vaped a few too many times." She reached forward. "Hold on to your stripes."

The world twisted, shimmered with golden light, then settled into a familiar place. Of course, just because it was familiar didn't mean it was any less awe inspiring. As they emerged onto the outer Core, with its linked squares of golden light beneath their feet and what might have been the entire Core flipped upside down and doming the space far above, Johnny heard half a dozen sucked in breaths. Even Dillac muttered, "Whoa, boz."

"Stay close together," Torres said. "Torg?"

"Nothing." His stripes tilted. "Let's hope they can't see us yet."

"Wobble, you ready if things go upslope?"

"Affirmative."

Johnny rolled over to Shabaz. "Sorry," he said, trying not to sound sullen. Snakes, he was terrible at this. "I snapped, I think. Shouldn't have done that."

She looked at him for a long moment, the distant gold lights from the sky reflected in her eyes. "Okay," she said, her lips twitching into a smile. "I might have done the same. We're all a little spare. Everyone's frightened of Betty, even the new ones."

"I don't think Torres is scared," Johnny smirked. "I think she's scary."

"Can you blame her?" When he grimaced, she added, "No, think about it. When we left them, the Skidsphere had been saved. The Thread might have been broken, might have been dangerous, but it wasn't on the verge of collapse. The skid she admired, Albert, was leading them and had stepped up his game. They felt they had a shot at finding Betty, who saved us all, who we all worshipped. Now Betty's gone spare, the Thread could end tomorrow and Albert's not there to lead her. She isn't scary, Johnny: she's scared."

That . . . made sense. After all they'd been through, hope mattered. That's what had led Johnny back to the Combine, that's what had made Shabaz start helping every skid she could in the games. And even though they weren't happy with everything and could feel the pressure of time pressing against everything they tried to do, they'd still had more than a year left to try and do it. The Skidsphere had been saved, it wasn't going anywhere. The Thread was so large, you couldn't imagine it collapsing. But now . . .

As if on cue, the ground rumbled. "Yeah, okay, scared it is. I get it." Although, Torres still had her manic grin and the light-swords. "Maybe a little of both." He considered the skid in question, his gaze lingering on her single orange stripe. "Interesting that she ended up in charge instead of Torg."

Shabaz chuckled. "Torg's great, but he's not going to lead a group of anything." She sighed. "Poor Torg. It might be worse for him than anyone. I think he really liked Betty."

"Yeah," Johnny said. An abrupt stab went through his heart. "And then there's Wobble."

"Yeah," Shabaz agreed sadly, watching the machine. She reached out and squeezed Johnny's hand.

"Okay," Torres announced. "We're about as ready as we're going to get." She took a deep breath. "Wobble, drop the shields."

There wasn't any warning. To Johnny it was as if Torres finished her sentence and then, instantly, Betty was sitting in front of them.

"So," the oldest skid in the universe said. "The gang's all here."

CHAPTER FIFTEEN

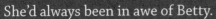

She'd always been in awe of Betty.

Sure, coming up through the Skidsphere, Shabaz had known about Johnny, who didn't? And sure, she'd had a couple of fantasies about a grind in the woods with the most popular skid in the sphere, something she was *never* going to tell him. Although, if she was honest, she'd always thought Albert was the sexier one—that brooding thing, the silver shine . . . yeah, she was never going to tell Johnny that, either. Nevertheless, she'd had her sense of adoration about the two leading skids of the day.

But Betty . . . she'd worshipped the idea of Betty Crisp. Any time a holla ran about the black and pink legend, Shabaz would stop what she was doing, watching out of the corner of her eye 'cause it wasn't cool to watch hollas of someone else, even if it was Betty-freakin'-Crisp. She remembered the day she'd stopped during the Rainbow Road—she'd been going to lose anyway—at the exact spot Betty had begun the Leap, the moment she'd been remembered for more than any other, even her record on the Slope, the moment that had been so famous GameCorps had created a game based on the feat.

Shabaz remembered angling an eye over the edge of the brilliant multicoloured road and immediately pulling it back. Beneath her, nothing but black. Okay, fine, there were the rainbow ribbons of the multi-level track far below, but they were *far* below, barely a thread in the eviscerating darkness. How the hole could you possibly hit one? And which thread to aim for? And how had she even known that she'd be allowed to do it; how had she known that the space in-between the threads above and below weren't going to just vape her like the blackness all around?

To do something like the Leap required a courage and imagination that Shabaz had never possessed. To do something like that . . . she'd never had that in her stripes. You had to be . . .

You had to be mad, Shabaz thought, years later, staring at her idol, the vast space of the Thread stretching out in every direction.

Betty sat there, looking as calm and assured as she had that first day they'd met her, in that lost node in front of her hollas. Muttered whispers of awe broke out behind Shabaz, the new skids feeling just like she had a few months ago. Betty sat on her treads like the only solid thing in the world. Why not, she was the skid who'd saved them all, the skid who'd survived ten times longer than any skid ever had, the skid who'd led them into battle and into the Core.

Of course, she was also the skid who'd put the Skidsphere into stasis to save it. There'd been a madness in her eyes when she'd done that—Shabaz remembered that.

That same madness was in her eyes now. In fact, if you looked closely, it was in more than her eyes: it was in the tension in her flat-black skin, it was around the edges of her single pink stripe, the edges blurring as if they vibrated at the wrong frequency, as if the stripe were a wire strung too tight.

On second glance, Betty didn't look solid. She looked like she was about to explode.

Shabaz tensed as Betty's gaze settled on Johnny. "I thought you went home."

Shabaz knew if there was one skid in the universe more in awe of Betty than she was, it was Johnny. She had no idea what he was feeling, but her heart ached at the expression on his face. The tension was horrible—she wanted to reach out and protect him from it, just a little if she could.

A small smile quirked at the side of his lips. It was a new trait, but one Shabaz already loved. "Turns out that's harder to do than you'd think."

The eye on Johnny stayed while a second looked out over the group. A smirk crawled across her lips, a very different smile than the one Johnny wore. "Poor Johnny Drop," Betty said finally. "Can't go anywhere without an entourage, can you?"

Shabaz stared at her, stunned. Before, Betty had teased them, sparred with Bian, even said the hard truths that hurt to be heard. But Shabaz had never heard her be mean before. Without even realizing it, she rolled forward and said, "Hey! That's not fair."

Slowly, the eye swung. "Ah, the complainer. How do you find competing with ghosts, Shabaz?"

For a second, Shabaz thought she was going to cry. Stunned, she sucked in her breath. She couldn't believe how cold . . .

She saw Johnny open his mouth to defend her and instantly all her emotions, warm and cold, coalesced into something hard along her stripes. Once, she'd flinched looking into the void. But she wasn't that skid any more, and as much as she adored Johnny for the thought, she didn't need him to defend her. Not here. Not now.

"Funny," Shabaz said stiffly. "I was going to ask you the same thing."

It was a dumb thing to say. Even as she said it, she realized that it didn't make any sense. Nevertheless, the eye on her widened then narrowed. "Fair enough," Betty said. The eye moved on, sweeping over Onna and the others, to settle on . . .

"Torg," Betty said softly.

"Betty," he replied.

She made a soft sound, hurt and disappointed. "You used to call me sweetlips. I liked that."

Torg gave her a long look, and then sighed. A little of the old Torg crept into his tone. "I liked that too. I live in hope that we may have an opportunity to do so again."

This time Betty's smile was genuine. "I hope so too."

"Do you?" Torres said, rolling forward. "Do you really?"

Betty's expression hardened once more. "I was going to say something about you missing someone . . ." She hesitated, watching Torres flinch, then she sighed and added, "But that would have been mean. And I'm not trying to be mean. I'm . . . I'm sorry, Shabaz, for what I said. You too, Johnny."

"Don't worry about it."

Betty looked at Torres. "You wonder if I still have hope that we can be friends. Of course I do. Please tell me you're here to help."

"Where's Albert?"

"How about you answer my question first, Torres."

"All we've ever done is try to help," Torres protested. "Where's Albert?"

Betty's lips quirked at the corners. "How do you know he isn't working for me? How do you know I didn't send him on some secret mission?"

It was Torg who broke the skeptical silence that followed. "Did you do that, Betty? Is that what happened?"

Betty held his gaze for a moment, then her eye dipped. "No," she said. "No, that isn't what happened."

"Where is he?" Torres said, her voice strained.

"That's not important," Betty said, drawing in a ragged breath. "We can still—"

"Where is he?"

"I AM FIGHTING A WAR!" Betty screamed, and somehow, in that wide open space, her voice boomed and seemed to echo off some far distant wall. The ground trembled. "You have no idea, you—" She stopped abruptly, her stripe hardening into a bar. "I'm not doing this again. If you won't help, I have too many things—"

"What happened in the Core?" Johnny said suddenly. He rolled forward. "I mean, after you stayed behind, Betty—what did you do? How did you survive?"

Shabaz was pretty sure the time for catching up had passed: Betty had that look she'd had when she'd put the sphere into stasis. Worse, there was a madness in her, and yet Johnny was asking for a history lesson. She was so baffled she almost missed it.

Ever so slightly Johnny's trail-eye twitched in the direction of Wobble. The one person who knew Betty better than anyone. The one person she'd steadfastly refused to look at yet. The reason they were actually here.

Wobble was supposed to be scanning Betty for information on Albert.

Shabaz had no idea how long that might take. It felt like they'd been stuck in this tension for hours, but it couldn't have been more than a few minutes. They needed more time. Making sure she didn't even glance in Wobble's direction, Shabaz rolled forward. "That's right—Betty, we don't know what happened. Can you tell us, please?"

"I'd be interested in hearing that," Torg drawled. The eye nearest her dipped a bit in recognition. "Come on, sugarlips, tell us a tale."

Betty drew herself back from whatever emotional precipice she'd dangled. She took another ragged breath. "Fine," she said. "I suppose you've at least earned that." She looked at Torg. "But only because you called me sugarlips."

She took a second, taking in the group, before looking back at the Core. She shivered. "After I closed you in," she began, "I dived as deep as I could. I wanted to get to SecCore, to stop him from interfering with you. It was . . . a close thing. I took a lot of damage, from Vies, from Antis. But I got through." She paused, the strain of that battle etched across her face. "I managed to embed myself in a part of the Core, then slowly, I began pushing SecCore out. It wasn't easy, but he's got his hands full."

Yeah, Shabaz thought, *defending the Thread*. SecCore might be a grease-bucket, but he was fighting for the same thing they were.

The tone in Betty's voice when she continued made Shabaz glad she hadn't voiced the thought out loud. "He's a cancer that needs to be cut out of the Thread," Betty said coldly. "We can't save the Thread until he's gone."

A long silence.

Then Johnny sighed. "Betty, I get it. You hate him and I understand why. Hole, he tried to kill you for fifty years. But isn't SecCore the Thread's defence system? Won't removing him make it worse?"

"Who says he's even defending the Thread anymore?" Betty insisted. "Didn't he try to stop you from repairing the Skidsphere?"

Johnny's eye dipped. "Sure. He's got some serious flaws. But Betty, I'll say it again: won't removing him make it worse? Isn't fighting him making it worse?"

For a moment, Shabaz prayed that she would listen to reason. She had to. She was Betty; she might go farther than any of them would, but she had to see the truth in the end. She'd never hidden from it before.

Then Betty's expression hardened and she snarled: "He is a *cancer*. He's a Vie. He's a dictator that wants power and nothing else. Everything he's done in the last fifty years—hole, maybe the last five hundred—has hurt the Thread, because he won't let anyone threaten his little corner of control. When someone tries to help, he kills them. Or don't you remember what happened to the other Wobbles? What happened to *him*?" Suddenly, a Hasty-Arm popped out, jabbing a finger at Wobble. *"You could at least look at me, dammit!"*

Slowly, gears and shutters whirred and Wobble's head rotated until two lenses faced Betty. The lids over his lenses were angled with a deep sorrow. "Empty beds and hallmarks in the rain-rain," Wobble said. "I-We am sorry-sorry, friend-Betty. You are hurting the Thread. You are hurting your friends. You are hurting yourself. Please."

Betty stared at him, her expression so intent it was

hard to look at. They'd known each other ten times longer than Shabaz had lived.

When she spoke, her voice was raw and stressed each word like it was a bruise. "Why won't you help me?"

The lens shutters angled a little more. "I-We are trying too."

Shabaz tried not to breathe. Surely, Betty had to hear, she had to understand. Shabaz felt like her heart was breaking; there was so much need in Wobble's voice—*how could a machine sound like that?* Surely, Betty couldn't possibly fail to hear that need? Without thinking, she glanced at Johnny, saw the same raw emotion she was feeling on his face, realized in that moment she might love him forever.

That was the moment that Betty said in a cold, cold voice, "Are you, Wobble? Is that why you're here?" Her eye swung towards Torres. "He's got what you came for. See if you live to use it."

A thousand Antis appeared in the sky.

CHAPTER SIXTEEN

He'd always been fast, so he saw it coming. He also had some familiarity with rage and betrayal.

So when Betty popped her Hasty-Arms at Wobble, Johnny very quietly popped his own. He heard the words that Wobble said, saw the look that crossed Shabaz's face, and wondered how there could be anyone—let alone two people—who cared so much. How could he have any hope of matching that caring?

Then he saw the look that came across Betty's face, and he knew that look. He had experience with that kind of rage. They'd come here to find the skid that had once made Johnny feel that angry. So he was already reaching for Onna and Akash when Betty said what she said; her words as cold as the Antis already falling from the sky.

He grabbed the two skids and pulled them in, even as he backed away from Betty, trusting Wobble or Torres to engage her. Out of the corner of his eye, he saw Shabaz grab Zen and shove Dillac back. Kesi was already backing away.

"Stay close," Johnny said sharply. "Don't let those white things touch you, try to keep me between them and you." He saw Wobble begin to transform. Torres ignited her light-sword. But neither of them were the first to hit Betty.

They'd all forgotten about Krugar.

A grenade landed at Betty's treads and exploded on contact. The concussion drove Johnny further back, even as a second grenade followed the first.

"We seem to be outnumbered," Krugar said, scanning the sky. "I take it those are bad guys."

"Depends who you ask," Johnny muttered. "Torres, we need an exit!"

"I'm working on it!" she yelled back. "I can't find it. Wobble, I need a door!"

"Negatory," Wobble said, even as familiar mounted guns appeared from compartments in his side, swung upwards, and unloaded on the Antis. "The signal is jammed."

"No," Torres said, her voice edging up to panic. "There has to be a door, there has to be—"

"Hey!" Krugar barked, bounding over to her in three long strides. The smoke around Betty began to swirl. "Plan A failed. What's plan B?"

Torres looked up at him, all three eyes filled with terror, looking ridiculously young. Which, of course, she was.

"All right, let's move!" Johnny said, pushing Onna and Akash.

"Where?" Onna said, frantically staring at the sky.

"Anywhere but here," Johnny said. "Everyone, follow me. Krugar?"

"On it," the soldier said calmly and fired another grenade into the smoke. *He must have caught her by surprise*, Johnny thought. He'd seen Betty take far more damage, but right now he didn't care. They needed space; they needed a plan. "Wobble, can you cover our retreat?"

"Affirmative," the machine said as the first Antis touched down. Wobble began to move at an almost unimaginable speed, saw-blades of fire swirling into each Anti as they landed.

"Right," Johnny said, and gunned it in the one direction he hoped Betty wouldn't expect: towards the Core.

"You sure this is a good idea?" Shabaz said, rolling up beside. She tapped an eye towards the Core. "Isn't that her home base now?"

"Any idea was a good one," Krugar said, pulling up on his light-stick. "We needed to move."

"Yeah," Johnny said, "but now we need a door. Torres, do you know another one?"

"No," Torres said, her voice filled with shame and anger and fear. "I mean, yes, but I don't know where it is."

"We need something," Johnny murmured. Behind them, a shape moved inside the smoke. The white shapes in the sky began to track them. "More speed, to start."

Something slammed him from the side, pushing him violently off course. "Hey!" he yelled, as he saw Kesi rebounding in the other direction. "What the—"

"You forgot about this the last time we took off from certain death." The teal-plum skid grinned back at him. "Thought you could use a reminder."

Despite the situation, he almost laughed. He had forgotten. Again. If he and Shabaz ever got back to the sphere, he was going to figure out a way to get some real action; he was game-slow, like thick grease.

"Come on, gear-suckers," Dillac cackled and rammed into Onna. "Bump and sprint, squi."

"You heard the man," Johnny yelled. "Bump and sprint." He banged off Shabaz, winking at her as he did. "Try to keep the less experienced skids between us." They accelerated, forming a winding, twisting snake that raced in the direction of the Core. White shapes landed behind, turned in that clean, sharp way the Antis had, and began to pursue.

More importantly, a black shape emerged from the smoke and began to accelerate in their direction. *Okay, now we need a plan.* "Torres, Torg," Johnny said aloud, "we could really use another door."

"The only ones we know about are on the far side," Torg said.

"How about ones you don't know about?" Shabaz said. "It doesn't matter where we end up right now, it just needs to be not here!"

"Wobble might be able to find one," Torres said. "Wobble, we need you!"

"Affirmative." The steady voice came over the com. "Incoming in thirty seconds."

"We might need him faster than that," Johnny murmured. They were holding ahead of the Antis behind, but only just. Off to their right, a massive jagged scar cut into the golden squares that sectioned the plain, stretching for miles. Johnny remembered it from the first time they'd approached the Core. Before, the scar had been a curiosity; now it was cutting off one direction of escape.

Behind them, Betty was gaining. Johnny had no idea how she was doing it without running into anyone; then again, he'd once seen her create jets out of her body and fly. He wondered why she wasn't doing it now. Maybe she knew she'd catch them.

Maybe she knew she didn't have to.

Far ahead, the light from the Core soared into the upper reaches of the sky. Against that light, shapes began to emerge and head their way.

"Johnny," Shabaz said.

"I see them."

"No. Not them. What do you see in the centre of that mass?"

Squinting, he scoped to his maximum. The white shapes gained definition and shape, gleaming with the reflected light of the Core. And in their centre, a round shape, heading their way.

Albert?

But the shape wasn't silver, and it didn't reflect light the way the Antis did. A sinking sensation sank into his stripe, as Johnny pushed his scope farther than he ever had before.

The shape was black.

With a single pink stripe.

Oh snakes, he thought. Betty was still behind them, gaining slowly. But in front, coming from the Core . . .

Far out in front, he could swear he saw the black shape grin.

"It's Betty," Johnny said, snapping his vision back. "She's vaping with us." He didn't understand how it was possible, but she was more experienced then all of them put together. She knew tricks he hadn't even thought of yet. She'd attached herself to the Core, which meant that when she'd met them she'd already been two places at once.

They really needed an exit.

The closest trailing Anti exploded and Wobble soared overhead. "Wobble," Johnny said, "can you find a door?"

"Negatory. Signal is still jammed." He screamed towards the oncoming Antis and their owner.

It wasn't going to be enough. There were too many already, with more still coming from the Core. Cut off forward and behind, it was left or right and right was cut off from that scar, still cutting through the plain.

That scar . . .

When they'd first come to the Thread, Betty had explained how everything was just a metaphor for the programs they represented: the way the Core appeared, the hallways they travelled, the skids themselves. Johnny remembered passing that scar in the plain, wondering just what it represented, how deep it went, where it led. . . .

"It just needs to be not here," he murmured.

He cut right.

"Everyone grab someone else!" he bellowed, popping his Hasty-Arms and clutching onto Akash as he rebounded in his direction. "Get tight and follow me!"

"Uh, Johnny?" Torg's voice came over the com. "I know it's been a while, but please tell me you're not thinking what I think you're thinking."

"If you have a better idea, I'm listening. Anyone?"

"Why, boz?" Dillac said. "What are we—oh, shiz."

"Wobble, slow them down. Then get back here, we might need a guide."

"Affirmative. Don't worry Cho-May, someone's got to run the Kessel someday."

"I sure hope it's us," Johnny said, squeezing Akash to his left and Zen to his right. He eyed Shabaz. "Please tell me you got a better idea. You're smarter than I am."

"You know, less than an hour ago I was thinking about the Leap. About how I never would've had the grease to try it. Lot changes in an hour."

Snakes, my girlfriend is as crazy as I am, Johnny thought. But a feeling for her surged through his skin like it was being driven by one of the pressure plates in the Combine. "I love you," he said out loud.

"Can we run the race we're in?" Kesi yelled.

"Yeah," Torres half-snarled, half-purred. "Save it for the woods." Apparently, she'd found her Torres again.

The scar grew quickly. Off to their right, Antis closed in, the original Betty gunning through them less than forty metres away. To their left, wave after wave of white, racing in from the Core. Wobble fired a final delaying shot, then turned and burned towards the line of fleeing skids.

Johnny suddenly remembered Betty's final words to Wobble: "You got what you were looking for." He hoped the machine knew Albert's location.

Then they hit the edge and, once again, Johnny was falling into the unknown.

CHAPTER SEVENTEEN

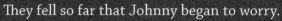

They fell so far that Johnny began to worry.

Three seconds, four seconds of falling; not into the black, just . . . falling. He felt that tightening surge in his stripe he felt any time he jumped off something particularly high; Up and Down was good for that, if nothing else.

Five seconds, six. The walls of the chasm raced by. Buried far inside them, the fractal grid that underlaid the Outer Core.

Okay, this is not too . . .

Black.

They plunged into the biting darkness, Johnny's hands reflexively clamping onto Akash and Zen, sending colour and names down the line. They could handle this. He didn't know where they were falling, and Crisp Betty he was tired of it, but they'd been here before, even the new ones, and they had Torres and Torg joining Johnny and Shabaz. He hated the biting sensation and he could feel Zen's horror, but they were all holding on. If Wobble caught up, they'd be all right.

As if on cue, a blaze of white appeared above and then dived below, matching speed just ahead of their fall. Wobble blazed a path through the inverted snowstorm of black shapes flurrying against his white light. No matter how long they fell, they should be able to—

Abruptly, the inverted snowstorm around Wobble vanished and, a heartbeat later, the biting sensation stopped.

What the—?

Then the snowstorm and biting returned. Then vanished. Then returned again, this time for a long stretch, although the severity of both lessened.

Then . . .

They fell through a darkness that did not attack.

"What the hole?" Shabaz said, and both she and Johnny realized she'd spoken out loud at the same time.

Ahead of them, Wobble remained the only light in the darkness. Over and over, he repeated the same words: "No end, this is the end, no end, this is the end . . ."

Off to their left, Wobble's light caught something. Then off to their right, and then again.

Then . . .

White light reflected off a clear surface that rushed up to greet them. At the last second, Wobble grabbed Johnny and blasted upwards, killing most of their momentum.

They still hit pretty hard.

Torg and Torres caught it the worst, each on an end of the chain, slamming into the surface with an impact that reminded Johnny of the time he'd won his second name. They weren't moving quite that fast—Wobble spared them the worst of it—but they both straightened their treads with a groan.

"I have most certainly not missed that particular aspect of the games," Torg sighed. "Is everyone okay?" He looked at Onna, who'd landed beside him. "You?"

"I'm fine," Onna said, shaking her eye-stalks and spitting blood. She glanced at Torres. "You guys got it the worst."

"Speak for yourself, squi," Dillac said, blinking rapidly as he popped a Hasty-Arm and flexed. "I think I sprained my chi."

"Pretty sure it was sprained already," Onna murmured.

Dillac gave her a look, then tilted his stripes. "True words."

Johnny rolled over to Shabaz. "You okay?"

A small smile. "I'd like to stop falling. Onto things, through things, over things. Seriously, can we do that?"

He smiled back and bumped her treads. "I'll see what I can do." He looked around. "Anyone know where we are?" Around them, complete blackness. No glowing lines, broken or whole. The white coming from Wobble was the only light, but it was bright enough to reflect off the surface of buildings that reached up into the darkness.

"No clue," Torres whispered, her eyes wide as she looked around.

They were on some kind of highway, the surface beneath them clear like black ice. A corridor perhaps; there were buildings on either side, stretching out ahead of them, maybe behind—it was hard to tell. Some of their surfaces reflected more light than others, what might have been windows: row upon row, column upon column. There was something vaguely familiar about the whole thing.

"Oh snakes," Johnny whispered, looking down. Wobble's light reflected off the glassy clear surface, but below that . . . below that, the light reflected faintly off another surface. And below that, very faint, another.

Johnny's eyes came up and he rolled over to one of the buildings. "Wobble, can I get a light over here?" The light swung and the building lit up in reflected ghostly glory, window upon window, stretching up until the light faded away.

Except they weren't windows. They were holla displays.

And they were all dead.

When they'd first fallen into the Thread, Wobble had found them and led them through a city of hollas. Now, they were in another one. Except the other city had been alive with light: thousands upon thousands of hollas, stretching up and down and along every corridor, enclosed by the sharp gold lines of the Thread itself, outlining every building. Here, the only light was Wobble.

"Crisp Betty," Shabaz swore. "Is this . . . ?"

"It's all dead-dead," Wobble said softly, his battered surface gleaming in his own light. "The archeologists just disappeared. All is silence-silence."

"All right," Johnny said, shuddering, "everyone stay tight, keep an eye out for Vies."

"What's a Vie?" Dillac asked.

"One of the spiky black bad guys."

"Unlike the knifey white bad guys or the spooky grey bad guys," Kesi said sarcastically.

"Or Betty freakin' Crisp, boz."

"Right," Johnny said, eyeing them both. "Starting to get it yet?" Kesi held the look for a minute, then rolled away, staring up at the buildings in awe. Johnny grit his teeth. He didn't need her to acknowledge him, but he did need her to get it. "Kesi, seriously, stay close, they can come right out—"

"They're not going to," Torg said, staring upwards.

"What?"

"I don't think we're going to see any Vies."

"Torg, every time we've been near anything broken . . ."

"This isn't broken." Torg popped an arm and ran a finger along one of the darkened displays. "This is dead." He waved the arm down the corridor. "The darkness was biting us, then it wasn't. Look around. Not one broken, sparking line of gold. Nothing. This is dead."

Johnny shifted nervously on his treads. "We still don't know if the Vies—"

"He's right," Krugar said abruptly, studying the buildings. "Vie stands for virus, right? Well, that means there has to be something alive for it to infect. There's nothing here."

"There's the buildings," Johnny said skeptically.

"They're just the shell, the bones. There's nothing here to infect."

Johnny peered down the corridors. The first time they'd seen the lit version, it had deeply disturbed him that the hollas ran but no one was watching. What that had meant for him, what it meant about the Out There. But if the hollas weren't even running . . .

"This is how it ends," he murmured, glancing at Wobble. The machine seemed to have shrunk in on itself, keening softly and rocking on its treads. Johnny rolled over and put a hand on its surface. "Wobble, are you all right? Does this hurt?"

Gears and lids spun. "No," the machine said. "I-We wish it would."

What could he say to that? Wobble was experiencing things on a level Johnny couldn't even comprehend. What could he possibly say that would make things better?

"Hey," he said, waving a Hasty-Arm around. "It doesn't have to end like this. The Skidsphere was in trouble, on its way to being just like this maybe." He shivered at the thought. "We stopped that from happening. We fixed it and you're a big reason why. We'll do it again."

It took some time, but slowly, the lenses shifted. "Thank you, Johnny-Johnny-friend."

Torres rolled over, her stripe twitching. "Wobble, I hate to do this, but I got to know: did you get it?"

Instantly, Wobble straightened up and his lenses spun as his metallic mouth split into a wide smile. "Affirmative! The hen clevered the fox! Wobble."

"Show me," Torres growled.

The lenses spun downward once more. "Inaccessible here-here. No maps. Regret and Listen waited-waited by the sea. Wobble."

"Oh," Torres said, deflating.

"That's fine," Torg said. "We'll find a way out of here and then we'll know. Right, Wobble?"

And the lens swung upward. "Affirmative."

"All right, all right," Torg said. He put a hand on Torres' stripe. "Don't worry, Torres, we'll find him."

"Right," Torres said. She grimaced, as if caring this much was embarrassing. "Good work, Wobble." She rolled back to the others and yelled something at Dillac.

Torg looked at Johnny. "She'll be fine. She's just been trying to do everything since Albert got captured." He sighed. "No one saw Betty coming. Not like this."

"How about you?" Johnny asked. "How are you doing?" Torg had always been the one who never lost his cool; the calm, collected drawl stopping fights in the sugarbar and making jokes in the middle of the craziest game. Now he looked like his stripes were weighing him down.

Torg chuckled. "You mean, aside from the fact that, if I don't die today, I die in less than two months, no matter what? I don't know . . . lately I've been having rather unhealthy dreams about me and a pile of sugar."

"Hey," Johnny said, "you don't know that. You don't know when you're going to die. Betty survived out here for fifty years. Maybe as long as you're out here, you'll do the same."

"Yeah," Torg sighed. It turned into a grimace. "'Course, that means I can't go home again."

Johnny blinked. "Did you want to? I mean, you stayed out here with Albert."

"'Cause I was looking for something. I knew what I wanted and Albert was the best shot." He paused, sinking into his treads as he looked around. "That's the thing that bugs me. I spent my life knowing what I wanted and what I was going to do. Sure, maybe I wasn't you or Albert, but I was pretty good and if that wasn't always good enough, well, it was a hole of a ride." For a brief moment, a grin stretched over his face that Johnny knew and loved. Then it faded.

"But now . . ." Torg examined the dead building above them. "I don't know how we get out of this. I mean, I know exactly what needs to happen: Betty and SecCore have to make peace, get out of each other's way if they can't find it in them to actually help each other. They do that, hole, who knows what happens? At least they got a shot at stopping the Vies. Maybe we can't save the whole Thread, but I bet they could save what's left. Look what we did with the Skidsphere."

"So how do we do that?" Johnny said. It had to be possible. Johnny had made up with Albert . . . kind of. He'd certainly worked with him. Hole, Albert had taken orders from Johnny when he'd hated Johnny's stripes. If Al could do that, if they could do that together, surely they could make Betty and SecCore at least talk to each other?

"I don't know," Torg said softly, his stripes sinking inward. "I was hoping, praying, that maybe if Wobble was there, maybe if I was . . ." He stopped, staring into space. "They've hated each other for fifty years. I thought I'd seen hate, but you and Albert have nothing on those two. I've never cared for anything the way Betty cares for things. And SecCore? We all think he's a jackhole, but he's, what, thousands of years old? Tens of thousands? What if he just cares too much? What if he just can't see it anymore?"

Johnny looked across the corridor to where Shabaz was talking with Onna and Akash. He thought of how different his feelings for her were from anything he'd ever felt before. How terrifying that feeling could be at times. And that was after only a few months. How would he feel after fifty years? After a thousand? Would he care less—would that feeling decay like the Thread had decayed? Or would it grow stronger? A thousand times stronger?

The enormity of the thought hit him and a jolt went through his stripe. At that moment, Shabaz swung an eye his way, so he slapped a smile on his face and tried to respond with . . . he wasn't sure what he wanted to show her, but it sure the hole wasn't the terror surging through his skin.

"Whoa, squid," Torg said. "You all right, Johnny?"

"Yeah," he gasped, sucking in a breath. Throttling the emotion down—at least he had some experience with that. Johnny appreciated how much his old friend was sharing his feelings, but Johnny sure the hole wasn't going to share this. "I'm good. So . . ." he added, deflecting, "we get them to talk. Or maybe Albert can."

"Looks like he already failed at that once."

"Failure doesn't always lead to more failure," Krugar said, stepping out from behind a building.

"Snakes!" Johnny said, jumping back. "Where the hole were you?"

"Scouting around." Krugar popped a single beam of light from his light-stick and took a seat. "Sometimes failure is a cycle. But sometimes you figure it out." He looked at Torg. "Your friend any good?"

"Yeah," Torg replied. "He's not bad."

Krugar bobbed his head. "Then maybe he can help us figure it out."

"Maybe," Torg said doubtfully, which Johnny could understand. The person most likely to help them do that, the person who had the last time, was the problem now.

"Hey, I get it," Krugar said. "That was another one of your friends we were talking to and two things are pretty clear: she's not your friend right now and she's pretty scary." He glanced at Johnny. "Is it me or was there more than one of her out there at one point?"

"It's not you."

Krugar absorbed this, then nodded. Johnny thought he'd say something else about Betty, but instead, the soldier cocked his head back towards the direction he'd come. "Had a look around. There's a break in the corridor floor, big one, about four hundred metres that way. Some real damage to the buildings. Let's call that north. Same thing to the west, little farther out. East might be good for a while, haven't checked south yet."

Torg and Johnny exchanged a glance. They hadn't been there that long; the speed Krugar could get around was amazing. "How'd you see anything?" Torg asked.

Krugar chuckled. "You think Wobble's the only one with a light? By the way, this place is definitely dead. Night vision doesn't read anything that isn't lit up from an external source. Thermal, infrared, ultra, nothing. Whatever this is, it's dead." He frowned. "I'm surprised it isn't colder."

"Uhh . . ." Johnny said, watching the cloud of breath coming out when he breathed. "Seems pretty cold, Krugar."

"We should be frozen solid. If this is truly dead, then there shouldn't be any heat at all." He shook his head with a bemused smile. "If I hadn't believed we were operating under different rules before . . ."

Torres rolled over with Shabaz. "We should move. If Betty thinks we know were Albert is, she might move him."

"Maybe she hasn't captured him," Shabaz said.

"Well, we're not going to find out here," Torres muttered. "Wobble, what's the best direction to get the hole out of here?"

"Negatory. They switched the poles, the dipper runs-runs over-over. Space cannot be determined, time is holding still. Wobble."

"Great," Torres spat.

"Krugar says east is clear for a while," Johnny said. He looked at the soldier. "Uhh . . . I don't know which way east is." Krugar smiled a small smile and pointed.

Torres looked like she might say something, then tilted her stripe. "Why not? It's not like anyone else has any bright ideas." She started rolling in the direction he'd pointed and the others followed her into the darkness.

CHAPTER EIGHTEEN

To Shabaz, it felt like they rolled for days.

For the first few hours, everyone talked nonstop about the size of the space they occupied— awed whispers with each ghost building they rolled past, startled cries of amazement the first time they saw damage: structures cut in half, broken holla screens topping them like jagged teeth, rifts in the corridor wider than the Combine. Wobble ferried them across each rift, two at a time.

Nothing attacked them. Shabaz had never been in a damaged part of the Thread where a Vie or an Anti wasn't coming out from behind something or dropping from the sky. It took her hours to relax. And when she finally accepted that they weren't in immediate danger, she almost broke down at the thought; they might be safe for the moment, but the lack of Vies was a sign of something gone horribly, horribly wrong.

Then, as the hours continued pass, vast space after vast space lit up like some underwater wreck, she became numb. They all did, the chatter dying away. Even Dillac shut up.

Johnny rolled over. "How're you doing?" It was the umpteenth time he'd asked, but it was sweet he kept doing it.

"Not a vaping clue," she said, passing a building where a single sliver remained—a shattered black needle glinting with white light until even that died out in the darkness above.

"Yeah," he said in a hushed tone. "It's gotta end sometime, right? How are the others?"

"Onna and Akash seem to be all right, last time I checked. As for those two," she poked an eye at Kesi and Dillac, "your guess is as good as mine."

He chuckled. "What about Zen?"

A thread of irritation trickled down her stripes. "Shouldn't you be the one checking in with him?"

He blinked. "What?"

"Johnny, you're the one who's been hanging out with panzers and squids for the past few months. Don't you think you'd have a better idea what's going on with them then I would?"

"Uhh . . . sure?" he said, backing up a tread. He stared at her for a second, then rotated on his treads. "I'll, uh, I'll go check on him." He got about three metres, then two eyes swung back her way. "Do we have a problem?"

She sighed. "No, I just don't know why you'd assume I'm checking in on everyone more than you are. I'm not Bian, for Crisp's sake."

"Whoa, wait," he said, rotating back on the treads. "What the hole does that mean? I wasn't assuming anything—what does Bian have to do with this?"

"Nothing," she said, flustered.

"You were checking up with them before, weren't you?"

"Yeah, well, just because I did something before, doesn't mean you should assume it's my job." Now, why had she said that? How the hole had they gotten here—she'd just been thinking he was sweet. There was a point she was trying to make, she knew there was, but she wasn't sure she was making it, or even what she was trying to say.

He stared at her for a long moment. "Fine," he said finally, swinging on his treads. "Whatever you say."

This time she stopped him. "Wait!" she said, popping a Hasty-Arm reflexively.

He stopped. Waited.

"Can we—" She bit her lip and started again. "Can we not do this? Not here?" She felt like all her stripes were trying to squeeze into one or tear into a hundred. "I don't know what just happened—I get we're both stressed, but can we not do this here? Please?"

He stared at her and for a moment she was terrified he was just going to roll away and she didn't know what she would have done if that happened. Then his eye dipped and he took a long, shaky breath. "Do you know what I was thinking a few minutes ago?" he said, blinking rapidly. "I was thinking how much I wanted to find Albert."

Okay, not what she expected to hear. "All right . . ." she said slowly.

"I think that's amazing. I hated him, so hard, for so long, and now I'm hoping we can find him so the jackhole can pull off something I have no idea how to do. Except that maybe we can pull it off, maybe we can get Betty and SecCore to talk after all. Because if I can end up wanting to talk to Albert after how much I hated him, then anything is possible."

She still didn't understand why they were talking about Albert. "Okay, that's a good—"

"But that's not the crazy thing," he continued, and the way he said it—the raw, startled surety of the words—caught her own response and held it in her throat. All three of his eyes swung towards her. "The crazy thing is that I care more about you than I ever hated Albert."

From her very core, a fierce bright warmth, exploding along her stripes. *The crazy thing is . . .*

Almost immediately, he popped an arm. "Sorry, I shouldn't have said that, that's not fair. Sorry."

Sorry?! That's what he was going to apologize for?

He stared at her, waiting for her to speak. When she couldn't, his eye bobbed. "Right, yeah, never mind." He glanced at Dillac and Kesi. "What's up with those two? Oh, right, not your problem. . . . I mean, I'm not saying—" he sighed and started to roll in their direction "—*vape it,* I'll go see what they're—"

"Hey!" she cried, finally finding her voice, rolling forward so hard she almost bumped him. She reached out and grabbed his Hasty-Arm, bringing him to a stop. "Hey," she said again, more gently, trying to think. "Don't . . . look, vape those two. Just . . . just stay here, all right?"

His hand was shaking. Finally, it settled a bit and an eye swung her way. "All right," he said, his stripe flushing. "Sorry, I shouldn't have—"

"Stop," she said. "You don't have to apologize, you don't—" She placed the palm of her hand on his stripe. "We're good. We're good."

They rolled like that for a while, one of her hands in his, the other on his stripe, as above them ghost-lit buildings soared past in silence.

"Okay," he said finally, giving her hand a squeeze as he let it go. "Okay." He was silent, then smiled a little Johnny smile and said, "That was intense."

The laugh that burst from her was loud enough for Dillac to turn his head. "Go vape yourself," she told him playfully, sticking out her tongue. The crimson skid blinked in surprise, then tilted his stripes and rolled on without saying anything.

"Intense, he says," Shabaz murmured, her eye-stalks shaking in disbelief. *The crazy thing is . . .* "Yeah, that's one way of putting it."

Johnny grinned. "That's nothing. Dillac just let a moment go by without one 'squi' or 'boz.' I think this place may finally be getting to him."

"Maybe. Although the minute I understand how that guy rolls . . ." She laughed again. "As for Kesi, I think she gets it, but that doesn't mean she's suddenly going to be on our side."

"Why not?" Johnny said. "Whose other side is there?"

She very deliberately did not roll her eyes. There were times he just couldn't see anything that wasn't the direct line. "Even if Albert and you hated each other, you respected each other. The hate was based on that respect; it meant you could work together. But Dillac and Kesi don't respect us, and they didn't respect us back in the Skidsphere. Plus, it's pretty obvious she was with Trist. They might not have had what we have, but his death just happened and it happened in a way she can't even comprehend. She's going to be confused and she's going to be angry. Who do you think she's going to take it out on?"

He thought about it. "I guess." Then he shuddered.

"If it even was a death. She's not the only one who doesn't comprehend what happened to Trist."

"Yeah," Shabaz said. "We need to find out what that grey is . . ." Her voice trailed off. "What's that?"

Far down the corridor to their left, a distant golden light twinkled against the dark.

CHAPTER NINETEEN

"Wobble?" Johnny started to say, even as he swung in the direction of the light.

"Hey," Kesi cried. "Look at that!" She banged off the nearest building and raced down the corridor. Dillac turned to follow.

"Kesi!" Johnny barked. Crisp, she was fast to react. "Get back here!" Glancing at Shabaz, he banged off a building; she did the same.

"That's just great," Torres swore, popping her swords. "Wobble!"

"To the rescue-rescue. I-We will defend." The machine rose into the air and screamed after Kesi.

Before Kesi even reached the first spark, Johnny saw others further down the corridor: a few single sparks, but then lines, followed by fractured buildings, all glowing with the light of the Thread. They were entering the end of the dead space and back to the merely broken.

Which meant . . .

"Hey," Kesi said, pausing by the sparking light, "this has got to be—"

Wobble screamed past her, four wheels of fire obliterating the four Vies that came out of the shadows. He flew another ten metres, landed, popped his cannons, and began pounding the darkness.

"You idiot!" Johnny yelled, passing Dillac and reaching for Kesi.

"*Zen!*"

Johnny spun, in time to see a Vie fall from the sky near the panzer. Far above, another spark of gold, flickering.

Johnny might have reached him—he cut that hard on the turn. If not, Shabaz might have—she was just behind Johnny. They might have crushed the Vie between them. But they didn't need to: Torres was coming, with Akash not far behind. Torres slashed through the Vie with her orange swords, tucking the One safely behind her as she screeched to a halt.

But now they all faced the wrong way.

"Kesi!" Akash yelled, plowing through the space between Johnny and Shabaz. Towards Kesi, who was just beginning to swing towards the Vie that emerged by her side.

Akash plowed into her, shoving her away as the Vie struck. He tried to use his momentum to rebound in the other direction, but a second Vie appeared in his path. He crashed into it and screamed.

"No!" Johnny cried, even as Torres roared and hurled her sword at the original Vie that had threatened Kesi. "Akash, hold on—"

For a heartbeat, Johnny thought he might. A horror came over the Three's face, then a hard look, his mint skin boiling like a storm. Johnny's hands strained as they reached out; if he could get to him like Shabaz . . .

But Shabaz had been a Seven who'd been nicked a few times; Akash was a Three who'd absorbed one completely.

He dissolved even as Johnny placed a hand on his skin. A third Vie appeared. Without even thinking, Johnny grabbed it and pulled it inside him. A second of biting darkness, then Johnny crushed it with colour and rage.

The next few minutes passed without thinking. He might have swallowed another Vie, he wasn't sure. At some point, someone pressed a gun into his hand. He emptied it screaming.

After a time, the sound of guns died out. Wobble reappeared. "All clear-clear. I-We brought the—" The machine's voice died and his lenses spun. "Numbers are too-too small. I-We have failed."

"You didn't fail, Wobble," Johnny growled. How could the machine think that—how many times had he saved them all? He glared at Kesi. "Are you happy? Do you get it now? This isn't a game?"

"Oh, wait," Kesi protested, "this is my fault? No one dies if the great Johnny Drop gets to go check out the light first? Look, I appreciate the squid—"

"*His name was Akash.*"

Eyes swung as Onna, her expression filled with fury, rolled up to Kesi. "He wasn't a squid. He wasn't a panzer. He was a Level Three, *and his name was Akash!*"

"Whoa, hey, boz—" Dillac said.

"Shut up!" Onna snarled. "Shut up or I will feed you to the next one of those things I see."

Dillac shut up.

"And *you*," Onna said, backing Kesi up against a building. "You don't want to respect me, fine, I could give a gear. You don't want to respect Johnny or Shabaz or their friends, then you're an idiot, but fine. But you *will* respect the skid who just saved your treads or I swear I will rip the stripes right from your skin. His name was Akash, and he was a Level Three. He got there with skills he learned at the Combine—skills he just used to save your sorry skin. Skills he learned from them." She stabbed a finger at Johnny and Shabaz. "So take that and shove it up your stripes."

She pointed in the direction of the lights sparking in the distance. "You want to take off on your own? The two of you? Go ahead. No one's stopping you. You can die together." Her voice grew cold. "You can die alone."

Kesi stared at her, then her own eye dipped. "I'm sorry. I—I'm sorry. I shouldn't have . . . he died because of me."

Onna glared back, then bumped off her treads, hard. "You're vaping right he did." She rolled away, her stripes shaking.

"What was her name again?" Torres murmured.

"I got it," Shabaz said to Johnny, rolling after Onna. "You deal with Kesi."

The fact that they'd had a fight about something like this a few minutes—hours?—ago wasn't lost on him. But right now he didn't care. He rolled up to Kesi.

"She's right," he said, and Kesi flinched. "Onna might have said it a little more bluntly than I would have, but she's right. You got Akash killed. Maybe he would have died anyway; maybe we'll all die out here. But in that moment, you got him vaped. I'll echo what she said— you don't want to respect me, vape it, I don't care. But you will respect Shabaz and Torres and Torg and Wobble. They tell you to do something, you vaping do it. And if you're going to remain here, then you might want to respect Krugar and Onna and Zen too. Because if you don't, more of us will die without needing to, and *that's not going to happen.*"

He waited until she bobbed an eye in agreement. She looked guilty as hole, but he didn't care. He'd really liked Akash. Johnny looked at Dillac. "What about you?"

"Sure, boz," Dillac said. It was the first time Johnny had seen him look subdued. "That was a jack way to die, rhi."

Vaping right it was. "Gimme a minute," he said to Torres. He rolled away, his head a mess. He considered going over to Shabaz and Onna, but Shabaz she had it, and besides, he needed a minute.

He didn't get much more than that before Krugar walked over. He stopped a respectful distance away. "Machine says we're clear but that could change. If this is a bad place, we should move."

"They're all bad places," Johnny said ruefully.

Krugar cocked his head to one side. "How're you feeling?"

How was he . . . ? Akash was dead was how he was feeling. The poor panzer had . . . "He came back. The first day. To the Combine. The first day he made Three and he came back." Krugar frowned and Johnny realized the soldier had no idea what he was talking about. None of them knew anything. "That place in the Skidsphere you found us is called the Combine. It's where Level Ones and Twos train. Trying not to die. No one helps them, they have to figure it out for themselves."

Krugar's frown deepened. "That's not how it looked when I got there."

"After Shabaz and I got back from the Thread, I started helping out. It was how I dealt with . . . it was how I dealt. That's what Kesi and Trist were all twisted up about. Onna, then Shev, started showing up to help out too, after they made Three and didn't need to be there anymore. Akash wasn't the first. But he was the first one to come back on his first day."

Krugar studied him, then looked out into the darkness. "There's never anything good to say in moments like this. But he died saving a life. It wasn't meaningless."

Johnny grunted. "And if Betty and SecCore tear it all apart? If everything dies? How much meaning will there be then?"

Krugar was shaking his head even before Johnny finished speaking. "Nah," he said. He looked back at Johnny. "You can't think like that. You can't think that big in moments like this, it'll just mess you up. Stay small or it will tear you apart. Focus on the mission at hand. We're going to go find your friend, right?"

"Yeah."

"He's going to help, right? Might not save everything, but we're better with him, right?"

Johnny slowly bobbed an eye. "Yeah."

"Then that's what we do. We move one step at a time."

There was a golden spark flickering just over the soldier's shoulder. Johnny watched it for a minute, then asked, "Isn't someone supposed to keep an eye on the big holla?"

"Yeah," Krugar grinned. "And, yeah, it looks like that someone might be you. But not now. Now we go find your friend."

Shabaz rolled over. "Onna's going to be all right, all things considered." She looked at Krugar, then Johnny. "How about you?"

Johnny smiled ruefully. "I think Krugar was just telling me to run the race I'm in."

Krugar's face broke wide open, his smile showing teeth. "I like that. That's a good saying." He looked back at the group. "Come on, we're due a win. Let's go find one."

They rolled for twenty minutes before they found an active door. Vies attacked twice in that span, but the group stayed tight and Wobble was able to handle most of it. What few Vies got through were dispatched by Krugar, Torg, or Torres.

"How do you shoot that well with only two eyes?" Torg asked blithely.

"I know a woman who can do it with one," Krugar replied. "Never figured out how she calculated the distance."

Once they went through the door, Wobble scanned the surroundings. "All quiet-quiet on the outer rim. Warm and fuzzy. We-We are safe for-for now. Wobble."

"Huh," Torg said, studying a holla in a way that Johnny had once seen Betty do.

"What?"

"We're near a hub. One way travel, but goes lots of places. If we move fast, we might be able get to Albert before Betty realizes where we are." He led them down a corridor lined with light.

"And where are we?" Shabaz asked.

Torg grunted again. "Long way from where we were."

The hub was a large room with a brilliant glowing ball floating in its centre. "Okay Wobble, show us where Albert is," Torres said.

"Cartographers and holla-hollas. We found Turge, it was there all the time. Wobble." The machine projected an image into the space.

"That looks familiar," Torres said, frowning.

Torg examined the holla, then groaned. "It's a sim. She has him in a sim."

"What's a sim, squi?" Dillac said, peering at the holla as if he could decipher its secrets.

"It's the type of program we come from. Same with Krugar." Torg sighed. "I would greatly enjoy not to going back to the jungle."

"Well, we're going," Torres said. "Wobble, lock in the closest path through the hub. Let's go."

Travelling in the hub was instantaneous and remarkably pleasant. "How many ways are there to travel through the Thread, anyway?" Johnny asked.

"Too many to count," Torres muttered. "We've figured out about a dozen, including at least three we never would have found if we hadn't seen how Betty took us to the Core that first time. Some, like the hub, actually make sense." She rolled her eyes. "Come on, it's this way."

They travelled down a series of hallways. They turned one corner, then another.

Bian and Peg were waiting for them after the third.

Oh sweet snakes, this day, Johnny thought, his heart sinking as Torres and Wobble plowed through the two skids. It wasn't until Johnny neared that they turned and fell in line with him.

"You shouldn't be here," Peg said.

"You can't be here," Bian said.

I am not doing this, Johnny thought. *Shabaz is right there. She just walked through you. I am not having this hallucination right now.*

"Johnny, you must stop," Peg said.

Nope.

"Johnny, there is nothing but death here," Bian said.

Just walked out of a place like that, still rolling. He picked up speed, trying to put himself in the middle of the pack. They accelerated and swung in front of him. Furious, he waited three seconds until there was a little space between him and the group, then hissed, "Go away. I am not doing this right now."

"Johnny . . ."

"Shut up, my girlfriend is right over—"

"She regrets this most of all," Peg said. "This isn't where you need to be."

"He's waiting, but doesn't know how long he can," Bian said.

"Stop that. For Crisp's sake, if you're going to talk to me, you could at least stop talking like Wobble and start talking like skids."

They stared at him for a moment, a great sadness in their eyes.

"We can't," Peg said.

"We don't exist," Bian said.

"What are you talking about, you're right—"

"Johnny?" Shabaz said, emerging between the two ghosts. "Why are you—?" She caught the expression on his face and immediately knew. "Oh, you have got to be kidding. Is she here? Where the hole is she?"

The second her gaze swung directly at Peg, both dead skids disappeared.

"They're gone," Johnny said bitterly.

"She better be—" Shabaz stopped. "What? *They?*"

"Bian," Johnny said. "It was Bian and Peg. Together."

Shabaz's eye widened to full. "Bian?! With Peg? Oh, that's just vaping marvelous, Johnny. Now you've got another dead ex stalking you?"

"Hey, Bian and I never—*snakes, you think I asked for this?* You think I like seeing her? You think I like hearing the crazy grease they say? Don't blame me for this, I told them to go away."

She glared at him. Not far ahead, Torg appeared around a corner. "All cool here?"

"We're cool, Torg. Catch up in a minute," Shabaz said. Torg, catching the tone, bobbed an eye and rolled away. "I believe you, Johnny," Shabaz said coldly. "I believe you told them to go away. Now, we don't have time for this. We're going to go get Albert and we're going to focus on that. But once that's done, you and I are going to have a long talk about your ex-girlfriend."

"I told you, Bian and I—"

"*I meant Peg,*" she snapped. "Know when you're winning." With that she turned and stormed up the hallway.

Sighing, Johnny followed.

CHAPTER TWENTY

Shabaz couldn't remember being this angry. She'd never been the type. Sure, she'd complained a lot, but it had been a petulant complaining, fuelled more by fear than by rage.

She had plenty of rage right now.

It was hard not to direct it at Johnny. Oh, sure, she believed him when he said that he'd told them to go away. She believed he wasn't asking for this. Consciously.

Bian . . .

Shabaz knew that Johnny and Bian had never hooked up, but she also knew that Bian had a thing for Johnny in those days after she broke up with Albert—if she'd ever gotten around to actually breaking up with him. She'd definitely played Johnny off Albert.

Bitch.

Taking a long, ragged breath, she tried to calm down. She didn't want to think of Bian this way. Hole, she liked Bian: she'd fought alongside her, been in awe of the way she'd died, by what she'd said at the end about

Johnny and Albert, about the skids in general. What Bian had said had been half the reason why Shabaz had done what she'd done once she was back in the Skidsphere.

Not so much with Peg. Was Johnny creating her? Subconsciously? Was he afraid to move on? Did Peg offer him something she couldn't?

The crazy thing is . . .

She refused to believe he'd ever said something like that to Peg.

The others were waiting for them by a door. "Snakes, you two," Torres said, grinning fiercely. "Can't you snug some other time?"

"Feel like eating that sword of yours?"

Torres blinked. "Okay, not in the woods then." Her gaze narrowed as Johnny pulled up. "Something I should know?"

"We're fine," Johnny said. "Let's just get hurry up and get Albert, all right?"

"Hurry up and get Albert? Now I've heard everything."

"Torres," Torg said, studying Johnny and Shabaz. "How about we get this party started?"

Her stripe tilted. "Fair enough."

Like the sim where they'd found Krugar, there was a symbol on the entrance: a square with vertical bars and dots embedded in the space behind. "There better not be a jungle behind that," Torg muttered as Torres opened the door.

It wasn't a jungle.

They emerged into another hallway, except without the familiar golden outlines. Wobble's light was the only illumination, shining over darkened surfaces. It reminded Shabaz of the dead part of the Thread they'd just recently left behind. "Snakes," she whispered. "Is this dead too?"

"No," Krugar said, blinking rapidly. He appeared to be examining something embedded in his eyes. "There's heat here. This sim is active." He hesitated, blinking several more times. "I think."

Wobble widened his beam, revealing a hallway very different from any Shabaz recognized. There was an overabundance of detail: the walls weren't completely flat, nooks and crannies abounded, with pipes hanging overhead. It made her think of a cramped version of the ghostyard. It wasn't a comforting thought.

"Anything moving?" Torres said, one of her light-swords out. "Wobble? Krugar?"

"Nothing," the soldier said.

"Negatory," Wobble said, gears whirring.

"Fine," Torres said, but she kept the sword lit. "Wobble, where is he?"

Wobble displayed an enclosed schematic with several floors. Krugar grunted. "We're on a ship."

"What?" Torres said.

"A ship. Transports people place to place."

"Uh, I don't mean to argue, boz," Dillac said, "but this looks more like a building, squi." They all looked at him. "What?" he protested, popping his arms and spreading them. "Don't it?"

"It is a building," Krugar said. "Just one that moves." He peered down the hallway. "Why don't you let me take point? This might be more my world than yours."

Torres glanced at Johnny and Torg, then tilted her stripes. "Go ahead. Wobble, can you pinpoint Al's location?" A dot of red light appeared near the centre of the holla. "All right, Krugar, after you."

Slowly, the soldier took them forward, his head following his rifle as he did. Nothing else moved except the skids and the light from Krugar's rifle and Wobble.

"If this building transports people," Dillac muttered, "where's all the people at?"

That was a good question. Shabaz had found the dead city of hollas creepy as hole, just like the ghostyard from the first time they'd been in the Thread. But this was worse. All she could see were shadows.

They rounded a corner. Shabaz stopped. "Betty Crisp," she swore. Behind her, nearly every skid did the same.

The left side of the new hallway was a window. And through it . . .

"What the hole are those?" Kesi breathed.

There were thousands of small lights against a black background. No, not thousands . . . millions. No, not millions. . . .

"They're stars," Krugar said, then paused when he saw the looks he was getting. "You know, twinkle, twinkle? You do have night time in your sim, right?"

"Yeah," Shabaz breathed, "but not like this." She'd never seen *anything* else like this.

"If this is nighttime, boz, where's the moon?"

Now Krugar looked amazed. "You have a moon but no . . . why would anyone do it that way?" He shook his head. "All right, look: you have a sun, right? I saw it."

"Yeah," Dillac scoffed, like only an idiot would believe in a world without a sun.

"Right," Krugar said, waving at the window. "That's what those are—suns. Trillions of them."

Trillions??

"How far away are they?" Torg said. Shabaz hadn't

heard him stunned too often, not even the first time he'd seen the Skidsphere from the outside.

Krugar chuckled. "That's a lesson way beyond the time we have. Let's go with: pretty damn far."

A trillion suns in the night sky. So far away that they looked like . . .

"Oh, snakes," Shabaz said softly. "Do you know what this is, Johnny?" She swung two eyes. "It's the Out There."

"No," Torres said firmly, although her own gaze was pinned to the view. "It's a program. Maybe this is what the Out There might look like but philosophy can wait. We have a job to do. Krugar?"

The soldier looked like he had a few questions of his own, but he shrugged and continued down the hall. They weaved down several corridors, descending stairwells twice. "Definitely bipedal," Krugar said.

Shabaz didn't know what that meant, but the stairs certainly weren't designed for treads. Kesi came up with a good solution when she molded skis and slid down. Shabaz might not like her, but she hadn't seen that many skids so instinctive with their treads.

After five minutes, Krugar held up an arm and stopped. "What—" Dillac started to say.

"Shut up," Krugar whispered. "I heard something. That way." He pointed down a long side tunnel. After a second or two, something shuffled past the far end. Shabaz wasn't sure, but it seemed upright; like Krugar, but with a bigger head.

"Not alone, then," Torg whispered.

"Doesn't matter," Torres hissed, rolling forward. "We're close. Let's get Al and get . . . oh, snakes." She stopped, staring at the wall.

At first, Shabaz couldn't see what was different. Then she realized that the section didn't glint in the light like the surrounding hallway. In fact, it didn't reflect any light at all.

It was flat grey.

Dillac inched forward to have a closer look, but Torres snapped a Hasty-Arm, clamping it down on his own. "Don't touch it," she hissed. "Never touch anything solid that's grey like that."

Behind them, Wobble began to quietly keen.

"Is this related to the things we fought in the woods?" Shabaz asked. Just looking at the flat grey made her stripes crawl.

"It creates them. Instantly. The moving grey are bad, but you could fight off one or two if they touched you. But this . . ." Torres shivered. "We have to get Al."

"Torres," Johnny said, staring at the grey patch with one eye and scanning ahead with the other, "if this whole place is like this . . ."

"We are not leaving without Al," Torres insisted. "Wobble, stop whining and show me the map again." The schematic sprang up, the red light indicating Al's position. "See," she said, "we're almost there. We just need to go down one level—"

The red light on the holla went out.

Immediately, the keening sound Wobble had been making rose in pitch. "Negatory, negatory! The Tuatha never-never existed. Oh friend-Albert."

"We are not leaving without Al," Torres snarled and sprang forward.

"Torres!" Shabaz cried, then pressed her lips together in horror, remembering the shape down the other corridor.

"Krugar?" Johnny said.

"On it." The soldier sprinted after Torres, his shadow disappearing down a stairwell at the next bend.

Shabaz stared after them. Wobble continued to keen, his light throwing shadows over the now empty hallway ahead. "Johnny," she said, "we can't leave them."

"Are you serio, boz?" Dillac protested. "What if those things are down there? What if that whole level done gone grey?"

"Then we die," Shabaz said. "Torres won't leave without Al and we're not leaving without Torres."

"She's right," Kesi said suddenly.

They all looked at her. All three of her eyes were wide with fear. She swung one towards Dillac. "What are we supposed to do, stay here? Go back? We might die anyway. And she . . . she saved us that first time in the woods. Torres saved me from that Vie after Akash . . ." Her plum stripes vibrated then swelled. "Shabaz is right. We go after her." Without waiting, she rolled towards the staircase.

So that's what it looks like when someone figures it out, Shabaz thought, bemused, before following the teal-plum skid.

"In for a spoonful . . ." Torg murmured as he and the others fell in behind Shabaz. Even Wobble, although he continued to keen.

As Shabaz slid down the stairs, a hand grabbed her and pulled her sharply left. "Careful," Krugar said, grabbing Dillac next. "You might've been fine, but that whole right side of the prison is grey."

"Prison?" Johnny said, hitting the bottom and swerving left.

"Yeah, that's where we are. Your friend Betty knew what she was doing."

"Where's Torres?" Shabaz asked. Down the central chamber she could see an orange light, disappearing and reappearing along the left side of the prison.

"Trying to open the cells. I don't think she knows which one your friend is in."

"*WOBBLE!*" Torres yelled, splitting the silence. "I can see you down there. Get over here and show me which one he's in."

"Negatory, negatory," Wobble keened.

"For god's sake," Krugar snapped. "Get over there and help her before she brings this whole place down. You can't make it worse." Wobble made a terrible noise, but he moved towards the flashing orange beams.

Torres had buried her light sword in a door, cutting it open. "I know you know which one he's in—tell me, dammit!"

"Negatory. Please-please friend-Torres, I-We-You must leave. Oh, friend-Betty why? *Why?*"

"Wobble!"

"Negatory, hope is dead here. The Calamari—"

"*Dammit, you vaping machine, tell me where he is!*"

Wobble made a final keening sound. His light narrowed down to a spot, landing on the door three cells away. Torres made a sound that scraped from her throat, rolled, and plunged her sword into the door.

"Torres," Johnny said softly, coming up beside her.

"Go vape yourself, Johnny, we're not leaving without him."

"We're not going to," Shabaz insisted, taking the other side. "We'll open the cell and grab Albert, but we need to be care—"

"I. Am. Not. Leaving . . ." Torres slammed her weight down on the sword with each word. On the last, the piece she'd carved out slammed into the cell. "Without Al," she finished, entering the darkness.

Shabaz glanced at Johnny and followed her in.

The orange glow of the sword lit up the chamber. Something in the corner moved. "Al?" Torres said hopefully, raising her sword.

A skid entered the light. It had three eyes and treads. It had a scar down one side of its body. But the body wasn't silver and it didn't reflect the light of the sword.

The body was grey.

CHAPTER TWENTY-ONE

He'd always been fast. And he'd always had an ability to see things coming.

He never saw this coming.

But he was fast, and so when Torres said Al's name—with an acute loss that Johnny never, *ever* wanted to feel—and started to roll forward, he immediately snapped a Hasty-Arm and grabbed hers. When she snatched it from his grip, he darted in front of her, glancing at Shabaz with one eye and keeping the other on the thing that had once been his enemy and his best friend.

"Torres, we have to go now." The grey thing shuffled forward and then hitched back, as if it couldn't remember how to use its treads.

"Get out of my way, Johnny," Torres hissed, pushing against him. "I'm not leaving without—"

"That's not Al," he said, pushing back. "Whatever it is, it's not him."

"Torres," Shabaz said. "Johnny's right, we have to get out of here." The thing corrected its hitch.

Torres tore her hand from Shabaz and raised her sword. "I said get out of my way."

He didn't have any choice. And he still had three years of skill on her, no matter what she'd learned out here. Faster than she could react, he snatched the light-sword, turned it, and touched her stripe. Not deep, but deep enough. She screamed, and in that moment when she couldn't think and probably didn't have control, he geared up as hard as he ever had from a sitting start and drove her back, even as the thing behind him reached out with a flat grey arm.

"Johnny!" Shabaz yelled, turning to follow. "The grey!"

Snakes. As hard as he'd shoved, he locked his treads and dug in before they spilled across the corridor to the half coated in solid grey.

"Let go," Torres hissed, grabbing the sword back. She lunged at him, and as he swerved to avoid the blade, she darted through the space he'd vacated. Johnny spun, terrified she would attack Shabaz, terrified that the thing that had been Al would escape—

Someone else was already blocking the door.

"Get out of my way, Wobble," Torres spat, raising the sword.

"Negatory." And given all the pain and sorrow Johnny had heard in the machine's voice before, that single word was the worst. "Please, friend-friend-Torres-Torres. Friend-Albert is not here. We-You must go."

"Wobble, I swear I'll kill you—"

"Then you'll kill all of us," Krugar said, stepping up beside Wobble, his rifle angled down. "I get it, he was your friend, and I don't know what happened in there, but whatever it is, your friend is dead. And if you don't think the machine hates having to tell you that, then you're insane."

A moment of silence except the sword, humming. Kesi's voice came from the stairs: "I think I hear something moving up there."

"Torres," Shabaz said gently. "We have to go. That isn't Al in there. I'm sorry, but it's not him. And if we don't get out of here, we'll all end up that way."

Another heartbeat, then the sword came down. "Fine," Torres said, strangling the word. "I'll clear a path for us out of here. Stay the vape out of my way." She turned for the stairs.

Shabaz made a soft sound. Krugar surveyed the group, then nodded. "I'll cover her."

"I'd stay out of her way," Torg murmured. "What happened in there?"

"You don't want to know," Johnny whispered.

"Al?"

He felt sick. He managed to grind-out the words: "It's all grey."

"Ahh, snakes," Torg said, the words collapsing from his mouth. "Is there . . . is there anything we can do?"

Tears were falling from Shabaz's eyes now. "We need to get out of here," Johnny said. "Can you gather the others, maybe make sure Krugar and Torres are all right? We'll be right behind you."

Torg hesitated, glancing at the space behind Wobble. Then he sighed and headed for the stairs.

Johnny looked up at Wobble, who had his back pressed against the space Torres had carved out. "Are you keeping him in there?" he asked.

Wobble's lenses shifted. "Affirmative."

Johnny bobbed an eye. "Can you . . . can you end it?" Nearby, Shabaz made another soft sound.

The machine didn't move. "Affirmative."

The longest moment of his life. But what else was he going to do? What else was he going to say?

"Okay," he said.

There was a whirring sound and the space behind Wobble briefly lit up. Then a loud keening sound, so much worse than anything Johnny had ever heard from Wobble before. Shabaz was weeping openly. Johnny . . .

He had no vaping idea how he felt. Not knowing what else to do, he turned to comfort Shabaz. "I'm sorry, I shouldn't have made you watch—"

"Don't you dare," she hissed, drawing herself up. "Apologize to Wobble if you have to, but not to me. If you could do that, I could be here to watch." She drew a harsh, raw breath. "You had to do that. He . . . he would have wanted that. Oh, snakes, Albert."

A loud half-screech, half-roar of loss and rage came echoing down the stairwell. "Wobble, you should go make sure Torres is okay," Shabaz said. Another cry. "Though she probably doesn't need any help." Without speaking, Wobble lifted off the ground, transformed into his knife-shape, and hovered towards the stairs.

Johnny stared at the open space leading to the cell. He shuddered. "I don't need to see that," he said, rolling after Wobble.

"Vape no," Shabaz muttered.

They found most of the others huddled around the top of the stairwell. "Um, Torres went up ahead, boz," Dillac said. He looked shaken, his stripes frazzled. "She was . . . rhi, I don't know what she was." A scream of rage came down the hallway, followed by gunfire. It sounded like it was coming from one floor up.

"Krugar told us to wait here," Onna said, looking no

better than Dillac. "He and Wobble followed Shabaz. Dillac's right, she looked . . . what happened down there?"

"Nothing good," Johnny said, drained. "Stay tight, we'll work our way up." He started to roll down the hall.

"Wait!" Kesi said. "Shouldn't there be someone else? I thought we were here to get Albert?"

An image came to him: a round shape, shuffling out of the darkness. Three dead eyes. A hitch in the gears, then a grey hand, reaching . . .

"Albert's dead," Shabaz said, her voice sounding as drained as his own.

"But how?" Kesi protested. "We saw that signal, how . . . ?" Her voice died as she read the emotion in Shabaz's expression. "Sorry. Never mind."

If he didn't move, he was going to scream. Johnny felt strangely flattened out, as if the world wasn't quite real. There was gunfire and screaming . . . abruptly, he chuckled.

Of course it wasn't real.

"Johnny?" Torg said.

The chuckle got louder. Of *course* it wasn't real. It was dead. Albert was dead, the one constant in his life. No, not dead, turned into something else—they weren't even here, he'd been like that since they'd saved the sphere, *why the hole had they saved the sphere?* He was laughing louder now. It was all dead: Albert, the Out There, there were trillions of abandoned suns. . . .

"*WHY DID WE SAVE THE SPHERE?!*" he cried aloud, and the laughter burst loose, out of control.

"Boss?" Onna said, rolling forward.

"It's all dead!" A whining of gears, a flash of light. Nothing they'd ever done mattered, it was all dead—

Shabaz appeared in front of him, all three eyes on his, her hands on his stripe. "It's not all dead. I love you. I'm right here. I'm right here."

"We're all dead already," Johnny said, the laughter curling into a snarl. "Black, white, grey, it's already killed us—"

"It hasn't killed me," a small voice said. Zen rolled forward. "I'm still here. I don't know why, I should be dead—I'm a panzer, that's what we do, right? We die. Well, this world is vaping Threes and Fours and Sevens and I'm still here. I don't know why, but I'm still here."

"Me too," Onna said fiercely. "And I know exactly why I'm here. I'm here because of you. You came into the Combine and picked me. Vape me if I know why, but it saved my life. You saved my life."

"Me too," Torg said. "Said it before, I'll say again. I'll say it however many times you need to hear it."

Whatever the hole was twisted up inside Johnny loosened a little. He glanced at Shabaz.

"You know you did," she said softly. Her hands were still on his stripe. "I'm right here."

A wave of grief washed over him and his whole body sagged. "Okay," Shabaz said, removing a hand from his stripe and taking one of his own, "let's get you out of here. Torg, Onna, take point. Watch out for grey patches. Kesi, Dillac, take the rear, yell if you see movement. Zen . . ."

"Yeah," the panzer said fiercely.

"Stay in the centre, stay breathing." When the indigo skid's gaze fell, she added, "You already saved a life today." Zen's expression brightened, then another screech echoed down the hall, this one several floors up. A scattered round of gunfire.

"All right," Shabaz said, carrying Johnny's arm. "Let's get the vape out of here."

CHAPTER TWENTY-TWO

They came across the first body at the stairwell leading up. Torg dragged it away. "The bodies you can touch," he said, sniffing in disgust. "It's just the solid grey that's instant."

Johnny stared at the thing as Torg and Onna tread up the stairs. It was larger than Krugar, but the same basic shape: two arms, two eyes, two legs. An elongated snout with teeth protruding from the upper jaw and claws instead of fingers. Its skin was pebbly and it was wearing some kind of three-quarter battle suit.

"That's major snaze, rhi," Dillac muttered, following Johnny. Treading up the stairs was a little trickier than sliding down, but they managed.

At the top of the stairwell, Shabaz tried to take his hand again, but he gently pushed her away. "It's all right," he said. "I'm . . . well, I'm not fine, but I'm not crippled."

She studied him for a moment, then reached out and gave his hand a squeeze. "Okay," she said, and rolled out front.

There were hundreds of bodies, every one of them a creature like the one they'd seen downstairs. "Thank goodness the hallways are narrow," Torg said, eyeing a pile of bodies. "If they'd been able to pack us into a corner . . ."

Like downstairs, Johnny thought. If they hadn't gotten out quickly, if the fight with Torres had gone wrong or she'd refused to leave . . . he shuddered.

They heard a few more sporadic bursts of fire, but no more screams of rage. Finally, as they mounted the final stairwell, even the gunfire died out. Krugar came running down the corridor, scanning every junction, his rifle pointed down. "I think we got them all. Thank god for Wobble, he stopped the one horde I saw. That machine's amazing."

You don't know the half of it, Johnny thought, as the machine in question came down the hall. His entire body was smoking and covered in grey matter. Now that the battle was over, he moved with his familiar hitch.

"All clear-clear. Wobble." The machine didn't look happy. Johnny knew how he felt.

"Boz, you got a little . . ." Dillac said, grimacing. He reached out to flick the biggest piece of grey off Wobble's shoulder, then shied away. "You know what, it's a good look, boz."

"Come on," Johnny said. "Let's go see how Torres is doing."

As they rolled towards the entrance, past the window with its trillion suns—he steadfastly refused to look, he didn't need the distraction right now—Johnny had a sudden spastic thought: they were going to find Torres, but her purple-orange skin would be grey, her eyes dead, and they would have to kill her too. Then they rounded the final corner and found Torres, alone, sitting by the exit.

Immediately, Johnny's heart filled with sorrow for the fierce skid. He'd gone a little spare downstairs—hole, he'd gone *a lot* spare downstairs. And, if anything, Torres had an even greater tie to Albert than Johnny.

Three months ago the thought would have made him laugh—how could anyone be more tied to Albert than Johnny? Half the stories the skids told in the Skidsphere had been about Albert and Johnny, their rivalry and their hate.

But then Albert had stayed in the Thread and the skids stopped telling stories about Albert and Johnny because Albert didn't exist. Not in the Skidsphere. Only in the Thread, where the first time they'd arrived—falling through a darkness that wanted to kill them—there was only one skid who hadn't been saved by Johnny.

Torres.

All three of her eyes were on the ground, the light-sword sheathed. Depressed into her treads, her stripe flat orange instead of its usual glossy sheen. "Torres?" Johnny said, stopping a respectful distance away.

Her body didn't even twitch. "I guess you got what you wanted. He's dead now."

He'd half-expected it, but it hurt nonetheless. Sweet snakes, it hurt. Behind him, he saw Shabaz open her mouth and he popped a Hasty-Arm. "It's okay, I got it," he said, even as he felt a surge of love for the combative look she wore. What had he done to deserve that support, to deserve what she'd done downstairs?

What he deserved was right here.

"Torres, I am so sorry."

A half-snarl, half-snort of derision. "Of course you are. Did you finish it? Did you kill him?"

"I didn't kill him." He had to stay calm here, but snakes it was hard—he felt like screaming at her or maybe joining her on the floor. "Wobble . . .Wobble finished it."

"Oh that's great, Johnny Drop. Blame the machine. You jack—"

"All right, Torres that's enough," Shabaz said, rolling forward.

"Shabaz, I said I got this."

"No you don't," she said, two eyes on Torres and one on Johnny. "Not this you don't. Not after what you had to . . .Torres, I love you like a sister, but you need to back up."

"Of course you'd defend him."

"Torres . . ." Torg said.

"*And of course you would defend him!*" she screamed. "His best friend and his snug-buddy! Aren't you glad he's back, Torg? Back with the winning team?"

Torg stared at her, his expression filled with sympathy and pain. "There are no teams, Torres. Just us."

"*Just you!*" She rose on her treads. "Admit it, none of you ever liked him. None of you ever listened to him, not you, not Betty, no one . . . *ever* . . . listened to him." She popped a light-sword. "*No one cared about—*"

A gunshot echoed down the hall. Johnny's trail-eye went wide as he realized it wasn't Krugar holding the gun.

It was Dillac.

"This is grease, squi," he said, his voice remarkably calm as he handed the gun back to Krugar. "You think boz don't care? Torres, what happened to you ain't right, but you ain't close to round on this. Boz don't care? Rhi, panzer went spare downstairs. I thought he was going to blow sug for sure."

"What's he talking about?" Torres muttered, staring at Dillac like he was mad.

"It's not important," Johnny said. "This isn't about me—"

"No, it is important," Onna said, coming around Shabaz. "Crisp, Torres, I can't begin to understand how you feel, but Johnny doesn't care any less."

"The hole he doesn't."

"Yes, he does. This guy was important to both—"

"This guy? *This guy?!*" Torres cried. "His name was Albert!" Her whole body went still, and then she wailed: "*HE WAS MY ONLY FRIEND!*"

The last word echoed down the hall, filled with loss and shame. As the echo died away, Kesi rolled forward.

"Sometimes your friends die," she said. "Sometimes when they shouldn't. Sometimes in ways . . . in ways they shouldn't." She looked at Torres and, for the first time, Johnny saw sympathy for another skid in her eyes. "We don't have to die with them."

Torres stared at her, then past her to Krugar and Zen. "Everyone else had their say, you two want in?"

"Just . . . I'm sorry about your friend," Zen said, blinking rapidly.

Krugar looked down at him, then nodded. "Yeah," he said, looking back at Torres. "That'll do for me too."

The silence stretched out, then the light-sword extinguished. "There'll be a hub somewhere nearby that will take us back to the base. Betty's probably waiting for us there, but I don't care anymore." She turned on her treads and rolled out the door.

"Give her some time," Krugar said. "She's tough, she'll come around."

"I hope so," Johnny said. "We need her."

"Well, we're due a win."

Johnny chuckled, although it was devoid of humour. "I thought we were already due a win before."

Krugar shrugged. "Then we're due two. Come on."

Torres was waiting for them in the hall. When they all emerged from the sim, she turned without speaking.

"I-We will find us a hub-hub," Wobble said, catching up with Torres.

They rolled in silence. Everyone gave Johnny space, although Shabaz kept glancing in his direction even as she went from skid to skid, checking in. The sight brought a brief smile to his lips. They'd had a fight over that. A stupid one. Then again, maybe all their fights had been stupid.

Then he thought about Peg and Bian. Okay, maybe that one wasn't stupid—he could understand why she was upset about that. He was upset about that. They were just one more thing that didn't make sense in a world that no longer made sense.

Albert was dead. *Albert*. And Betty had killed him, or least put him a place where he would die. A place where they might follow him and die as well.

Johnny had a real nasty suspicion about how they'd found Al. About how that red light indicating him had gone out when it did. Sure, maybe he'd been alive until then; maybe that was the moment Albert had turned grey. But there hadn't been any of those grey things in his cell. Maybe there had been some of the solid grey, but the rest of it had been on the other side of the prison.

They'd gone to the Core to steal information about Albert from Betty. What if Betty had given it to them?

He remembered wondering why she didn't catch them when they were on the plain, why she wasn't using her jets. How Krugar had taken her out with a grenade—come to think of it, how the hole did she miss Krugar being there in the first place? There's no way she should have missed that.

What if the whole thing had been a play to get rid of them all? If Torres fought him down in those cells for one minute longer, if those things trapped them down there, with one side of the prison gone to grey . . .

She regrets this most of all.

Peg had said that. He'd thought she'd been talking about Shabaz—he'd just said something about her—but they'd been just outside the sim. What if she was talking about Betty?

Of course, Bian had also said something about how he was waiting but didn't know how long he could, so maybe Albert had been alive at that moment. Of course, if Al was in a prison, he wasn't exactly waiting, so why would Bian use that particular . . . ?

"Ugh," he groaned.

"Everything okay?" Shabaz said, dropping back.

"What? Oh, yeah, I was . . ." He did not want to start a fight again. Then again, not talking about it hadn't helped before. "Vape it, I was thinking about Peg. And Bian."

"Oh," she said warily, her stripes tightening.

"Listen," he said, "I know this bothers you, I get it, I'm not mad that it does. I don't know why I keep seeing Peg—I have no idea why Bian started to show up and spout nonsense—but I swear, I'm not creating them myself."

"Okay . . ."

"I mean it, Shabaz. I miss Peg, sure, I always will. And yeah, the last time we were all here, I was probably still a little nuts about her. But I'm not with her now. It's like you said back in the prison: I'm here. With you. I don't want to be with anyone else."

The edge of her lips quirked. "You know, I know I said I wanted to talk about this, but I wasn't really serious."

He laughed. "Sure you weren't."

"Not to be caught eavesdropping," Torg drawled, dropping back, "but did I hear you say that you're still seeing Peg? And now Bian?"

"Uhh . . ." Johnny said, eyeing Shabaz. This was already a touchy subject; he didn't want to make it worse.

Shabaz tilted her stripes. "It's Torg, we're here."

Johnny sighed. "Yeah, I'm seeing Peg. And sometimes Bian."

"And they're talking to you? As in, you're having conversations? I thought Betty said that wouldn't happen."

"Betty said lots," Shabaz muttered.

"True," Torg said. A sadness crossed his face. "It has occurred to me that she might have led us into that prison."

"I was just thinking that a minute ago," Johnny said grimly.

"You mean so that we ended up like . . ." Shabaz's voice trailed off, her eyes going wide. "That's horrible."

"One of the things Peg said right before we went inside was: *she regrets this most of all.*"

"Peg said that?" Torg said. "That's rather cryptic."

"It's not like we have a normal conversation," Johnny said. "They show up, say something weird, then disappear. They don't talk like skids; they talk like Wobble. It's all: *She regrets this most of all*, and: *He's waiting, but he doesn't know how long.*"

"Who's waiting?"

"I don't know, Torg!" Johnny protested. "I don't understand anything they're talking about, except the bit about how to fight the grey."

"Peg told you how to fight the grey?"

"Uhh, no," Johnny said, glancing at Shabaz. "Bian did. She, uh . . . she told me the grey wasn't like the black, and that I had to fight slower."

Shabaz's gaze narrowed suspiciously. "Just when was this?"

"When we fell through the grey the first time. It was the first time Bian showed up. Well, just her voice, really. It was the only time she made any sense at all." His voice trailed off as he saw the look in his girlfriend's face.

"You said you thought that up."

"I, uhh . . . I don't think those were my exact words."

An awkward silence, then Torg coughed. "Wow," he said. "You're really not getting any better at this, are you?"

Thankfully, that got a smile from Shabaz, even as she glared at Johnny. He looked back at her with what he hoped was the appropriate amount of innocence and shame.

It must have been close, because she did laugh. "Fine," she said. "Here's the deal, sir. The next time your friends show up, you tell me." When he started to protest, she added, "I'm serious, Johnny. No more secrets. I won't be mad at you, unless you keep hiding this from me. Either of those two show up, you let me know."

"I don't suppose there's any chance you won't want to talk to them."

"You don't suppose right," she snapped. "Seriously, if she's got some message for us, she can share it with the group."

"What else exactly did she tell you?" Torg said thoughtfully, looking up ahead.

Johnny sighed. "I don't know, Torg. Like I said, except the bit about fighting the grey, it was all one liners and cryptic grease. Someone's waiting. Something about something coming. That's helpful."

"You said they sounded like Wobble," Torg said. "We know that he's tied into the Thread in ways we can't even comprehend. There are times when he sounds like he knows everything that's ever happened to the Thread. Including the future."

"Okay, that's a little . . ." Johnny stopped. Wobble did sound like that sometimes.

"What if Peg and Bian aren't Peg and Bian, but they're some part of the Thread?" Torg said.

"You think the Thread's trying to talk to me?" Johnny said. "To me directly—'cause let's face it, no one else is seeing them. So it's got to be me it's talking to." He laughed. "Crisp, Torg, I've got an ego but that sounds like something Betty might have thought."

"Maybe you're just the messenger."

"If that's the case," Shabaz said coldly, "then the Thread can vaping pick someone other than Johnny's ex-girlfriends to do it."

Johnny considered pointing out that he'd never been with Bian, saw the look, and decided to keep his mouth shut.

Torg's stripes tilted. "Got our attention, didn't it?"

CHAPTER TWENTY-THREE

They found a hub and travelled through it. The entire time, Shabaz kept looking behind her, expecting ghosts and feeling pissed.

Not long after, Torres had Wobble take them through a pulse. However, when the purple skid immediately started taking them down an unbroken hallway, Torg grunted and said, "I'm putting a stop to this." He rolled towards the front. "Torres?" he called. "Torres!"

"What's wrong?" Shabaz asked, scanning the corridor. Everything looked fine. She liked it when the hallways were empty.

"We're travelling stupid," Torg said. "We might as well be wearing a sign. *Torres!*"

The skid in question ground to a halt. "What?" she snapped.

"This is dumb. We don't travel like this and you know it."

"This is the fastest way back to the safehouse."

"This is the fastest way to let Betty know where we are." Torg's voice softened. "Torres, I know you're in pain, and maybe you're right: maybe Betty's waiting for us back home, maybe she's watching us right now. But if there's a chance she doesn't know where we are, then you know how we roll."

Torres looked like she was going to explode again, but instead she grew still and growled, "Fine."

"Thank you," Torg said. "Wobble, find us a broken path."

Poor Wobble, Shabaz thought, as she watched the machine's head rotate back and forth between Torg and Torres. He was getting torn apart by everything: the Thread, Betty, and now his friends. Nevertheless, he turned and after a moment found them a door, its edges frayed and sparking. They formed a chain, except for Torres. She glared at Shabaz's proffered hand, then snorted and plunged through the door. Shabaz was pretty sure Krugar was right, Torres would come around. But it wasn't going to be any time soon.

Once everyone was through, however, Torres did take the lead again. Torg watched her roll out front. "Could be a good sign."

"And if she's right?" Johnny said. "If Betty's waiting back at the safehouse?"

Torg's stripes took on a bitter tilt. "Wouldn't be the first time I was wrong."

They rolled in silence for a while, Johnny slowly dropping to the rear. Shabaz considered joining him, but given how bad he'd been hurt by Albert's death, she wanted to give him some space. She had no idea if this was the right thing—all this was screwed-up new emotional territory—but she had to trust her instincts. He'd chosen to create some space, so she'd give him space.

But if he got that look on his face like he had company…

Stop it, she thought, angry at herself. Johnny had said he'd let her know if the girls showed up. It wasn't his fault—she honestly didn't believe he was creating them out of some kind of repressed love. They were something else, although she wasn't ready to concede Torg's theory. Then again, Johnny had said they sounded like Wobble. And Wobble did seem at times . . .

On a whim, she rolled over to the machine, who was drifting off to one side. "Hey, Wobble."

Lenses spun, and remarkably, the metallic face split into a familiar broken smile. "Friend-Shabaz. Warm and fuzzy. Claw-clacks and press to send-send. Don't tell-tell Indira she's my favourite."

"Right," she laughed. Snakes, it was nice to see him smile. "I see you cleaned up a little." He still looked battered, but at least he was no longer coated in dead-matter.

The grin widened, his single loose sheet-metal tooth flapping on its faulty hinge. "Broke-broken doors take the grey away-away. Dillac spoke true words, Wobble looked gross. Wobble."

"Yeah, he's a shaman," Shabaz mused, then bit her lip. She had something she wanted to say, and then something she wanted to ask. But she was afraid the first would take the machine's smile away and, with the second, she was just afraid. "Wobble," she said, taking a deep breath. "I just wanted to thank you for what you did for Albert. What you did for Johnny."

The smile did, in fact, fall away. Gears whirring, Wobble said, "Friend-Betty betrayed us all-all. No-no-no one should die alone. There were no teddy bears."

"Yes, there were," Shabaz insisted. "You were there. You saved Torres from herself, maybe all of us as well.

Then you put Albert to rest. It was the right thing to do. It was grease you had to be the one to do it, but it was the right thing, Wobble. Albert didn't die alone. He had you."

Wobble's lenses angled into grief and he stared at her for a long moment, no gears whirring at all. Finally, he said, "Thank you, friend-Shabaz. You should ask your questions."

A shiver right through her stripes. There were times when Wobble didn't sound broken at all. "Uh, okay," she said, swallowing. She hesitated—but if she wasn't going to ask, why had she rolled over? "Wobble . . . can you see the future?"

Immediately, Wobble's head spun and rotated like a gyroscope. "Danger, danger, Robb became his own son, Yzz-pac sold the clampionship. This is not a safe mode of inquiry. The answer-answers already happened-happened—he is waiting, they are on the way. She shouldn't have asked, she never did." As abruptly as his head began spinning, it froze, staring at her. "You will part."

The shiver became a stab. Unbidden, her Hasty-Arms popped and she covered her mouth, even as tears sprung. Because there was a second question she'd been going to ask.

She'd been going to ask if she and Johnny were still together.

"Okay," she said meekly, backing away. Her eye-stalks shook and she wasn't sure she wasn't going to pass out. She was such an idiot. He was right, that was stupid, she shouldn't have—*why did she ask?!* "I'll just . . ." She wanted to flee, but where the hole was she going to flee to? She started to turn away. . . .

"*WAIT!*" Wobble cried, arms out-stretched. "Untoward.

They don't know the whole truth, so help you god. The genie fools-fools them all." He rolled towards her. "Do not give up hope. Clutching the flotsam, Homer came home. He-She saved each other. The Thread is greater than you could ever imagine." His head spun once, then stopped, staring into her eyes. "There are a trillion suns and each one knows of love."

She was going to pass out. How do you survive emotional swings like this? *Do not give up hope.* Her stripes felt like they were burning. *There are a trillion suns....*

The crazy thing is ...

She gulped a breath. Then another. Another. "Okay," she said, looking up into lenses that had no right to convey pain or hope but nonetheless did. "Okay," she said again. On an impulse, she placed a hand on the side of Wobble's head. Gears whirred and the machine broke into its broken grin. "Okay," she said a third time. "I won't give up hope."

"Hooray!" Wobble hooted, then rose from the floor, transformed into his knife form, and darted forward through the group. Shabaz stared after him, stunned into bemusement.

"Interesting conversation?" Krugar said, stepping up beside her.

"That's one way of putting it." Her stripes were still vibrating. She took a ragged breath.

Krugar cocked his head. "You all right, Shabaz?"

Snakes, she must look a mess. "Yeah," she said, sucking in air again. She blinked rapidly, her eyes still full of tears. "Just asked a question I probably shouldn't have asked."

"I'm sorry," he said, taking a step back. "I shouldn't have intruded."

"No," she said, reaching out. "It's okay. Seriously, I'm okay."

The soldier smiled. "Good. I was on my way to sweep up front, but it looks like he's got that covered. I'll just head back." He turned, then caught the look she was giving him. "What?"

"You're pretty cool, Krugar."

"Thank you." His eyes crinkled in surprise. "What brought that on?"

"You did. You got thrown into this world; I don't even know what we must look like to you. You don't know any of us, you don't know what's going on more than anyone else, and yet you haven't complained once."

Now the smile intensified. "Nah," he said. "I complain lots. I just do it when you're not looking."

"Krugar," she said flatly. "We have three eyes. We're always looking."

"Well, that's true." He shrugged. "Could be worse."

"It could?" she said incredulously.

"Yeah. I mean, sure, the situation is pretty bad. I'm still not sure I understand all of it, but it's bad. I'm sorry about your friend."

"Thanks," she said, her eyes dipping with sorrow.

Krugar gave her a moment then continued. "But the situation is only half the thing. The other half is who you're with." He cocked his head. "You want to know what you look like to me? I don't understand the world you're from, I don't get how your lives work, but you all seem pretty cool to me."

"Really?" she said. "Even Dillac?"

"He the one that talks like he got hit in the head a few times? You should see some of the trubs we get in basic. Besides, he stood up for Johnny. That's something."

It certainly was, she thought.

"For all that talk when we first got here about how you all don't help each other, that yellow guy taking off . . . you all came around faster than I expected. I thought that one over there—Kesi, right?—I thought she was going to be a problem." He shrugged. "Sometimes people surprise you."

Sometime they surprise themselves, she thought, remembering what she'd been like, remembering how useless she'd felt until, suddenly, she'd stopped making excuses. She glanced back at Johnny. She remembered the moment he'd saved her life—him and Albert—and then that moment that she'd helped, that moment when she realized that she wasn't useless after all. Another thought followed.

Krugar caught the look. For a creature with two eyes, he caught a lot. "What?"

"Nothing," she said, flushing.

"Is this about one of those questions you probably shouldn't ask?"

Caught way too much. "Nevermind. It's stupid."

"Shabaz . . ." he drawled. For a moment, he sounded exactly like Torg. "I'm a pretty tough man. If your question bothers me, I'll choose not to respond. Ask your question."

She shivered. That was a little close to what Wobble had said. "It's about . . . you said you had a woman you loved?"

Krugar nodded. "My wife. Laleh."

Now she felt like an idiot. This was mean; she was better than this.

"You're worried you're going to hurt me because of the way I talked about my wife back in that place with all the holograms. When I said I thought she wasn't real."

"Krugar, it's okay, I shouldn't have—"

"Don't worry about it. I changed my mind about that."

She blinked. "What?"

"Yeah," he said, nodding. "Laleh, Aden, Huma—that's my son and daughter—they're real. I decided that."

"You decided that?"

"Why not?" He rapped a knuckle off the nearest wall. "Look, I get it now, I think: we're programs in a giant program. So we could all just curl up and say none of this matters, none of this is real. If you thought about it one way, I never met my wife, she never existed, she's just a program inside a program. She's just another layer. Just another thread, I guess."

Shabaz couldn't believe how matter-of-fact he was, how quickly he'd come to grips with the Thread. She'd been out here twice and still didn't like to think about it.

"But the thing is," he continued, "I got over twenty-five years of memories of my wife. Eighteen years of my son, sixteen of my daughter. And they're real." He shrugged as if it were the most obvious thing in the universe. "They're real. The way Laleh's favourite smell was orange blossoms. The way Aden took *way* too long to learn how to walk—Christ, we were worried. The way my daughter is smarter than I ever will be." His face scrunched up and for a moment he looked away. "Sure, maybe I don't get to see them again, and that . . . that's horrible. But they're real. They're alive." He looked back and tapped his head. "Up here."

She really didn't want to cry. "That's a beautiful way of looking at things, Krugar."

He shrugged. "Nah. People obsess about the wrong details too much. That friend of yours that died back there . . . did he matter?"

Albert, with Johnny, saving her life . . .

"Yes," she said. Apparently, she was going to cry after all.

The soldier smiled. "Then that's it. I'm sorry I made you cry."

She laughed, shaking her stalks to clear her vision. "That's okay. Given everything that's happened, I probably needed it."

"I'd offer you a handkerchief, but I'm afraid they didn't make it out of the jungle."

"That's okay, I don't know what a handkerchief is."

"Well thank god for small mercies," he said exhaling sharply. "'Cause there's a ton of things about your world that I don't understand at all. How the hell can you have a moon but no stars? That just ain't right." He looked back at her. "How come you wanted to ask about Laleh?"

"I was going to ask how long you guys had been in love," Shabaz said, still trying to blink her eyes clear. "But you answered that already. Have you really been in love for twenty-five years?"

"Twenty-eight, actually. Why, how long have you and Johnny been a thing?"

She flushed. "Three months." It seemed such a pitifully small amount of time.

"Aww, see," Kruger said. "You're just getting started. You'll figure it out."

"Krugar, three months is the longest relationship most skids have."

He stared at her. "I swear I don't get your world at all."

"We live fast, die fast."

"Right. Five years. You're all under five." He shook his head in disbelief.

"But I don't want my thing with Johnny . . . I don't want it to be like that. I want it to last. Can . . . can you really love someone for twenty-eight years?"

His head curled back, as if for the first time he understood. "Every day," he said. "And every day until I die."

"How do you do it?"

He barked a laugh and exhaled again. "Ohh, there's no manual." He caught the need in her expression and winced. "Uh, I don't know . . . don't expect it to be perfect? He doesn't need to be perfect, you don't need to be perfect. I'd tell him about the toilet seat, but I guess that doesn't apply." He made another face and she almost laughed; it was the first time she'd seen him stymied. She was also hanging on his every word.

"I guess," he continued with a shrug, "I guess, I'd say . . . when times are good, don't take it for granted. And when times are bad, kinda like *this*—" he made a motion to encompass the whole corridor "—just . . . just cut the other person a little slack. You know, help them get through."

She stared at him. "Cut the other person a little slack?" She was thinking of the first place they'd seen him, a warehouse in the jungle. A speech she had made.

"Uhh . . . sure?"

Her face broke into a huge grin. "I think that's beautiful advice, Krugar."

"Yeah? I'll try to remember that one, then."

She laughed again. Impulsively, she leaned over and gave him a peck on the cheek.

"Oh right," he said, grinning. "And don't do that in front of him too much. Guys are stupid about stuff like that."

"I bet you could take him."

He gave her a funny look that said—*uh . . . yeah*—then shrugged again. "Speak of the devil," he murmured, as Shabaz swung an eye to find Johnny rolling forward to join them.

"I think we're almost back to the safehouse," he said. Then he frowned. "Did I just see you give him a kiss on the cheek?"

Shabaz looked at Krugar, then burst out laughing.

CHAPTER TWENTY-FOUR

Johnny rolled towards the front in a puzzled daze. He really wasn't sure what just happened.

It was good to hear Shabaz laugh like that. They needed a few laughs. Whatever Krugar had done, it was good, probably deserved a peck on the cheek. No need to be jealous. After all, it's not like they could hook up.

He stopped. They couldn't, could they?

"The race you're in," he muttered, but he surprised himself by smiling. Shabaz had been laughing. And that *was* a good thing, he thought as he joined Torg and Torres.

"So what do you want to do when we get there?" Torg asked the purple skid.

"Oh, you're asking me now?"

Torg sighed. "Torres . . ."

She popped an arm. "All right, fine, we're here. I get it." She glanced at Johnny. "I'm not apologizing."

That sounded like the old Torres. "I wasn't expecting one. We've all been through—"

"Don't," she snapped. "I'm sorry for what I said, just don't play the sympathy game. We don't have time."

"Uh, okay," he said, trying not to smile. So much for not apologizing.

Torres glared at him, then looked back at Torg. "We'll go in, sweep the area, see if Wobble reads any hostiles. Then we enter the safehouse." She grimaced. "Won't matter. It's probably rigged to explode the second we go in."

"I'm sure it is," Torg said. "That's why we're going to send Dillac in first." Even Torres had to chuckle at that.

"Rhi, boz, I heard my name, what goes?"

And that was that. All the absurdity and tension and pain came to a point and they exploded with laughter as the crimson skid rolled up and stared in confusion at the three skids contorted in the hall.

After a minute, Torres half-giggled, half-snarled to Johnny, "All right, you win. You're still a jackhole, but Al definitely would have hated him more."

"Hey!"

"Relax, Dillac," Johnny said, blinking his vision clear. "Albert still would have hated me more than anybody. A little." He suppressed another laugh.

"Oh," the confused skid said. "True words, then."

"What are true words?" Onna said, rolling up with Zen. Shabaz and Krugar trailed, with Kesi bringing up the rear.

"We were just debating who would be hated more," Torg said.

Onna blinked. "So who won: Johnny or Dillac?"

Which of course set them off again. When Dillac looked like he was going to protest, Johnny reached over and slapped his side. "Seriously, Dillac, don't worry about it."

The chocolate stripes tilted. "Just don't like coming in second, squi."

"Okay," Torres said. "Since we're all going spare, the world is literally falling apart and we're probably vaped anyway . . . let's get to it. Wobble?"

They crossed through a broken door—a short, scrapey transition—and emerged into the black and gold grid-space that surrounded the block of the safehouse. "Okay," Torres said, popping her light-swords, "scan the area Wobble." She looked like she was hoping for a fight.

The machine took long enough with his scans that Johnny got nervous. Finally, Wobble said, "Negatory hostiles. All scans-scans are clear. The Cleag must have gone through-through the Crown."

"Still probably going to blow up when we walk in," Torres muttered, sheathing the swords. She glanced at Dillac, then tilted her stripe and went in first. They followed her inside. The building didn't blow up. "All right," Torres said, as the hollas sprang to life. "Thread knows what we're going to do now, but let's get a look at—"

A row of Antis rose from behind a holla-bank.

Even before several doors slid open and more Antis poured through, Torres had re-ignited her swords. "*I told you!*" she screamed, as Johnny's heart sank and he reached for Zen.

"PLEASE STOP. WE COME IN PEACE."

They did stop. It was something in the unfamiliar tone of a very familiar voice. That and the fact that the Antis didn't move once they floated into the room. "They are here for my defense," the voice said, changing its pitch so that it no longer filled the space. "They will not attack."

A figure emerged from behind the Antis. It looked a little like Krugar, except it had molded white skin and its legs were inside some kind of floating device that resembled a modified knife.

"Please," the figure said. "We come in peace."

Johnny stared, not trusting his ears. It was Shabaz who said it first. "*SecCore?*"

The figure raised a hand, palm out. "Please. We come—"

"In peace," Torres snapped. "Yeah, we got that. What the vape are you doing here?"

"We require assistance. We will offer assistance. The interloper is—"

"You mean Betty," Johnny said.

"Yes. Betty Crisp is winning—correction: no one is winning. I am in danger of being removed from the Core. We require assistance. We will offer—"

"Sweet snakes," Shabaz breathed. "She's winning . . ."

The molded white head turned in her direction. "No one is winning. Our battle is damaging the Core. Our battle is damaging the Thread."

As if on cue, the ground trembled. *Yeah*, Johnny thought, *you could say that*.

"Why don't you surrender, then?" Krugar said. "Give up the Core, retreat, stop the damage."

The head swung and shaped itself into a look of distaste. "You are not where you should be, little avatar."

"No one in this room is," Johnny said, keeping one eye on the Antis. "Answer his question."

"We are SecCore. We cannot defend the Thread if we are removed from the Core."

"Then why don't you let Betty defend the Thread?" Shabaz asked.

"Like grease she will," Torres muttered.

"Betty Crisp cannot defend the Thread. If we do not exist to defend the Thread, the Thread will die."

"Rhi, you sure you're not just saying that 'cause you're losing, boz?" Dillac said. When Torg, Torres, and Shabaz all looked at him, his stripes swelled and he added, "What? We ain't allowed questions too?"

SecCore's head turned his way. "We are saying that because we are losing. We are also saying that because it is true."

"See," Dillac said, sniffing indignantly. "True words."

"If you're losing," Johnny said, "then why are you here and not there, fighting her?"

"We are in the Core and we are here. We exist in many places, as does the Core. You have seen this."

They certainly had. "And now that Betty's gotten into the Core, she can do it too."

"Yes. We require assistance."

"As much as I'd like to vape that jackhole's stripe," Torres said, "why the hole would we help you? You've tried to kill us as often as you've tried to kill her."

And yet the Antis still didn't move. Whatever was going on here, Johnny thought, SecCore wasn't trying to kill them now.

"We will offer assistance in return. We already have done so."

"How?" Shabaz asked.

The head turned again. "We observed your actions in what you refer to as the outer Core. You are no longer allied with Betty Crisp. When you escaped—" The head froze.

Then remained frozen.

"Uhh . . ." Johnny said.

The head came back to life. "We do not understand what transpired there. You fled, then ceased to exist. You chose to cease to exist. Then you returned to existence elsewhere, through a means of movement we do not understand."

"When we figure it out," Torres muttered, "we'll let you know."

"Please do so." SecCore's face molded into distaste. "We do not like the failure to understand." The face returned to its neutral expression. "When you returned to existence, we immediately launched a full scale assault on Betty Crisp."

"Huh," Krugar grunted.

"What?" Johnny said.

"Focus her attention," Krugar said. "Keep it away from us."

The head turned. "You are correct, little avatar."

"Wait," Torg said. "How soon did you do this after we . . . returned to existence?"

"10-25 seconds upon your return."

"Snakes," Torg swore. "So she might not know we survived."

"We had not yet focused her attention on us. It is likely she is aware of your return to existence."

"Great," Torres said. "And she knew we were going after Al."

"Yeah," Johnny said slowly. "But she might not know what happened there. She might think we're dead." He worked it through in his head. "So you're saying that after that split second we returned, she hasn't been able to track us at all?"

"That has a high probability of truth."

"So wait," Shabaz said. "If you're so busy distracting Betty, how'd you know when we'd get back here?"

"We did not. After your return to existence and at the moment of our assault on Betty Crisp, we sent a portion of our selves here to speak with you upon your return. We have been waiting."

"You've been waiting . . ." Johnny breathed. He glanced at Shabaz and Torg and saw the same stunned expression on their faces. Slowly, all three of them swung two eyes in the direction of the creature sitting quietly in the corner of the room.

Wobble.

"Ah," SecCore said, his head turning. "The traitor."

One of Johnny's eyes swung back. "You know, if you're looking for our assistance, you'd better find something else to call him. Right now."

A pause, then . . . "Apologies. We have made . . . errors in judgment."

"You're vaping right you have. And I'm not the one you need to apologize to."

"You are correct. Greetings, Wobble."

Wobble didn't even twitch. "Hello."

"Apologies, Wobble. We have made errors in judgment. With regards to you, they have been substantial."

Ever so slightly, the lids over Wobble's lenses opened further apart.

SecCore's head turned back to the room, stopping on each of them. "In defending the Thread, we have made errors in judgment. This has caused damage to the Thread. We find this difficult to say."

Johnny was amazed he was saying it at all. SecCore had never sounded like this. And he was pretty sure Betty had never heard him sound like this.

"These errors have caused a proliferation of the infection you call Vies. It has caused an increase in the corruption you refer to as the grey. It has resulted in a failure to repair areas of the Thread in need of repair.

We have failed in our task. We have failed to defend the Thread. With regards to you, Wobble, our errors have been substantial. We should not have destroyed the other of your kind. We should have considered your advice. We should not have . . . we are uncomfortable saying this. We should not have damaged you in the manner in which we damaged you. It was . . . unkind."

With each thing SecCore said, Wobble's lids continued to widen. At the last, a gear whirred and he said: "Thank you, father-father. You spoke-spoke of assistance. The court is frozen. Why-why did they trust the Belarai? Wobble."

"I have spoken of assistance and assistance I have rendered."

"Yeah," Johnny said, "but that's not why you're here. You said you wanted our help, but there's no way we can take on Betty directly. So what else you got?"

The head never turned away from Wobble. "We should not have destroyed the others of your kind. We did not destroy the manner in which to create them again."

Instantly, Wobble's shutters snapped all the way open and his head spun like a gyroscope. He rose on his treads and pressed forward. "Coronas on the horizon and Farsi got them home. *You will tell me now.*"

"Oh my," Torg breathed.

"What?" Johnny said, his eyes swinging, not sure where to land. "What are they talking about?"

"He's talking about the Wobble factory," Torres said, her gaze filled with need and fire.

"What?"

"Al had a theory," Torres explained. "He said it was possible that SecCore destroyed the other Wobbles, but not the factory itself."

"The little silver skid was correct."

Wobble surged forward. "You will tell me now."

The molded head froze. Remained frozen. Unfroze. "Very well."

Wobble came to a dead stop. Then, slowly, the lids over his lenses closed and then opened again. "Thank you, father."

"Hold on a second," Shabaz said. "Does Betty know about this?"

Both machine heads turned. "No."

"Oh my," Torg said.

CHAPTER TWENTY-FIVE

They raided the stores and geared up to move.

"Take everything you can carry," Torres said, strapping ammunition belts and power packs over her torso. "If this doesn't work, we're not coming back. If it does . . ." She grimaced. "Vape it, let's not jinx things. Take it all."

"Bam your gears," Dillac said, hoisting a huge gun that Johnny thought looked familiar.

"Unless we're going to be falling," Torg drawled, "that one isn't as much fun as you'd think." He went still, then looked at SecCore. "Please tell me we will not be falling."

"It is unlikely."

"Good," Torg and Shabaz said together.

"There are, however," SecCore continued, "factors of which you should be aware."

"Of course there are," Kesi muttered, looking for a place to put her grenades.

"We will not be able to travel with you. Nor provide you with Antis for protection. The probability of either course of action entering Betty's awareness is too high. If we return our attention to the Core we will be able to sustain our assault, which raises the probability of Betty remaining unaware of your course of action."

"That's fine," Johnny said. "If you can keep Betty off our trail, we should be able to handle ourselves until we get to the factory."

"There are other factors—"

"Of course there are," Kesi muttered again, giving up on the grenades.

Johnny sighed. "All right, what's the trap?"

SecCore's head turned. "You are aware there is a trap?"

"Why would this be easy?"

The head froze, then unfroze. "I do not understand your kind. Why would you wish it to increase in difficulty?"

"SecCore," Shabaz said impatiently, "just tell us the danger."

"The final path to the hub you refer to as the factory is singular. We eliminated all other paths. The path is broken and undefended."

"Which means Vies," Shabaz said grimly. She grabbed another power pack. "Great."

"There are other factors—"

"Oh, would you just say it all at once?" Johnny protested. He would've rather had this conversation with Wobble, but the machine had gone still and Johnny didn't want to mess with whatever preparations he was making.

"Apologies. We left an attachment of Antis within the factory for security. They can be deactivated with a code." The head froze. "However, there is a probability that time and the damage we have sustained from Betty will have caused the Antis to go rogue. In this scenario, their power must be cut from the central power source."

"And that would be in the centre of the factory, then?"

"Correct."

"So Vies, then Antis," Johnny said ruefully.

"Par for the game," Shabaz grinned.

"Hey," Krugar said, emerging from the back. "Are we looking to attack or defend?"

"Looks like mostly attack," Johnny said.

"There are other—"

"*Oh come on!*"

The face formed into an expression of distaste. "The assault on Betty is not going well. This is uncomfortable to say. Should she counterattack and further access the Core, there is a possibility that she may become aware of the factory's existence."

"A possibility or a probability?" Johnny said suspiciously.

The head turned towards Krugar. "You should prepare for both."

"Fair enough." The soldier disappeared into the back room. Five minutes later, he emerged with a large pack strapped across his shoulders.

"Snakes, Krugar," Onna said. "You're going to carry all that?"

"Nah, this ain't bad. Better to have and not need than need and not have." His head cocked to one side. "I'd kill for battle armour, though."

"All right," Torres announced. "Everyone got everything they can carry? Let's gear up. Wobble?"

Immediately gears whirred and Wobble rose on his treads. "Affirmative. Let's go-go for a ride."

"Vapin' right," Dillac said, heading for the door.

"Hold on," Johnny said. He rolled over to SecCore. "I just want to say this: I don't like you. You've been responsible for killing skids. I don't like what you did to Wobble. And if you'd figured this out sooner and accepted Betty's help in the first place, the Thread might have been fixed by now."

The molded face remained silent. The entire time the security program had been here, the rows of Antis hadn't moved once.

"But," Johnny said, "coming here took courage. Asking for help took courage. And apologizing to Wobble was the right thing to do. You keep Betty off our backs and we'll get this factory going. And then we'll come back and help you get the rest of the Thread right."

The face remained silent. Then: "That would be acceptable."

"Good," Johnny said, turning away. "Then give her the gears."

As they streamed through the door, SecCore called out. "Wobble?"

The machine hesitated by exit.

"Make him admit the truth."

Now what the hole did that mean? Gears whirred, but Wobble didn't speak before rising on his treads and going through the door.

Johnny was the last one out. As he rolled past the exit, his trail-eye blinked. When it opened, SecCore and the Antis were gone. Johnny snorted derisively.

The guy was still a jackhole.

Then again, he'd given them hope. If he hadn't showed up, Johnny had no idea what they might have done. And he'd accepted the offer of help with fixing the Thread, and that might have been even more impressive than Albert and Johnny working together.

Al would have liked that, Johnny thought, and a pang ran through his stripe. The silver skid should be going with them. He was the one who'd remained in the Thread, for reasons just like this. Of course, Albert's first course of action had been to search for the skid who eventually vaped him, the skid who still might cause it all to fall apart.

"Hey you," Shabaz said, rolling up after Wobble led them through an unbroken door.

"Hey you," he said back.

"So, here we go again. Except, did we switch sides?"

He chuckled. "I was just thinking about Betty. Who would have thought SecCore would become the reasonable one."

"So you think he meant what he said? At the end, that bit about accepting help even after this is done?"

"I don't know. But he seems like a pretty rigid program. That was the whole thing with Wobble, he couldn't handle all the angles. I don't even know if he's capable of lying."

"Maybe," she agreed. "What do you think he meant by: *make him admit the truth?*"

"Beats me. Sounds like something Wobble would say."

"Or . . ."

He gave her a look. "They're not here."

"'Cause this is the kinda time that they tend to be."

"Shabaz," he said, firmly. "I haven't seen Peg or Bian. And if I do, I'll let you know."

She let her gaze linger, then smiled. "Okay." She rolled quiet for a moment, then said, "And the Albert thing? You going to be okay?"

He chuckled. "I was just thinking about him too. About how he should be here. It's weird . . . I miss him. I mean, I sort of did before, back in the sphere, but I never thought I'd remember him fondly." He shook his stripe. "He *was* a jackhole, right? It wasn't just me the entire time?"

She took a little longer with the answer than he would have liked before she said, "Well, you both had your moments." She nudged his tread. "What do you want me to say? You both saved my life."

"Yeah," Johnny said, staring down the hallway, the golden lines quietly glowing their glow. "Nope," he sighed after a minute. "Still weird."

They came to a travel hub. They moved through that one directly into a space with another, then repeated that several times. "Okay," Torres muttered after the forth hub, "now I believe he's keeping Betty occupied. Two days ago and that last one would have been filled with Antis."

They entered a long, wide hallway, wider than most of the corridors they'd seen before. It stood several skids in height. They rolled down that for a long time before Wobble pulled up. "I-We are near. Bao-Hai-Huu was right, that-that's a lot of Kromans. Wobble."

Beyond the machine, the hallway stretched for another hundred metres before the first break in the gold began on the left. A little beyond that, another break on the right. A few sparks, here and there. After that, more and more breaks, the shattered golden lines of light fading into the darkness. And after that . . .

"That is a lot of Kromans," Torg murmured.

The darkness seethed. Occasionally, a flash of gold, but mostly it seemed as if the hallway ended in a writhing wall of black.

"Oh, this is snaze," Dillac said, his eyes wide. "This is real not round, rhi."

"Okay," Torres barked. "Wobble, in front. Me and Johnny right behind. Shabaz and Torg bring the rear. Everyone else, uh, Kesi and Dillac behind Johnny, Onna behind me . . ." Her gaze fell on Krugar. She sighed. "Like I'll tell you where to go." Her lead-eye looked up the corridor and she sighed again. "You do this, right? This is your thing?"

"Yes," Krugar said, his rifle resting easily in his arms.

"Okay," Torres said, conceding. "What should we do?"

"You were thinking right," he said, stepping forward. He looked at Wobble. "How wide a path can you keep completely clear? I mean, total kill zone, nothing gets through."

Wobble's gears whirred. "Three metres, sir, yes, sir."

That got a chuckle. "Good enough. Torres and Johnny take a corner of that area, but angle out a bit. The rest of us tuck into the space created. Shabaz, Torg, keep the rear." He studied Onna for a moment. "It's better if I can rove a bit, support where it's needed. Can you hold down a side by yourself? We'll keep it tight."

Onna bobbed an eye. "No problem."

"Good. Take the right; Dillac, Kesi take the left. Zen—"

"I know," he sighed. "I'm in the middle."

Another chuckle. "Pretty sure you're going to get to fire the gun, kid. Shade towards Onna, but look everywhere. Hallway's pretty tall, watch anything getting in from above."

"They'll come up from the floor too," Torres said.

"Well, that's great. All right, watch for that too. Stay tight, keep the perimeter." He paused. "Now, this last thing's the most important: we keep moving. We keep pace with Wobble and we never slow down. Someone stumbles, they catch up on their own. We lose more than one, rotate where I tell you. We lose me, go where Zen tells you, he's got the best seat."

"Oh," the Level One said, his stripe going pale.

"I repeat: *we never slow down*. There's no cover, no breaks in the enemy, so we run until we get there. Anyone got anything else to add?"

"Forget bumping," Johnny said. "It'll just cause chaos. And you can take hits and survive. Think of your name and the colour of your stripes. They're scary but they're not tougher than we are."

"Damn straight," Krugar said. He took a final survey, then nodded. "All right then. Wobble?"

"Affirmative." The machine rose from the floor and transformed into his knife form. "I-We bring the end."

"Heh," Krugar said. They fell into formation, then followed Wobble towards the writhing dark.

Wobble slowly accelerated until they were moving at a good pace. Not Johnny's top pace, but fast enough. He glanced at Zen, impressed. The One was moving way faster than a One should have been able to tread. Then again, given the look on his face, he didn't look like he was about to fall behind.

They crossed the last hundred metres in three seconds flat. In the final second, Krugar roared, *"Fire at will!"* What seemed like a hundred weapons sprouted from Wobble and opened up as they plowed into the wall of Vies. Johnny opened fire and didn't let up.

When they'd assaulted the Core, it had been mad. But that had been more like the madness of the Slope, bobbing and weaving through the chaos, taking out any Vies or Antis that got past Betty. This was like Tag Box stuffed with every living skid and they all had swords. There were Vies *everywhere*. Johnny couldn't possibly pick targets, they just mowed ahead. He could feel a biting in his treads, but he pushed it back and plowed on.

He kept one eye angled up for Vies, but Krugar quickly dispatched anything that came from above. The soldier rode with the glowing stick pressed between his knees and the end of his rifle constantly spreading fire in short, controlled bursts: a burst here, a burst there, a burst *there*. Johnny tilted his upper-eye to check on Shabaz. Her stripes had swelled up half her body and her gun moved almost as fast as Krugar. Her skin was relatively clear.

The same couldn't be said for Zen, just in front of Shabaz. The Level One was emitting a constant roar, as if he could scare the Vies from touching him, and even though he hadn't slowed at all, Johnny could see black splotches in the indigo skin.

He had no idea how far they had to go.

"Eye's front, Johnny," Krugar barked, and Johnny's upper-eye snapped forward.

Five minutes passed. Then ten. More. The biting in his treads never went away—it was as if the floor were made of Vies. They'd all selected high load weapons, but he still had to change power packs. Every time he did, he got tagged. He could handle a few hits—Torres, Torg, and Shabaz could do the same—but he was starting to feel nauseous. And it was only a matter of time until they took one hit too many, or one of the others got hit square.

"Incoming," Wobble cried. "Four square in twenty."

Twenty what? Johnny thought. Even seconds felt too long—Zen was starting to look strained, everyone had blooms on their skin.

Suddenly, he heard a roar of pain. On the periphery of his vision, he saw Dillac eat a Vie full on. Before Johnny could even begin to swing the eye, the crimson skid's skin turned black, swirling furiously as he roared again. For a second, Johnny thought Dillac might have it, then his left tread hitched and he fell out of formation, disappearing into the chaos.

"Dillac!" Kesi screamed, starting to turn.

"*Stay in line!*" Krugar roared, moving to cover.

Wobble abruptly slowed and rotated. "Door," he keened. "Run, run, run, I-We will hold!" His guns began firing back through the group; somehow, he didn't hit anything but Vies.

"Go," Johnny yelled at Torres, shoving her through the door. Next was Zen, then Kesi, Torg and Shabaz. Krugar followed her and Johnny turned to follow him. "Wobble, we're clear!"

"*Don't you close that vaping door!*"

From the hurricane of Vies, Dillac stormed out of the darkness—his skin black, gun in each hand spitting fire, roaring with defiance and rage. "*This . . . is . . . treadgrease!*" he screamed as he hurled the guns away and dove past Wobble, who snapped the door shut behind him.

Johnny had no idea what kind of space they'd entered; it was as black as it had been through the door. The only light came from Wobble and Krugar. They could have been back in the dead city again, for all he knew.

Dillac staggered in the edge of the light, his expression wild. Johnny reached for him, but the skid stuck out an arm. "I got this, squi," he said, and a wave of crimson bloomed against the darkness in his skin. Then it faded, and he sagged on his treads. "Nope," he said weakly. "Need a hand."

Johnny lunged forward and dove in.

It was like Brolin all over again: biting black everywhere. Except he heard screams of rage and defiance as he gunned for the core: "*DILLAC! DILLAC! DILLAC!*" Johnny broke through, stunned. He'd thought he'd experienced rage, but Dillac fought for his life like he was being ground against the spikes in Tunnel.

A crimson wave pushed out against the black, then fell back towards the crimson core banded by six chocolate stripes. It pushed back out, but then fell in again, closer to the core. Dillac was losing strength fast. Johnny didn't even think about what he was supposed to do. He just got behind the next wave and pushed. A surge of triumph and rage—snakes, had he ever been this angry? The wave plowed outwards with a final roar: "*MY NAME IS DILLAC, SQUI!*"

Johnny reeled back from Dillac's body, blinking his vision clear. Just in time to see an Anti emerge from the darkness.

Are you kidding?

The Anti aimed for Dillac, but before Johnny could move, a teal flash raced by and plowed into the Anti's side. Kesi screamed—Johnny knew how bad that felt. The Anti bounced ten metres, turned—

Wobble came out of his own light and blew the Anti to shreds.

Johnny realized he could hear gunfire everywhere. "Wobble!" Torres cried. "Get to the centre and turn these things off. We'll hold them here!"

"Negatory," Wobble said, fire-wheels spinning out from his carriage to pierce the darkness. "Follow-follow, I-We will—"

"Dammit, Wobble, we don't have time, you have to get—"

"*NEGATORY!*" For the first time ever, Johnny heard anger in Wobble's voice. "You-You will follow. *NOW!*"

Another wave of fire-wheels, then the machine turned and took off into the darkness. Johnny reached for Dillac, but he and Kesi were already racing after Wobble. Johnny followed, the last in the line. They didn't go far, but Torg still got tagged and snarled in pain. Flashes of light popped in the darkness. *How many vaping Antis did SecCore leave?!*

Wobble reached a door. "Inside," he ordered in a voice that did not offer debate. He shoved Johnny in last.

"Nice," Torres breathed. "Go shut them down."

"Negatory," Wobble said fiercely, spinning in the doorway. "I-I have another idea. Stay-stay here." Then, remarkably, a grin split the knife-like shape. "Torg, you are kind of cute."

The doorway shut behind him. As the sound of thunder began to come from the other side, they all stared at it, stunned.

CHAPTER
TWENTY-SIX

"Well," Torg said. "That was something." Then he sagged on his treads. "Whoa," he said. "Give us a minute."

Johnny could relate. Nausea from helping Dillac rolled under his skin. He could probably use a minute of his own to recover, but he wasn't sure they had one. "Head count," he yelled. "Tell me how you're feeling. Krugar, I need to see everyone."

"Hold on." A beam of light twisted, then widened out. "How's that?"

Fortunately, the room wasn't that big; Johnny could see them all in the dim light. "Shabaz?" he said, trying to sound calm.

"Like Torg," she replied, her voice strained. "Need a second." She groaned, but her skin cleared. "Okay, I'm good."

"Me too," Torres said. "I'm sick as sugar, but good to go."

"I don't think I am," a voice said weakly. Zen's indigo skin was almost all black and he was deflated on his treads.

Him first then, Johnny thought. "Kesi, Onna, hold on."

"I'm fine," Onna said, although she didn't sound fine. Kesi just groaned.

Hold on, Kesi, he thought, and reached for Zen. "Shabaz, get over here. Someone else needs to learn how to do this in case I ever can't." He peered at his girlfriend in the light, hoping it was just shadows he saw on her skin. "Can you do this? You don't—"

She put her hands on Zen. "What do we do?"

Snakes, he loved her. "Follow me," he said and dove into Zen.

He'd been terrified Shabaz was still infected, but she was a strong wave behind him. They dove for Zen's core together, where they found him barely holding on. Given the extent of the infection, it was a wonder he was alive at all. For a Level One, he had crazy fight. *First Dillac, now him.* Like Shabaz the first time, there was strength in the most unexpected skids.

And none of them wanted to die.

He had a brief flash of Makaha, vanishing in the woods without a chance to fight. *The race you're in,* he thought, banishing the image.

Taking one side of Zen's core, Shabaz took the other. It took two tries, but Shabaz learned fast and, on the second attempt, Johnny felt Zen join them as they pushed the black out. "Whoa," Shabaz said, rolling back from Zen as they emerged. "So that's what that feels like on the other side."

"Come on," Johnny said grimly. "Kesi next."

"Hold on," Torg said, rolling over. "Take a tread, Shabaz. I want in on this."

"Me too," Torres said.

"Okay," Shabaz said, sounding a little relieved. "Johnny, are you okay to keep going?"

"However long I have to. Okay, Torg, you help with Kesi; Torres, you'll help with Onna. Onna? Can you hold on?"

"I think I sprained something," the Level Four groaned weakly. "I'm good for five. Maybe don't make it ten."

Torres moved towards Onna. "Maybe I should—"

"Wait for me," Johnny said firmly. "We won't need five." He hoped that was right.

Kesi wasn't in great shape, but she was in better condition than Zen or Dillac and, like the others, she had lots of fight. Johnny might have been able to handle it himself; instead, he backed off and let Torg take the lead to learn more. Torg instinctively supported Kesi and after a few attempts they pushed the virus out.

As they emerged, Kesi's eyes went wide. "I am *so* sorry. If that's what you've been doing for other skids, that was incredible. Thank you."

"My pleasure," Torg drawled, although it was an exhausted drawl.

"*Johnny!*" Torres cried, and he swung an eye in time to see Onna collapse into her treads.

Oh, snakes, Johnny thought, gunning it. Torres already had her hands on the completely black skin. Not a shred of white or red left. "Her name and her colour," he said to Torres. "Hold on, Onna."

Somehow, Onna was even worse than Dillac. Of course she was, Johnny thought, furious with himself. She'd held up an entire side of the formation alone, for Crisp's sake! Who knows how many times she'd been tagged. And she was only a Level Four, why the hole had he allowed—

Hey! The race you're in! The thought came clear and angry as a purple streak passed Johnny, heading for

Onna's core. Johnny swallowed the guilt and followed Torres down. They arrived to find a white core already covered with black spores, the red stripes in shreds. Johnny could feel Onna fighting, but there was so much damage. One of the stripes tore away . . .

ONNA! Torres screamed, plowing into the virus. *YOUR NAME IS ONNA!* Then she stunned Johnny by diving into the core.

A second where everything went still: the core, the stripes, even the black. Then the stripes reformed like a whip and two voices roared—*ONNA, ONNA, ONNA!*—and tore into the black. Johnny, suddenly finding himself along for the ride, slipped in behind to support, but the virus never really had a chance.

They emerged and Johnny rolled back from Onna with a bemused expression. Her white skin was flawless, her four stripes thick and strong. Torres grunted, as a bloom appeared and vanished from her skin. "You all right?" Johnny asked, amazed.

"Yeah," she said, spitting. "My stripes feel like they've been scraped, but I'll be fine in a minute."

"That was incredible," Onna said, staring at them. "Thank you so much. Both of you." Although she had two eyes on Torres. "Thank you."

Torres caught the look. Despite the grimace on her face, her stripe flushed. "No problem. You . . . you would have done the same for me." She coughed awkwardly, then swung an eye at Johnny. "So that's how that's done."

"Uhhh . . . yeah," he said. Torres had gone right into Onna's core. "That's how we do that." He backed up a tread, studying Onna. "Glad you're good." Rolling away, he chuckled.

Right into her core.

Shabaz rolled up. "I'm fine," he grinned, reading the look on her face.

"Are you sure? You just did four skids, one after another, including Dillac by yourself. You've never done that many before."

"I'm a little nauseous, but I'll be okay."

Krugar walked over. "I don't know what the hell just happened, but whatever it was, it was impressive."

Johnny's stripe twitched. Right into her core. "Torg and Torres did most of the heavy lifting on the last two. I just helped a little."

"Helped a little," Shabaz said in disbelief. She bumped his treads. "You're an idiot."

"Hey, I just saved four lives, I think that makes me heroic."

"Except Torg and Torres did the heavy lifting."

"You helped too."

She smiled at that. "Good answer."

Krugar was looking at Onna with one of the most intense expressions Johnny had ever seen on the soldier's face.

"What?" Johnny asked.

Pursing his lips, Krugar said, "If we're all programs in a giant program, then didn't you just do some programming?"

Johnny barked a laugh. "Wasn't it you who said you can't think that big?"

"No," the soldier said, examining the other skids. "I said there are times when you can't."

"Like when there are an unknown amount of Antis out there trying to kill us?"

Krugar chuckled. "Fair enough. A thought for later, then." He looked towards the door, as the pounding sounds of battle continued outside. "I'd offer to help Wobble . . ." The pounding stopped and one of those full-mouth smiles split Krugar's face. "But it appears he might have it under control."

A moment passed, then the door slid open and a battered Wobble rolled in. Johnny had seen the machine damaged before, but this was ridiculous. His whole body smoked, charred black in dozens of places, twisted and scarred in a dozen more.

"Snakes, Wobble," Torg breathed. "Maybe you should have let us help."

"Negatory," the machine said, and his face broke into a huge shattered grin, multiple teeth dangling. "Max-Max told the story. One thousand men enter-enter, one man leaves. Wobble."

"Well, at least you managed to shut them down," Onna murmured, staring at the smoke rising from Wobble's carriage. Remarkably, his twisted parts were slowly moulding back into shape. The charring slowly faded.

"Negatory. Antis gone rogue-rogue. Too random to shut down, no one jumps that-that worm. I-We eliminated the problem. Wobble."

"Eliminated?" Johnny said, staring. "You mean you wiped out all those Antis?"

"Affirmative. You-We know what we bring."

Johnny leaned over towards Torg. "Is it me or were there an insane amount of knives out there?"

"One would have thought. Although machines count a little different than we do."

"Yeah," Johnny said. That was one way to put it.

"Come," Wobble said, spinning on his treads. "We-I will find the lights." Even though he still had his stutter, there was a purpose behind Wobble's words Johnny had never heard before. Wobble was always excited, but Johnny had never seen him *driven*.

As they rolled out into the still darkened factory, Johnny tensed, half-expecting an Anti to loom out of the darkness. But he began to relax after they rolled down corridor after corridor in peace. The light from Wobble and Krugar lit off brilliant white surfaces, sometimes disappearing into the darkness. Wherever they were, the space was huge.

Dillac rolled over. "Hey, boz. Thanks for the save back there. Tight game, rhi."

Johnny's stripe tilted. "No problem. You did a lot of the work. And the way you survived falling out of the formation, that was . . . that was something." He chuckled at the memory of Dillac, from the storm of Vies, screaming, "*This is treadgrease!*" When most skids ate a Vie, they died. Dillac must have eaten dozens.

"True words." Dillac held up a splayed hand, fingers pointed out. Johnny blinked and stared at him.

Dillac rolled his eyes. "Tap'em, boz." When Johnny awkwardly tapped his middle finger against Dillac's, the crimson skid rolled his eyes again. "Squi's got moves like bam and still don't know the know." He rolled away, shaking his stalks.

"Looks like you disappointed him," Shabaz murmured, rolling up.

"Apparently I got moves like bam but still don't know the know."

Her gaze narrowed and then, abruptly, she burst out laughing. "That might be the best description of you I have ever heard," she giggled.

Bumping her treads, he said, "Shows what you know about the know." A gleaming white loomed out of the darkness. "I wonder how far we have to go to find the lights?"

"We-We are here," Wobble announced.

"Well . . . all right then."

"Warning, warning," Wobble said, his head spinning with barely contained enthusiasm. "The Sim could not chill. This— this may be . . . impressive. Wobble." A gear whirred and the lights came on.

It was impressive.

"Vape me," Kesi whispered and Johnny couldn't blame her for cursing. He'd expected big. After all, they'd already rolled a fair distance and it was a factory.

He just hadn't expected this big.

The pentagonal space they occupied was larger than the central hall of the Combine, rising up, level by level. Everything gleamed a smooth white, like the surface of an Anti. On each of the five sides, a corridor extended into the distance.

"It's like a ghostyard," Shabaz breathed, rolling towards the centre of the space, her eye-stalks stretched out in three directions.

"It can't be that big," Johnny murmured, but he wasn't certain. He tried to scope to the end of a corridor and failed.

Pods lined each of the five corridors, presumably for the creation of other Wobbles. Just how many had been made? Johnny had been thinking in terms of hundreds, but now that he saw this space he realized that he'd been thinking way too small. He'd seen thousands of Antis before—hole, he'd felt like there'd been that many waiting for them in the unlit factory. If SecCore had tried to make as many Wobbles as there were knives . . .

"Agendas and departure windows," Wobble said. "I-We must repair-repair before We-I can return the hub to active-active status." His head never stopped spinning. "This will require time-time." He started towards one of the hallways.

"Whoa, hey," Johnny said. "What will take time? Time where?"

"Follow." Wobble didn't even break stride.

Johnny stared after him, then looked at Torg and Shabaz. "I guess we follow," Torg said.

Not far down the corridor, they came to another, extending off to the side. More pods lined the walls. Wobble reached out and one of the chambers opened: an empty, glowing space about twice the size of the machine.

Wobble's head spun as Johnny and the others pulled up. "Pit stops and lasers under light. I-We must repair." Johnny had never heard the machine so excited. "We will be some time."

"How much time?" Johnny demanded, not even sure what Wobble was going to do. Was he just going to shut himself inside the chamber for—what? Hours? *Days?*

"Uncertain. But repairs must-must occur if more Wobbles are to be created. Do not fear, We-You found the map. Try the one on the left. All will be Teddy Bears." Without any other warning, he rolled into the chamber. A clear cover emerged from the top and turned opaque as it sealed shut.

"Huh," Krugar chuckled. "Well, I guess if it's all going to be teddy bears, it can't be that bad."

Johnny slowly swung a skeptical eye. "You know what a Teddy Bear is?"

"Sure. I'm pretty sure Huma still has mine from when

I was a kid." He ran a hand over the chamber, which softly pulsed with light. "Still . . ."

"Still what?"

"Well," Krugar said. "He was pretty much our big gun. What happens if something other than a teddy bear shows up while he's inside this thing?"

"Uhhh . . ." Johnny said, staring at the softly pulsing chamber. "Hope it's willing to wait?"

CHAPTER TWENTY-SEVEN

Shabaz watched Wobble's pod seal tight with mixed feelings.

She was thrilled he was finally getting a chance to repair the damage that had haunted him for so long. But Krugar had a point: he was their big gun. Shabaz had gotten so accustomed to having the machine cover their stripes; now that he was gone, she felt exposed. Not only that, but Wobble was the only one who knew anything about where they were.

"So," Onna said, staring at the pulsing chamber. "What just happened?"

"It would appear Wobble will be indisposed for a time," Torg drawled.

"He couldn't have waited a bit?" Kesi said. "He could have at least shown us around first."

"Hey!" Torres barked. "Wobble gets to decide whether or not he plays tour guide. If he wants to get repaired first—you got a problem with that?"

Kesi sighed. "Look, I'm not shredding your friend. That guy saved us all a crazy amount of times. But Krugar's right, what are we supposed to do now?"

"We look around ourselves," Shabaz said, rolling back to the main hallway. She understood Kesi's concern, but Torres was right. Mixed feelings or not, after everything Wobble had been through, he could do what he wanted.

"Is that safe?" Zen said, glancing at Krugar.

"I'm pretty sure Wobble wouldn't have left us if he thought there was still any danger. He took care of the Antis, Betty doesn't know we're here, and I doubt any Vies are getting in. Look at this place, it's spotless."

"Yeah," Kesi said, "but Wobble didn't say we could look around."

"Didn't say we couldn't, rhi," Dillac said, nudging her tread as he rolled past. "Let's go see where at's at."

Shabaz led them back to the main hub. She couldn't believe the size of the factory—how were they supposed to get something this big up and running? Could Wobble do it all by himself? If he could get it going, could they create enough Wobbles to clear the Vies that surrounded the facility? Could they create more?

For the first time since falling back into the Thread, Shabaz felt a surge of hope. They'd had disaster after disaster, but this place was so immense and it was untouched by Vies or corruption. No black, no grey. Nothing looked broken. It might not be working yet, but when it did . . .

"We could win," Shabaz said softly.

"Well, we're due," Johnny said, rolling up and giving her a nudge. "Right, Krugar?"

"Amen," the soldier said, his gaze sweeping the entire factory. "This is a good idea. We find out what else is here; maybe find a place to defend, if necessary."

"Why?" Onna said. "Betty doesn't know about this place, right?"

"Yet," Krugar said. "But SecCore sounded like that wasn't guaranteed forever." He pointed up. "I'll see if I can't get to the upper floors, find some lines of sight."

"All right," Shabaz said. She looked at Johnny. "What do you think?"

A grin split his face. "Hey, this was your plan. Point me in a direction."

She loved cocky Johnny, she really did, but some things deserved a response. Which is why she said, "All right, we'll go in pairs. Stay in touch. Find anything, report it over the com." She pointed at one of the corridors, and added in her sweetest tone, "Why don't you and Dillac take that one, Johnny?"

The grin faded a bit, then, remarkably, intensified. "Absolutely, boss-mama-sir." He jerked an eye. "Come on, Dillac, let's go see where at's at."

Okay, she was definitely going to get him later for the boss-mama-sir thing. That and the smug whatever-you-can-dish-out look in his trail-eye as he rolled away. She tried to ignore the way her heart seemed to be accelerating as his eye remained on her.

"Shabaz?" Torres said, but there was a little smile on her lips. "Any other pairs? Or was that it?"

"Shut up," Shabaz murmured, although it was good to see Torres smile. On a whim, she said, "Okay, why don't you and Onna take that one?" The two skids glanced at each other and their stripes flushed almost in unison. *Thought so.*

"Sure," Torres said.

"No problem," Onna said, with the same flustered edge. Together they rolled off.

"That was nicely done," Torg drawled.

"I don't know what you're talking about," Shabaz grinned. "How about you and Zen go together?"

Torg gazed at the Level One. "You promise to take it easy on me?"

"Okay," Zen said, his eyes a little wide.

After they left, Kesi said, "So I guess that leaves us. Didn't trust Dillac and me together?"

"Not at all," Shabaz said easily, studying the remaining skid. "I just thought Johnny had it coming." She was pleased Kesi laughed at that. "And besides, we haven't had a chance to spend much time together."

"No," Kesi said, hesitating. "I guess not." She considered the two remaining corridors. "So which one do we take?"

They both looked the same: gleaming white and impossibly long. She was going to let Kesi pick as a peace gesture when Shabaz remembered something Wobble had said, just before he'd entered his repair pod. "Let's try the one on the left."

The hallway was lined with pods, stretching up into the heights. Shabaz counted thirty levels before she finally gave up. At a certain point, the uniform white and the haze from the glow made everything blend together. Same thing with the corridor: if it had an end, she couldn't see it.

"You really love him, don't you?" Kesi said suddenly.

"Hmm?" Shabaz said, squinting into the distance. "You mean Johnny?"

"I know you guys are together—everyone knows that—but you're different around him. You guys don't . . . you act different than other skids who get together. That thing where you sent him off with Dillac;

he'd just said he was going to follow whatever you said. Why'd he have it coming?"

Shabaz chuckled. Explaining this, when she'd barely begun to understand what she and Johnny were going through herself, would be interesting. "Johnny sometimes gets this look when he thinks he's doing something noble, like letting someone else lead. And given how much he likes to lead, it is kind of noble. But he still gets a little cocky. Which I like." She grinned. "But I can't let him get too cocky."

Kesi bobbed an eye in understanding, then a spasm of grief crossed her face. "Hey," Shabaz said, rolling closer. "Are you all right?"

The teal skid popped a Hasty-Arm. "I'm fine."

It took her a second before she got it. *Oh*, Shabaz thought, feeling a wave of empathy. So that's why Kesi was asking about her and Johnny. "Kesi," Shabaz said gently, "is this about Trist? Were you—?"

"No," Kesi said sharply. "We were just going to the woods. That's it. He was just a snug."

Shabaz studied her. "Was he?"

They rolled in silence for the next few hundred metres. Just when Shabaz thought Kesi wasn't going to answer, the teal skid said, "He was different."

"Trist?"

"Yes." Kesi's gaze wandered over the pods, her eyes full. "Crisp, this place is big." Another silence, then she sniffed violently. "I don't know exactly what it was, but Trist . . . thought different. I liked the way he was willing to stand up to you and Johnny. Lots of skids didn't like what you were doing." She glanced at Shabaz. "I think I get it a little now, although I'm still not sure how I feel about what you did."

"It's okay, Kesi, you don't have to apologize."

She sniffed again. "That's nice. And if you were hanging out with skids when they died . . . I guess that was pretty nice too."

"Thank you."

"But I only say that because now I know about all this." Her eyes swung around the corridor, shaking in disbelief. "Back in the sphere, no one knew why you and Johnny suddenly started doing what you were doing. Especially you. With Johnny some skids thought it was just a Ten thing, but you . . . no one could fathom why you'd quit at Eight. I sure couldn't." Her gaze narrowed. "Although you're not really an Eight, are you?"

Shabaz grimaced. "It's complicated."

"Right. Okay." Kesi stared at Shabaz's eight stripes, then shook her stalks. "Anyway, lots of skids complained but Trist was the only one who did anything about it. He was the one who said if we went and told you to cut it out together then we'd have a better chance. Funny, but when I think about it now, he was helping other skids. The same thing we were mad at you for."

Shabaz smiled. She'd said something similar to Johnny not long after Trist and his gang first showed up.

"So yeah," Kesi continued, "I guess I felt . . . I mean, we weren't like you and Johnny but . . . I liked him. More than the other guys I'd been with." She took a long ragged breath. "But I guess that doesn't matter."

"Oh, Kesi—"

The Hasty-Arm thrust out again. "Don't. Please, just . . ." Her hand clenched into a fist, which she banged off one of the empty pods. "Crisp Betty, I'm doing it again. Whine, whine, whine. It's like that's all I've done since I got out here. Even Dillac isn't complaining as much as me. When did that happen? I swear I'm not usually like that. That's not the skid I am."

Shabaz chuckled. "I was."

"Sorry?"

"The complainer. That's exactly the kind of skid I was for most of my life. Hole, the first time we fell into the Thread, I never stopped moaning. Sometimes I think it's a miracle Johnny and Bian didn't vape me."

"Who's Bian?"

"Ahhh. . . ."

That was dumb. She did *not* want to think about Bian. Or Peg. Or Bian and Peg. Or Johnny and . . .

"That's also complicated," she said, then bit her lip, angry with herself. "No . . . no, it's not. She . . . she was one of the skids who was with us the first time we were out here. She was my friend."

It must have been in her face, because Kesi hesitated before asking, "She died?"

"She did. Saving the Skidsphere."

"Oh. I'm sorry."

"That's okay. Anyway, I spent most of my life complaining. About everything. If I lost in a game, I complained. If I got to the sugarbar and didn't get a booth I liked, I complained. And once we were out here . . ." She winced, remembering the entire time leading up to meeting Betty. "Seriously, it's a miracle Johnny didn't kill me."

"What changed?"

Shabaz smiled. "He saved my life instead."

"Oh, like how you and him did with us?"

"Yeah. It was Johnny and Albert." A small pang went through her heart at the thought of the silver skid. She took a ragged breath. "I was certain I was going to die—

another skid just had, right in front of my eyes—and then . . . they saved me. And I helped. And that's when I realized that maybe I didn't have to be a victim. Maybe I'd never been a victim. I mean, there were all these skids, even the little ones like Torres and Aaliyah,—" another pang "—all feeling overwhelmed, all beat up and half-vaped . . . but they were doing something about it. So I decided that maybe I should do that too." Her stripes tilted. "And that was it."

Kesi bobbed an eye. "Yeah. Maybe I should start doing that."

"Hey. You geared up for Torres in that prison sim. And besides, you and Trist and even Dillac weren't complaining in general." She stopped. "Okay, maybe Dillac was." She smiled and was rewarded with a smile in return. "You guys had a specific problem: Johnny and me. Even if I think you were wrong at the time, you were trying to do something. And as for what you were like when you first got out here . . ." She swept an arm across the immense hallway. "Everyone gets a little vaped by the Thread."

They rolled in silence, past pod after pod. Then Kesi smiled a little smile and said, "Thanks."

"No problem. We're all in this together."

"Yeah. So . . . are we supposed to be looking for anything in particular?"

Shabaz laughed. They'd already rolled over four kilometres. Every five hundred metres, there was a side corridor that looked like a slightly smaller version of the first. "Beats me," she said. "I guess it's like Krugar said: get an idea of what this place looks like, maybe find a spot we can defend if we need . . ." Her voice trailed off as she stared down the hall.

"What?" Kesi said, swinging a second eye out front.

"Hold on." She couldn't believe it, she'd just been talking about her. Shabaz turned on her com. "Johnny?"

"Hey babe," his voice came over the com. "Is your hallway as exciting as ours is, 'cause we've been rolling—"

"Don't care. Drop what you're doing and get over here."

"Uh, that's a pretty long haul back. Is there a reason—"

"Your girlfriends just showed up." She couldn't believe it, but there were two smears of colour in the distance: one pink, one red.

She half-expected Johnny to say something about Bian not being his girlfriend, but instead there was just a short pause and then: "I'm on my way."

"What's going on?" Kesi said, as they continued to roll. "Johnny has other girlfriends?"

"Do you see anything down this corridor?"

"Uh . . . no? But I might not scope as well as you."

I'm not scoping. Ahead of them, she saw the pink and red shapes turn. "Hey!" she yelled, gunning it. "Don't you dare!"

After about thirty metres, she geared down. She was not going to do this. She was not going to chase Bian and Peg—*vaping Peg!*—down a hallway to hole knows where. She'd follow, but she was not going to chase them.

"Uh, Shabaz . . ."

"Listen," she said, "I know what this looks like. I just need you to trust me, all right? And if you do see anything, let me know." *It'll mean I'm not vaped off my gears.*

"Okay," Kesi said sceptically. But she did follow.

Several times, the pink and red smears disappeared and then reappeared. *Not playing, ladies,* she thought, although that was a little absurd because she was following. When she caught up to them . . . well, she wasn't really sure what she was going to do. She was chasing ghosts—she might not be racing after them, but she was still following two dead skids.

She wasn't sure who made her more angry: Peg or Bian. She wasn't sure it was sane to be angry at dead skids, but then again, they refused to stay dead.

"Okay," Johnny said over the com. "We're in your corridor. Be there soon."

The flashes disappeared and reappeared again. "No rush," Shabaz muttered to herself. "We're having a grand old time."

She suddenly realized that the smears of colour had stopped. As Shabaz and Kesi approached them, the corridor came to an end. They'd traveled ten kilometres from the central hub.

Shabaz stopped about twenty metres away from Bian and Peg. The ground trembled, but she ignored it. The two skids sat there, just shy of the end of the corridor. They didn't shimmer or fade in and out. She couldn't see through them. Bian looked alive and well, although Shabaz noticed that she was missing the arm that had been lopped off when they'd invaded the Core. Peg didn't look nearly dead enough.

When they didn't say anything, a surge of impatience went through her stipes and she said, "Well?"

"We will wait for Johnny," Peg said.

"Sweet snakes," Kesi said, rolling back a tread.

Shabaz couldn't help but laugh. "See them now?"

"Yeah," Kesi said, her eyes wide. "Yeah . . . okay."

Welcome to the circus, Shabaz thought as she turned back to the ghosts. "Johnny's going to be a minute. Why don't you tell me what you want?"

"We will wait for Johnny," Bian said.

"Well then you should have shown up in his vaping corridor!" she yelled, her anger echoing off the walls. She rolled forward a tread. "Seriously, it's nice to see you again, Bian, but unless you both got some reason for being here, unless you got something to say, you can scram. So speak up."

"You will not lose him," Peg said.

"You will lose each other but you will not be lost," Bian said.

"And talk sense!" she screamed again. Snakes, she hated this. She glared at Peg. "You're vaping right I won't lose him. I'm not you." She was pretty sure this wasn't fair—she actually had no idea how Peg had died—but she didn't care. "And as for you . . ." Her eye swung towards Bian. "I loved you like a sister, but stop talking like Wobble and talk like Bian."

"We can't," Bian said. "He didn't remember doing this."

"He will," Peg said, "but there isn't time. They're coming."

With her trail-eye, she saw a powder blue smear appear, then a crimson one. Johnny was booking it top speed. Behind them, another two skids appeared: Torg and Zen.

"Yeah," Shabaz said, "I can see that." She rolled right up to Peg. "So before they get here, let me tell you something. You want to talk to my boyfriend, you talk to me first. Are we clear?"

Peg didn't respond. She silently met Shabaz's gaze until Johnny rolled up, slowing as he got near. "So . . ." he said, in that way he had when he tried to sound casual. "How's everyone doing?"

"Like sugar," Shabaz said, backing away from Peg, holding her gaze. "The ladies here were just talking about getting lost."

"Easy to do in this place," Torg said, arriving with Zen. "Any of you check down those side halls? It's like a maze." He looked at Shabaz. "Heard over the com. Thought I'd come and see this for myself. Bian, Peg. You're looking good."

A faint smile graced both their faces then faded. "We are sorry, Torg. They are coming."

"You said that before," Johnny said, inching forward. "Who's coming? Who's they?"

"The stars grow narrow and fall," Peg said.

"The Core is falling," Bian said.

That sent a chill down Shabaz's stripes. "Explain that," she snapped.

"We can't," Peg said. Now that others were here and she wasn't quite so worked up, Shabaz realized they both looked sad. They'd carried a sense of sorrow from the moment Shabaz and Kesi had arrived. "There's no time. He would have shown you, but there's no time." She looked at Johnny. "This will be the last but one." Before Shabaz could react with the anger that surged again, Peg's gaze spread as if to encompass them. Bian did the same.

"We love you all," they said together. Then they disappeared.

Where they'd been sitting, a door appeared at the end of the corridor.

CHAPTER TWENTY-EIGHT

"What's going on?" Torres said, rolling up.

"Johnny's ex just showed up and disappeared again," Shabaz muttered, looking shaken. "Bian was with her."

"Bian?"

"Forget it," Johnny said, two eyes on Shabaz. "Long story."

The ground trembled beneath his treads, but he didn't care. Right now, he just wished the others weren't there. He had no idea what was going through his girlfriend's mind, but it couldn't be good. Why Peg and Bian had decided to appear to her, he had no idea. What they'd been talking about, he had no idea. He knew that there was probably something important about the door that had just appeared, but right now he just wanted to talk to Shabaz alone.

Apparently, he wasn't going to get to do that. "Hey," Onna said, rolling forward and examining the door. "That's interesting."

"What's interesting?" Johnny sighed.

"Wasn't one of these down our corridor," Onna said. She eyed Torres. "Was there?"

"Kind of hard to miss," Torres said.

"You got to the end of your corridor too?" Torg said. He winked at Zen, "Apparently, we were dawdling, sir." Zen grinned in return. Johnny was glad Shabaz had put them together.

"We, uh . . ." Onna stammered, her stripes flushing. "We made good time. We were . . . racing a bit."

Now why would they have done that? Johnny and Dillac had only been five kilometres down their hallway when they'd heard Shabaz's call. Dillac had talked largely nonstop the entire time, mostly about how weird all this was, and about how he was sad about Trist, and a lot about Kesi. Johnny suspected Dillac might have a thing for her. Although with the way Dillac talked, it was hard to be certain.

"Yeah," Torres coughed. "We even got to . . . look down the side halls a bit. Didn't see anything like this."

"Well, Bian and Peg wanted us to see it," Shabaz muttered, glancing from Torres to Onna and back again.

"Might have been nice if they'd left us the code to open it," Torg said, rolling over to the door, reaching out. "Without Wobble—"

As he touched the door, it disappeared, leaving an empty space in the wall.

"Oh," Torg said. "How about that?"

They all looked at Johnny. "Hey," he said, hoping to make peace, "Shabaz picked the corridor." A weird look crossed her face, although it didn't seem to be directed at him. He waved towards the door. "After you?"

This time she smiled. "All right then," she said, rolling forward.

They rolled down a short hallway, then into a single room not much larger than the room Wobble had locked them in when he'd fought the Antis. A single pillar sat in the centre of the room. And the walls . . . the walls were strange. They didn't look like the rest of the factory. In fact, they looked a little like . . .

"Is it me," Shabaz breathed, "or is the entire room a holla bank?"

"I was just thinking the same thing," Torg murmured, contemplating the central pillar. He rolled over. "Huh," he grunted. "Give me a minute." Popping his Hasty-Arms, he laid them over the surface of the pillar. "Now where are . . . ah."

The room lit up.

"Whoa, boz," Dillac whispered.

Whoa boz is right, Johnny thought. The room stunned everyone into silence, as streams of information flashed by. Everything from still pictures to moving hollas; schematics, blueprints, and diagrams; seemingly random shapes and lines; what looked like code . . .

"What are we looking at?" Torres said finally, staring.

"I'm not sure," Torg said, studying the walls, then looking down at the pillar where a light seemed to wrap around his hands. "Whatever it is, it's huge."

"True words," Dillac murmured.

"I just can't quite tell . . ." He stopped. "Huh." His eye swung away from the pillar and examined the room. Not the walls—the room. And then the doorway. "Huh," he grunted again, looking back at the lights around the pillar.

"What?" Johnny said.

"I don't think this room is part of the factory."

"*What?*"

"If I'm scanning this right," Torg said, "this room and the factory haven't existed for the same amount of time. The room is newer."

"So SecCore added it after he built the factory?" Torres asked.

"Maybe," Torg said, scowling.

"He would have shown you, but there's no time," Johnny said softly, glancing at Shabaz.

She was already there. "Wobble," she said. "They were talking about Wobble. Wobble built this room."

"Then why didn't he tell us about it?" Kesi said. "If we're supposed to find it, why didn't Wobble tell us himself, before he went into that repair . . . uh . . . thingy."

"SecCore did a lot of damage to Wobble years ago," Torg said, his hands moving constantly around the pillar. "Wobble needed him to tell him where the factory was. Maybe he didn't remind Wobble about the room he built."

"Or he didn't know about it," Johnny said, the realization catching him off guard. "SecCore didn't know about this room," he whispered, following the thought. "Torg . . . what does this room do?"

"I need more time."

"Pretty sure someone said we didn't have that," Dillac said blithely. When Torg glared at him, Dillac tilted his stripes. "What? That's what the crazy disappearing lady-skids said, boz. Serio, what's up with that?"

"Torg," Shabaz said, "can you give us your best guess?"

"I think it might be a map. Of the Thread."

Johnny stared at him. "The whole Thread?"

"*They found the map*," Onna breathed. "Wobble said that right before he went into the repair . . . thingy." Her stripes twitched. "Is this freaking anyone else out? 'Cause I'm a little freaked."

"You and me both, rhi."

"All right," Torres barked. "Let's give the man his time, whether we have it or not. I don't know what good a map will do us, but anything we can get, works. Let's go. Torg?"

"I'll let you know when I have something more solid," he said, all three eyes on the holla-walls.

As they rolled back out into the main corridor, Krugar floated down on his light-stick. "Sorry I'm late to the party. What did I miss?" They filled him in. "Huh," he grunted. "Can't hurt having a map in the long run." He sucked on his teeth. "That's the second time someone's told us we're running out of time. I'm not a big fan of psychics, but ignoring two warnings might be kinda dumb. Probably time to start making this place defensible." As if on cue, the ground trembled.

"How do we do that?" Torres said.

Krugar jerked his head back down the corridor. "This place has more nooks and crannies than you realize. Near the centre, side corridors connect the big ones; further out, there's a lot of twists and turns. I've got some stuff in my kit that can do some damage." He grimaced. "I bet this place has a defence system, but without Wobble all we have is what we have. If that SecCore guy was right and he can't hold off Betty, and she shows up with a few thousand Antis . . . even if Wobble wakes up repaired, I doubt he's bringing friends."

"What if she can't bring that many Antis?" Onna asked. "How many does she have, anyway?"

"Who knows," Torres muttered. "If she kicks SecCore out, she might have them all."

"Yeah," Shabaz said. "But she might not be able to bring them here. It's not like we're that close to the Core, right?"

Krugar grunted. "Like I said, lots of twists and turns. Anyone coming in has to go through the centre. We could lead them on a chase up the levels—up sucks for attack. We could do some damage." He paused. "It would help if we had a rabbit."

"Is that like a Teddy Bear?" Kesi said.

"He means give her a target to chase," Torres said. "Draw her focus while the rest of us do the damage." Suddenly, she chuckled, somewhere between a true laugh and a snarl. "Oh, snakes, Al would have loved this." She swung an eye at Johnny. "Guess who gets to play hero again."

"Me?" Johnny said. "Hey, I'll do whatever, but you and Torg and Wobble are the ones who've been a gap in her treads for the past three months."

Torres was already waving her stalks. "No. You saw what happened when we confronted her at the Core. I barely existed to her. It's you. You've always been her favourite. Even when Al was around, it was still you first."

"Okay, hold on," Shabaz said. "A) Torres, that's not fair. And B) no one is doing anything against Betty alone. We can take turns leading her."

But even as she suggested the idea, Johnny knew it wouldn't work. He didn't like to admit it— which was amazing given how self-centred he'd been just three months ago—but Betty did fixate on him. Maybe if Albert was here he could've split the duties, but now there was really only one skid that could get under Betty's stripe. He sighed. "Torres is right. It should be me."

"Johnny . . ."

"No, really. I'm not saying she's right to fixate on me, but she always has. Me and Albert. And Al . . . isn't here. So it's me. I'll keep her attention, she'll underestimate the rest of you and you get to do the damage. Until Wobble wakes up or Torg . . . I don't know, maybe that room is a defence mechanism."

"All right, that's the plan," Krugar said, spinning on his stick. "Let's get back to that centre hub and I'll show you what we can do."

As they rolled back, Johnny saw Torres lingering in the rear and fell back. "Hey," he said.

"Hey."

He rolled in silence beside her for a minute, then said, "You know I don't really want to be a hero, right?"

She let out a long ragged sigh. "Yeah, I know. Well, no, I think that's half treadgrease . . . but only half. And that's fine. It's not like Albert didn't want to be a hero. Hole, he was a hero." Her stripe grew pale. "No one should have to die like that."

"Yeah."

"No really. We've seen some pretty gruesome things out here, but that . . ." Her expression hardened. "If I could, I'd kill her."

He wasn't really sure what he could say to that. He'd admired Betty for so long; he'd watched her save the sphere—sure, he and Albert and the others had been the ones to repair the damage and make it whole, but if Betty hadn't put it in stasis, if she hadn't saved all of them dozens of times, if she hadn't led them into the Core, none of the rest would have happened.

"Torg seems to think we need both her and SecCore."

"Torg's in love," Torres snorted. Then she winced and said: "No, that's not fair. He's thinking about her as clearly as anyone could. I don't know who this whole thing was harder on—him or Wobble." Her whole face flinched as the ground rumbled. "I just don't understand.

I get what the Vies are, I get SecCore and the Antis, I kind of understand the grey, but I don't understand what happened with Betty. *Why would anyone do that?*"

With all her brash confidence, with all the times she'd taken the lead since they'd returned to the Thread, it was easy to forget just how young Torres was. But hearing the anguish behind that last question, the complete inability to understand how someone so driven could get driven the wrong way . . .

Johnny looked at her single orange stripe. Three months ago, she'd been a panzer. She wasn't anymore, but that didn't mean she wasn't still too young to understand what fifty years of rage could do. Hole, Johnny was too young to understand it. "I don't know," he said, staring down the hall.

They rode in silence past side corridors and empty pods. Then Torres pulled out her light-swords. "Here," she said gruffly. "You should have these."

"Torres, I can't take—"

"Betty has them. If you're going to taunt her, you might need them to stay alive. Take them."

Gently, he took the swords from her. He lit one, looked at the orange blade for a moment, then extinguished it again. "Thanks," he said. "I appreciate it."

"You better," she muttered. Then she glanced at him sideways. "We're good, Johnny."

He felt a surge of affection for her, as the ground rumbled again. "I'm glad." He held the look for a moment, then added. "Panzer."

"So's your game."

They arrived back at the hub. "All right," Krugar said, opening his bag. "We'll try to keep drawing her up and away from Wobble. Those little alcoves you see every twenty pods? Those are lifts. Blue circle takes you up, clear circle drops you down. Now, the first thing—"

The ground bucked hard to the left, throwing all of them against the walls. It was the biggest corpsquake Johnny had ever felt.

"WARNING, LITTLE SKIDS," SecCore's voice boomed into the factory. "WE ARE FAILING. THERE IS A HIGH PROBABILITY BETTY CRISP HAS BECOME AWARE OF YOUR LOCATION."

Oh snakes. "SecCore!" Johnny yelled. "How long do we have?"

"UNKNOWN. THE CORE HAS BEEN COMPROMISED. WE ARE FAILING."

"We need more time. You have to hold her there."

"NEGATIVE. BETTY CR—" the voice cut away "—AINED ACCESS TO CRITICAL ASPECTS. WE AR—" Another massive quake rocked the factory and SecCore's voice cut away completely.

"Okay, people," Krugar said, grabbing his bag. "We move on the fly. Let's go."

"Where do you want me?" Johnny said. A surge of fear shivered though his stripe. He half-expected a hundred Antis to come through the walls.

"If she's alone, keep her here. Try to keep them on this level as long as you can. If she's in the centre hall, I have line of sight. When we're ready, bring her up. We'll hit and run for as long as we can."

If she's alone ...

Johnny's eyes swung up and he yelled: "SecCore! SecCore!"

No response.

He decided to take the shot anyway. "SecCore, if yo' can, prevent her from bringing Antis with her. Lock out from what she can do at the Core." Johnny had no idea if that was even possible.

For a long moment, no response. Then, the ghost of an echo: "—IRMATIVE."

"Good idea," Krugar said, nodding. "All right, people, let's move." He sprinted for the lifts.

The others followed, each giving him a sympathetic look. "Don't lose those swords," Torres said, "they're the only ones I got."

Shabaz rolled over, her eyes bright and wide with concern and fear. She bumped his treads hard. "I know," he said roughly. "But you can't. One rabbit."

"Yeah," she said. She bumped his treads again, then kissed him full on the mouth, a long, hard kiss. "Don't you vaping die, Johnny Drop. Or I'll find your ghost."

He grinned back. "Okay."

The ground shook again. "Right," she said, and spun on her treads.

Leaving Johnny, standing in a vast empty hall. He wondered what was happening in the Core. "Too big," he murmured. SecCore would have to take care of itself. Although, he did wonder what they were going to accomplish here. Even if SecCore kept everything but Betty out, even if Wobble came back repaired . . . they were going to defeat Betty? Johnny didn't know how fast the factory could make Wobbles once it was running— certainly it looked like it could make a hole of a lot of them—but he assumed it wasn't instantaneous. He wondered what Torg would find. He wondered if it would matter.

"I wonder how long I have to wait," he said aloud, tensing instinctively.

Nothing happened.

He'd honestly been expecting her to show up right then and there. Betty had a tendency to do things like that. There was a reason why there were a thousand stories of her in the sphere. There was a reason why she'd been the one to save it.

"Snakes, Betty," Johnny muttered. "What are we doing?" How had it come to this?

Down one of the halls, possibly the one they'd used to enter the factory, a black and pink skid turned a corner. It paused, scoping his way, then seemed to bob its eyes and move in his direction.

He'd already decided to wait and let her speak first. If the whole point was to stall for time, he'd take as much as he could. He swallowed, trying to ignore the queasy feeling in his stripe.

She took her time. Stopped about ten metres from where he sat. When he didn't say anything, she swung three eyes around, examining the centre hub, then each of the five corridors. Finally, two of her eyes came down and settled back on him.

"So," she said casually. "Here we are."

CHAPTER TWENTY-NINE

"I see you found the Wobble factory."

"We did." He considered staying silent, but this wasn't about looking cool or establishing some kind of status. He wasn't going to beat her at that. He was just thankful she was alone.

She let her gaze wander. "We looked for this for over thirty years. I'd started to think that maybe the gearbox destroyed it all. We never came close to finding it. Of course," she added, pursing her lips, "we never had help."

The ground trembled. Now, *that* was her style. "Betty—" he started to say.

"Don't." She popped an arm. "I don't care. How it happened, what your excuse is, don't care."

She didn't sound like she didn't care. Her whole body was tense, her pink stripe so tight Johnny expected it to hum like the barbed wires sometimes did on Tunnel. "Your little ally is still fighting the good fight," she continued, "but it's only a matter of time. He's going to lose. I'm finally going to vape that jackhole."

"And you really think that's going to help?"

She ignored the question, swinging an eye back to the corridor from which she'd come, then back again. "Neat trick keeping me from bringing any friends of my own. Seem to be missing a few other tools as well. It's been awhile since I felt like this."

It's been three months, Johnny thought. That was it: three months. Sure they'd all changed, but did she honestly think it had been that long? She'd been alive for fifty years, for Crisp's sake.

"Where's the gang?" Betty said, her trail-eye wandering but the front two staying on Johnny. "Where's Wobble?"

His heartbeat spiked and he fought to control the wave of anxiety that rushed through him. He needed to stay calm. As casually as he could, he said, "They're around."

She laughed at that. "Priceless. Still Johnny Drop." She inched forward a tread. "You think you're important. You think you still matter. Why? Because you saved the Skidsphere? That's nothing. It's a drop. Do you have any idea how insignificant the sphere is?"

He stared at her. "You used to think it was significant."

"That was before I started fighting a *war*." The ground rumbled again.

She *was* doing it deliberately. Except, if the ground was shaking, then that was the Thread taking damage. She was damaging the Thread just to make a point.

"I'm more impressed that you found this place," she said. "Now, I don't know what you're doing to mess with my scans, but where are the others? *Where is Wobble?*"

Her scans weren't working? He was pretty sure they didn't have anything to do with that. Still, it was a good question—where was everyone now? On a whim, Johnny opened his private com to Shabaz, praying it wasn't a mistake. Betty might be lying about her scans being down. He found Shabaz on the third floor, moving—he had no idea if that was a good sign.

"You know, I'm not a real fan of being ignored," Betty said. "Or have you just gotten that slow?"

Something in Johnny snapped a bit. Maybe she was his idol, maybe she could destroy him, and maybe he had gotten slow compared to her, but this was grease. Inching forward, he said, "You know, for someone who thinks she's so vaping fast, you've spent an awful lot of time in the last two conversations we've had trying to put everyone else down. Afraid of something, Betty?"

A cruel smile split her lips. "Really? You think I'm afraid of you?"

"I'm just trying to understand why you're talking this way."

"I am fighting—"

"A war," Johnny said, inching forward again. "Got that. Why? Why are you fighting everyone, Betty? Aren't the Vies the enemy? Isn't fixing what's broken the goal?" He popped an arm and waved it around. "Who cares how we found the factory—isn't the important thing that we found it? That we get it up and running? Why won't you help us? SecCore helped us, for Corps' sake, why won't you?" A surge of anger and loss came welling up from deep inside. *Why would you kill Albert like that?*

For a second, he thought maybe he'd gotten through to her. Regret flashed across her face, a deep mournful sense of shame. She had to see it, didn't she? She was Betty, surely she had to see? But then the look went away, replaced by a pensive gaze.

"Why don't you have it up and running?" she murmured.

His heart fell. She couldn't see it. She wasn't even thinking like that anymore. He remembered the time in Krugar's sim, when she had Wobble vape one of the mems there, and Albert, furious, saying they weren't going to do that anymore, even if the mem would get resurrected later. That was the Betty that was here. Krugar had spoken about what thinking big could do to you in the wrong situation, and here was proof: Betty could no longer see the small picture. She was lost in her grand vision. That, and her hatred for SecCore.

One of the eyes focused on Johnny swung, and she spoke as if she were alone in the hub. "I'm not Wobble, but I've been around and this doesn't feel like a place gearing up. The lights are on, but that's it." Her eye stopped. "That's it . . ." The eye came back to Johnny. "That's why you're out here. Stalling. You don't have Wobble for some reason. Where is he?"

She rolled towards one of the corridors. As it happened, it was the one that had Wobble's repair chamber. "Hey!" Johnny shouted.

"You don't matter, Johnny," she said, still rolling. "All your little friends went and hid and they thought you could keep me from finding Wobble. Nice try."

If she hadn't done what she'd done to Albert, he might have let her find him. After all, Wobble had been her best friend for almost forty years. It was inconceivable that she would do anything to harm the machine.

But what she'd done to Albert was also inconceivable.

"Hey!" he yelled again, as he quietly opened his com to Shabaz. *Babe, this is going downhill fast. Are you guys ready?* Betty still didn't turn.

A brief pause, then Shabaz replied, *Krugar says we need another minute.*

Well, we don't have one. Whatever's going to happen, it's got to be now. "Hey!" he yelled a third time. "You know how everyone says your name?"

Betty rolled another few metres . . . then stopped. Another pause, then her trail-eye settled on him. "All right, I'll bite. Yes, Johnny?"

He couldn't help it. She was probably going to kill them all and the whole thing was so tragic he could scream, but he was still who he was and he had her. "Johnny Drop," he said, in the cockiest voice he could, the one he knew used to drive Albert spare. "That's my name. And in another ten years, hole, maybe five, that's the name they'll be saying. Not yours. Mine. They won't be saying your name at all." And then, because if there was one thing he knew how to do was get under another skid's skin, he pulled out Torres's light-swords, ignited them, and added, "Or if they do, they'll think of you the way you think of SecCore."

Rage flared across her trail-eye and then the upper-eye swung his way, as she turned on her treads. "Oh, this is going to be rich. I'm fighting on more fronts than you could imagine, but I can find time for this. You think because you've got the panzer's toy you can take me? Please." She popped both her Hasty-Arms and a sword ignited in each, pink like her stripe. "You couldn't take me on your best—"

The rocket came from above, and she had her upper-eye on Johnny so she never saw it coming. She screamed with fury as a smoke bomb followed.

Time to go, Johnny. The corridor on your forty-five. He didn't even wait to see how much damage they'd caused. He gunned it for the corridor.

First lift left, Shabaz continued. *Dillac and Kesi are waiting on the second level, get off on three.*

Behind him, he heard a roar and saw Betty emerge from the smoke, spot him, and pursue. He found the lift and the circle of force flung him upwards. He passed the second floor cleanly, and zipped out at the third. As Betty passed the second floor, the area around the updraft exploded. She screamed again, as the lift's force carried her up past Johnny.

"Not so much legend, boz!" Dillac howled from below.

But now Betty was one level up and Johnny had to keep her attention focused on him. He found another lift and zipped upward, as a roar came down the hall to his left. "Hey!" he yelled, and was rewarded as a black and pink shape, slightly battered, came around the corner. "Eyes on the prize."

He wasn't sure how much damage she'd taken, but she did look pissed. They couldn't kill her, Johnny was pretty sure of that. After all, most of her was still in the Core fighting SecCore. But maybe, just maybe, they could hurt her enough that she'd lose what she had here, make it so she couldn't come back to the factory.

Johnny, come straight on and take the third right.

He took off, keeping an eye on Betty to make sure she followed. Bouncing off the walls to gain speed, he careened around the corner Shabaz had indicated with Betty right on his treads. She didn't need to bounce off anything.

She was reaching for Johnny when the mine behind him caught her. Johnny caught a flash of white and red pulling away, Onna in retreat. Betty screamed incoherently—the ground trembled—but she emerged from the blast and smoke, her expression angry and set. "You think this is doing anything? I'll vape you all!"

He hated this. Not because his life was in danger, not even because it was his hero who was trying to kill him. He hated it because he still didn't even know why he was racing away from her, what they were going to accomplish, how they had gotten here. For the next five minutes, he streaked through the factory—up levels, down levels, back and forth—barely ahead of Betty, and only because at this corner or that a blast would knock her back, slowing her down.

And why? What were they going to accomplish? Was Wobble suddenly going to show up and—what?—talk her down? Vape his oldest friend? The blasts Betty took might be slowing her down momentarily, but there was no sign of her stopping, no sign of any real damage. And even if they could hurt her, even if Wobble showed up and they somehow kicked her out of the factory and sent her back to the Core and got the factory up and running, what then? Live to vape her another day? Take a thousand Wobbles and start another war, with Betty on the verge of taking out the one defence system the Thread had already?

He was racing for his life and probably shouldn't be thinking of the big picture, but the ground was shaking and Betty was here and if someone wasn't—

Okay, Johnny bring her to the fifth level, right here. A blip appeared on his positioning system. *Krugar says we've going to take the shot.*

He didn't know what shot that was supposed to be, but he hit a lift, flying up two floors, then sped down a hallway. He emerged onto a platform jutting out into the central hub, thirty metres wide.

Where the vape was he supposed to go from here? Three hallways led back away from the hub; other than that, three sides of empty air. Betty rolled onto the platform as he slowly backed towards the edge. "All right," she said, waving the two light swords. "You've had your fun. Now it's my turn. You first, then the rest of the traitors. Any last—"

The others burst onto the platform: Dillac and Shabaz from lifts on the left; Onna and Kesi from ones on the right; Krugar zipping down on a rope from above. They all opened fire as they hit the platform—Krugar was firing as he dropped. Torres emerged from one of the hallways with a gun like the one Torg had once used in the Core.

Betty screamed, bombarded from all sides, as the hub echoed with pounding detonations. Johnny stared: he'd never seen such violence at close quarters, even the race through the Vies to get into the factory hadn't been this concentrated. Betty's swords went flying; no one could survive this, this was a slaughter—

Then the scream became a roar and Betty's Hasty-Arms popped out farther than Johnny would have ever imagined possible, growing to ten times their size, sweeping the platform. She slapped Shabaz and the others off the sides, plucking Krugar out of the air where he'd leaped to avoid her and hurling him out into the factory.

"You jackhole," she cried, surging towards Johnny, her arms retreating back to their normal size. He raised a light-sword to defend himself and she snatched it from his hands with almost contemptuous ease. "You think you're saving anything here?! I'm the one trying to save everything. For the last fifty years, I'm the only one who's been defending the Thread." She flipped the sword around, blade down, pointed at Johnny. "And I'm going to vaping save it, with or without your help."

"Then maybe you should have a look at what you're saving," a voice said. And, even as the light-sword descended, a flash of magenta and gold darted in front of Johnny.

"Ahh, sweetlips," Torg said, staring at the sword embedded in his torso. "That hurts."

He reeled back on his treads, towards the edge. As he did, his Hasty-Arms fell to his side and something tumbled out from one of his hands, skidding away. Then he went over the side.

"*Torg!*" Johnny and Betty both cried, racing to the edge. Far below, Torg's body lay crumpled on the floor of the factory. It lay there for a moment, then evaporated.

A quality of anger that Johnny had never felt before surged through him. She'd killed Torg. She had *killed*— all three of his eyes swung towards her, to see a fury that matched his own. "I'll vape you," she hissed, reaching forward. "I'll vape you with my own—"

"*HEY!*"

Betty and Johnny swung an eye.

Not far away, Zen sat on his treads, holding the device Torg had dropped in his hands: a small, square box with a single button. The Level One had all three eyes on Betty, each one flat with anger. "I'm only seventeen days old. I don't even know who you are. But I *liked* Torg." He held up the device. "I wonder what this does?"

Betty lunged forward. Zen hit the button.

And the factory exploded with light.

CHAPTER THIRTY

Shabaz hit the floor of the factory and refused to get vaped. She refused to even slow down.

She had to get back to Johnny.

If that last assault hadn't even slowed Betty then she had no idea what she could do; they were geared unless Wobble showed up. Didn't matter. She had to get back to Johnny before someone got vaped.

Then, as she found the correct lift and vaulted upwards, a magenta body dropped in the other direction with an orange gleam embedded in its nine gold stripes, and Shabaz realized she was too late.

Oh, Torg . . .

She hit the fifth floor in time to hear Zen's words—*what was he doing, they'd told him to stay out of the fight!*—to see Betty reaching out, and then the Level One pressed a button on some kind of device.

And the entire world turned into a holla bank.

Every single surface became a platform for hollas: the walls, the floor, the floor of the platform—hole, they were even hanging in the air surrounding them. Still and moving images; landscapes and panoramas; diagrams and charts; highlights, portraits, collages; words and symbols and lines and lines and lines of golden light. She remembered the first time she'd seen the Skidsphere from outside; this was a thousand times more, a million . . . more.

A trillion individual hollas flashing to life.

Except they weren't all individual. Some of them were shifting places, connecting: this line lining up with that; images grouping together and then grouping together and then grouping together again.

It was the most beautiful thing Shabaz had ever seen.

"What . . . ?" Betty said, her hands dropping away from Zen, the oldest and youngest skid staring out with equally stunned expressions. "What is this?"

"It's the Thread," a bitter voice said.

Shabaz's gaze came away from the miracle around her to settle on Johnny and her heart collapsed. He was still by the edge of the platform, the spot where Torg had gone over the side. One eye on the hollas, but two on Betty.

She'd seen him angry before, in dozens of different ways. She'd been nervous of his anger at first, and still hated it when it was directed at her, but she'd come to see how he used it, how it drove him. Not the only thing that did, but nonetheless, one of the forces that helped make him who he was.

She'd never seen him angry like this. It was like it was drenched into his skin; it was so deep and hurt and sad.

"It can't be," Betty whispered, all three of her eyes flailing about, desperate to somehow take it all in, failing utterly. "It's too big."

"And you know something bigger?" Johnny said harshly, rolling forward. "It's the Thread, Betty. The whole thing. This is what you've been trying to save."

"But this is . . . even SecCore doesn't know . . . no one could save this. It's too big, no one could grasp—"

"Well, you better vaping try," Johnny snarled. "Because this is why you killed Albert. *This is why you killed Torg.*"

Around them, hollas continued to merge and merge again. One of her eyes came down from the sight. "Oh," she said, seeming to deflate. "Torg."

"Yeah. Oh . . . Torg." Johnny drove every word home. "He died so you could see this. Do you think it was worth it?"

She sat there, staring at him, as images flashed off her glossy black skin. Then her eyes dropped. "I've made a terrible mistake."

"*YOU THINK?!*" he screamed, popping his arm, the fingers spasming out.

A long moment. "I'm sorry."

Shabaz held her breath as Johnny stared at the skid who was once his greatest hero. "Are you still fighting SecCore?"

Her stripe flinched. "Yes."

"Stop it. Right now."

"Done." The ground beneath them stopped trembling— Shabaz hadn't even realized it was still shaking, she was so geared up.

"Get the vape out of the Core. Right now."

Shabaz didn't even know if that was possible, but after a brief hesitation, Betty swallowed and said, "Done." She paused and added, "It's just me now, here." Another pause. "You can kill me if you'd like."

He might do it, Shabaz thought. She saw it cross his mind, there was so much pain there.

"Johnny," she said, rolling forward. "Johnny, please." With agonizing slowness, an eye swung her way.

"Johnny, look around. Look at all this. You're right, this is the Thread. The whole thing. And it's still broken."

She popped an arm and pointed at section of hollas that had merged into one. She wasn't exactly sure what she was looking at—some kind of blueprint, a little like the one Wobble had shown them on the prison ship—but one thing was obvious: part of it was missing. There was jagged, empty space near the bottom of the holla.

"I don't know what that is, how big a part of the Thread it's supposed to represent, but it's broken, Johnny. And it's not the only one."

She could see it now. Just as when they'd dived into the Skidsphere, at first all you could see was the active hollas—a trillion flashes of light—but once you started to adjust, you could find breaks everywhere. An entire section of the far wall remained just that: a wall.

"We can't keep fighting each other," she said, swinging all three of her eyes towards the skid she loved. "Betty's right, it's too big. We need everyone we can get."

He looked back at her like he was losing something with each flashing holla. "So we just forgive her?"

"Not a chance," Torres said, sliding off a lift. Krugar and Onna followed. "She killed Al. She killed Torg. We don't forgive that. But Shabaz is right: if we kill her, she doesn't get to make up for it." Her eyes narrowed as they centred on Betty. "And she's going to."

Betty held her gaze for a moment, then bobbed an eye. "I'll try."

"No, you won't." Torres closed the distance between her and Betty in a heartbeat. "You won't *try*. You will vaping make up for it or I'll kill you myself." She popped her light-sword. She'd retrieved it from where Torg fell.

"True words," Dillac said, rolling off a lift behind Kesi.

Betty stared at Torres. "Okay," she said finally. As Torres backed up a tread, she added, "Is there any way we can turn these off? I . . . I get the point, I'm just finding it hard to think straight." She looked at Zen. "Can you do that? Please."

The Level One stared back at her. Shabaz wondered if Zen had been telling the truth about only being seventeen days old. She suspected it was the truth.

The blue stripe tilted. "Let's find out." Zen punched the button again and the hollas vanished. "How about that?" he said, tossing the device at Betty. "Hit that button again if you forget your promise."

"I will," Betty said. She started to swing an eye then swung it back with a small smile on her lips. "My name's Betty by the way."

Zen glared at her. "I'll let you know when I care."

The smile faded from Betty's face. "Okay. That's fair." Swallowing, she looked back at Johnny. "What now?"

"Vape if I know," he muttered. "I guess we wait for Wobble to finish getting repaired. Then we see if you can make up for what you've done."

"SHE CANNOT."

The voice echoed through the factory, and, suddenly, SecCore and dozens of Antis appeared on the platform. "SHE HAS DONE ENOUGH. BETTY CRISP WILL PAY FOR HER CRIMES."

"Don't you have a Core to repair?" Betty muttered.

"Betty, shut up," Johnny snapped, and the most powerful skid in the universe flinched. "Don't say a vaping word unless you're asked a question." He swung an eye towards SecCore. "And as for you: enough skids have died today. No more."

The white body didn't move. "BETTY CRISP WILL PAY FOR HER CRIMES. SHE HAS DAMAGED THE CORE. SHE HAS DAMAGED ME."

"She's damaged a lot of people," Johnny said. "But Shabaz and Torres are right. We need her, and she needs to make up for what she's done."

"SHE DOES NOT. SHE WILL PAY FOR HER CRIMES. SHE HAS DAMAGED THE THREAD."

"Oh, for . . ." Shabaz said, rolling forward. She was emotionally exhausted and sick of complainers. "You know what—who hasn't at this point? Betty damaged the Thread from the moment she broke out of the Skidsphere; that was your original problem with her, right? Well, you know who else did that kind of damage: *all of us.* Krugar dragged his damage right into the sphere. Sorry," she said to the soldier.

"Nah," he shrugged. "That's probably right."

She offered him a quick smile and returned her attention to the program in front of her. "You said she damaged the Thread. Well, Betty only showed up fifty years ago. How was the Thread doing before that? How were you doing, defending it?"

The white face turned towards her and took on an expression of distaste. "SHE WILL PAY—"

"For her crimes," Shabaz sighed. "Snakes, you're worse than panzers. You hurt her, she hurt you, let's all kill each other until there's nothing left. Let it go, SecCore. Let her help."

"WE DO NOT NEED HELP."

"Really?" Johnny said, rolling forward. "Because I don't remember that being what we agreed on. We agreed to help you, and you said you would let us continue to do so once this was all over. Or is that just a broken promise?"

A long pause, the molded face unnaturally still. "WE DO NOT NEED BETTY CRISP'S HELP. WE WILL ACCEPT YOURS, IF YOU DO NOT INTERFERE. WE WILL JOIN WITH OUR SON AND CREATE MORE OF HIS KIND. THIS WILL BE SUFFICIENT TO DEFEND THE THREAD."

"NO, FATHER, IT WILL NOT."

The voice filled the factory, and Wobble rose over the platform's edge.

His body gleamed. Shabaz had seen him repair himself, but she had never seen him without any scars at all. Like the Antis around him, but three times the size—was he bigger?—Wobble shone like he was new. Sliding smoothly onto the platform, his body seamlessly transformed— gears humming, each movement like clockwork—into his upright form. Settling onto perfectly aligned treads, his head spun above a body with four fully functional arms. His gaze came to rest on SecCore and he opened his mouth to speak. Remarkably, he still had a single loose tooth.

"You-I know We-We cannot do this alone," Wobble said in a voice crisp and clear. "Enough death. Swords sheathed and Ignelde placed his palm in the sand. We-You-They will defend the Thread together."

"WE DO NOT NEED BETTY CRISP. WE CAN FIX THE THREAD ALONE."

"Can you?" Wobble's head spun. "Friend-Betty?"

The pink eyes filled with tears. "Okay," she said, and the smile on her face was so grateful, Shabaz couldn't help but forgive her a little. Betty lifted the device in her hands and the hollas filled the factory once more.

Wobble remained silent for a moment, the light flashing off his flawless body. "Eyes wide and claws entwined in prayer. Guen saw the web and said this must not be. Father, is not the Thread greater than you ever dreamed?"

The molded face remained still, glimmering with reflected images, for a long moment. "IT DOES NOT MATTER. WE CAN DEFEND THIS THREAD."

"You are untrue, father. You will look again."

Another moment, then the face opened to speak.

"Father, you have not answered Friend-Shabaz's question."

The face froze.

"How was the Thread doing before Betty Crisp left the Skidsphere?"

This time it seemed like the face was frozen forever. Shabaz glanced nervously at the Antis. For all she knew, Wobble controlled them now, but if he didn't and SecCore insisted on killing Betty . . .

The face unfroze. "VERY WELL. BETTY CRISP WILL BE ALLOWED TO LIVE."

"Actually," Johnny said slowly, looking from Betty to Sec-Core and back again. "You might need to do more than that." He pursed his lips, taking his time. "You both have had access to the Core. You both work differently. Imagine if you worked together."

Even as Betty gasped and said, "Johnny . . ." SecCore's face molded into the most expressive face Shabaz had seen yet.

"NEGATIVE. WE WILL NOT SHARE THE CORE WITH—"

"AFFIRMATIVE." Once again, Wobble's voice filled the factory, before returning to its normal volume. "Friend-Johnny is right. Two strengths become one. This is the best way to defend the Thread."

Slowly, the face turned towards Wobble. "Son, do not make me do this."

Wobble didn't move. "Father, you are making an error of judgment."

The face froze, then fell. "Very well." It turned to Betty. "We will be in the Core. When you are ready, we will merge." It turned to each of the others, rapidly, settling on Johnny. "Thank you. We accept your assistance."

SecCore and the Antis disappeared.

"That was bam-tense, boz," Dillac said to no one in particular.

"Friend-Betty?" Wobble said.

"What? Oh." She pressed the button on the device and the hollas disappeared. She stared at it for a long time, then handed it back to Zen. "It's okay," she said. "I won't forget." She took a deep breath. "So, just so I understand . . . did SecCore just agree to merge with me in the Core? To defend and repair the Thread?"

"Affirmative," Wobble said.

"And if I don't want to do that?"

Shabaz felt a surge of irritation and opened her mouth to speak, but Torres beat her to it. "Zen, give her that box back," the purple skid said flatly.

"Okay, okay," Betty said, waving an arm. "I didn't mean—kinks, I'm no good at this." She sighed. "Okay, whatever you want. I'll go, I'll . . . do what I can." One of her eyes swept over all of them, settling on Johnny. "I'm really sorry about Torg. And . . . and Al."

Johnny stared back at her. "Prove it."

An eye bobbed. She took a deep breath. "Fair enough." Then she vanished.

"Friend-Betty has returned to the Core," Wobble said. "She is merging with father. Lights in the distance."

"All is Teddy Bears," Torres muttered.

Wobble's head spun. "Negatory. They are coming. But lights in the distance mean different things. Come." And his face broke into a familiar broken grin, one tooth flapping. "We—I will show you how we cook."

CHAPTER THIRTY-ONE

Wobble transformed and floated off the edge of the balcony. The skids entered the lifts one at a time and followed him down to the floor. As he landed, Wobble transformed back and spread his four arms wide. "Science is magic. Abracadabra." Then he turned to Shabaz and winked and she felt her heart startle with anticipation. "Wobble."

Instantly, a hum like ten thousand gears filled the factory. From every major corridor, a single pulse of light, which faded but not completely.

"Do you feel that?" Krugar whispered.

"Affirmative," Wobble said, his head spinning. "I-We-You bring the beginning."

"Not for everyone," Johnny whispered.

He was sitting twenty metres away, on the spot where Torg had fallen. Tears stained his face. "He might have died a month from now, for all we know," Johnny said, his voice rough with grief. "Doesn't matter. This is the worst."

Her heart aching, Shabaz raced over to him, popped an arm and placed it on his stripe. "Hey, it's okay, it's . . ." She stopped. "No . . . I guess it's not. I'm so sorry."

IAN DONALD KEELING

Torg was dead. That seemed impossible. More than Johnny, more than Albert, Torg had been a constant in the sphere. Even these last three months when he'd been absent—struck from any records or memory—it hadn't seemed that way. She'd started comforting the skids dying at five years old because she'd wondered what Torg might have done in her place. He was like the Spike, the quiet centre of their world.

Torres rolled over. She popped an arm of her own, resting it on Shabaz. She didn't say anything, but together, they wept for their friend. It lasted for some time and the others left them alone; even Wobble kept his distance. Finally, when the last sob choked from Shabaz's throat, the machine rolled over. "Rain falling and pipes on the bridge. Some loss is complete. I-We am sorry. Friend-Torg was my friend."

A surge of warmth broke through Shabaz's tears. Wobble gleamed like the most fearsome knife there was, but he still had a Wobble way with words.

"Yeah," Johnny said, sitting up on his treads. "Mine too."

"Yeah," Torres said. Suddenly, she chuckled. "At least he got his wish. He was the one who insisted that Betty and SecCore had to work together." She sniffed violently, her eyes refilling with sorrow. "I hope he was right."

"He probably was," Krugar said, walking over. "He seemed pretty smart to me."

"Yeah," Zen said. "He was really nice to me." The look on his face broke Shabaz's heart a little. Seventeen days was way too young to learn this particular lesson.

"Boz was real all right," Dillac agreed. "True he ruled the Pipe, squi?"

"Ha!" Johnny laughed, a laugh straight from the heart. "True words. Slow down, son, you're trying too hard." He

290

shook his stalks and chuckled. "Snakes." He looked up at Kesi. "But we don't have to die with them, right?" Then his eyes filled again and he popped an arm and said in a rough voice, "Nope. Uhhh . . . maybe give me a minute."

"Come on," Shabaz said softly, "let him breathe." She let a hand trail across his stripe as the others respectfully backed away. "We'll be over there. Take all the time you need."

As she started to turn away, his hand shot out and grabbed hers. "No," he said, looking up at her. "Not you. Don't ever leave me."

And now she was crying again. "Okay," she said, bobbing an eye. "Okay."

They sat like that—his hand encircling hers, neither of them speaking—while the others waited. After a time, his gaze came up and he took a ragged breath. "Ohhhh-kay," he sighed, blinking rapidly. He looked at the ground. "There should be a rock here. Right here."

"Maybe Wobble can make him one," Shabaz said. She lifted his hand and kissed the back of it. "It's a good thought."

"Yeah," Johnny said. "We get back to the sphere, I'm making him a vaping boulder." He sniffed. "Okay, let's go see what's going on." They rolled back to the others, still holding hands.

"Guys," Torres said as they rejoined the group, "you have to hear this. Wobble, how many other Wobble's does this place make at a time?"

"Five hundred thousand," the machine grinned.

Shabaz stared at him. "How many?" Johnny said.

"Five hundred thousand Wobbles," Wobble said. "With exception, I-We have decided to call them Knives. There is only one I-We-Us." His head spun.

"You can say that again," Onna murmured, peering down the corridors in amazement. "How often does this place produce that many?"

"Punching clocks and The Salvinu lazed it smooth. As I-We begin, one production run every twenty hours. With assistance, productivity will increase. The boss will be pleased."

Every twenty hours. This time tomorrow, there were going to be half a million Wobbles. Shabaz couldn't even wrap her stalks around numbers that high, there were never more than seventy or sixty thousand skids in a given *year* in the Skidsphere. "Half a million," she murmured.

"And they can help repair the Thread?" Johnny asked. "Not just kill Vies, but actually put together broken pieces?"

"Affirmative." His head continued to spin with glee.

"That's great," Johnny said, and smiled for the first time since Torg had died. "Well, I don't know what we can do in the face of half a million Wobbles, but whatever we can do—"

Wobble's head stopped spinning. His flaps lowered into a saddened expression that they knew so well. Gears humming, his head slowly looked from Johnny to Shabaz and then back to Johnny again.

"You-She will do enough."

Before Shabaz could even react to that, Onna cried, "Hey guys!" They looked down the corridor to where she was pointing.

Far down the hallway, a smear of pink and a smear of red.

Great, Shabaz thought, her heart sinking as she glanced at Johnny. *Just great*.

CHAPTER THIRTY-TWO

Johnny did not want to go down the corridor. Every single time Peg or Bian showed up, something was either going sideways or it was about to. At the very least, something significant would happen.

Johnny didn't want anything significant to happen. He was drained from the loss of Torg, elated from the Wobble factory coming to life, and just emotionally burnt out in general. Thank the Thread for Shabaz. Without her . . .

She was looking at him now. A half-smile he'd grown to love played across her lips as her stripes tilted. "If we don't go, they'll just show up somewhere else."

"We-You must go," Wobble said, as he turned and began moving down the corridor. "They are coming. It is time."

"Bam, that's not ominous at all, rhi," Dillac said.

True words, Johnny thought. But Shabaz was right—there wasn't much point in ignoring them. Sighing, he geared up. As Shabaz fell in beside him with the others trailing behind, she grunted. "What?" he asked.

"This is the one corridor we didn't explore. I took the one on the left. This is the one on the right."

A shiver went through his stripe. Not ominous at all.

As they approached Peg and Bian, the two ghosts turned and started back down the corridor. Johnny and Shabaz exchanged another glance, but continued to follow Wobble. They rolled in silence, except for the faint hum of the factory surrounding them and filling the world.

Finally, they came to a blank wall. Bian and Peg turned.

"Is it time?" they said together.

Wobble rolled forward. "It is time. This conversation is happening now. Pieces of chalk and a billion species crawled from the sea. They are coming."

"They are," Bian said.

"It is time," said Peg.

Behind them, a door appeared. Johnny was about to make a comment about having seen this trick already when he stopped. The door didn't look like the one that had led to the map room, but it did look familiar. Where had he . . . ?

"Oh, snakes," Shabaz whispered. "Johnny, it's a door to a ghostyard."

"No," Peg and Bian said together. "There are no more ghosts."

Peg looked at Shabaz. "This is the last time. We are sorry for any pain we have caused. We are sorry for your loss."

Bian rolled forward. "We love you all." Then, for a moment, her expression changed, and it was Bian—their friend—sitting before them. She swung an eye, looking at each of them in turn, lingering on Wobble, Torres, Shabaz, and Johnny. "I love you all."

Then her expression changed back and she and Peg said, "We love you all."

They disappeared.

Johnny stared at the door. His stripe felt like it was on fire—he no longer felt drained, not one bit. All his life, he'd looked up and wondered . . .

Wobble rolled forward. Reached out with an arm. "Come," he said, turning to Johnny as the door opened.

"The universe is waiting."

The glow faded, taking Shabaz with it.

Darkness enveloped them, although, unlike the biting black of the broken Thread, this darkness didn't attack.

It did, however, persist.

What the hole is this?

Not sure, boss, Onna's voice echoed in his head.

Not much to look at, Torres murmured.

All right, Johnny thought. If this was how they were going to explore the Out There, then quite frankly, this sucked. *Be really nice to see something—whoa.*

The black vanished instantly and Johnny's senses whirled. It was like he was viewing the entire ghostyard, but with a hundred eyes looking in every direction.

They had to be looking out from the ship; it made sense that a moving body with no windows had some kind of eyes. The view reminded him of the feeling he'd had in the outer Core, when he'd felt like he was looking at the Thread from all angles, inside and outside it at the same time. The ghostyard seemed brighter, the edges more precise.

Off to the side and slightly below, a soldier and five skids: four staring at the ship in anticipation, one with a look of dread. Johnny yearned to shout her name just one more time—

The view shifted and Johnny fought off a wave of nausea as he heard—felt?—thoughts of surprise from

Torres and Onna. Shabaz and the others dropped away, then held . . . as the ship floated, hanging in space above the cluster of skids in the ghostyard for what felt like forever and yet not long enough. Because suddenly, too soon, the view swung, drifted, swung again, and then with a stunning rush the group plunged into the distant behind—the ship accelerating to speeds faster than Johnny had ever hit, even on the Drop—the ghostyard mashing into a blur of colour with a small window of clarity forward and back, snapshot hollas at each end of the kaleidoscope. The front showed a small hole of black past kilometres of machinery that began to expand, growing wider and wider and wider until, less than twenty seconds after they'd started to accelerate, they were free of the yard.

Would you look at that! Onna breathed, as the ghostyard fell away to be replaced by a 'scape of stars.

Johnny had always thought he'd been aware of his surroundings. It was his secret strength: he might be faster than most skids, he might be more aggressive or daring, but the main reason he'd been so good in the games was that he saw everything. By the time he'd hit Level Six he'd figured out a way to overlap the peripherals of his three eyes so that he could take in a whole game at once.

But now he realized that wasn't true. He'd never taken in everything: he didn't look at the ice directly beneath him on the Skates or the sky in the Pipe. He certainly didn't examine the incline under him when he was on the Slope. Moreover, even though he'd had a three hundred and sixty degree field of vision, much of that was still on the edges of what two eyes could see—more like suggestions of things instead of clarity.

Now . . . *everything* was crystal clear and overwhelming.

For a second, Johnny thought he might go mad. It was like the window into the Out There in that prison they'd found Albert, except this view expanded in every direction. The scale was too grand to process, there was depth in those points of light that hit him on some instinctive level: each point was a different distance away—*how could a trillion things all be a different distance?!* There was no direction, even as they looked every way around them. And every direction was either empty or so much farther than they'd ever dreamed—how could it be this empty? How could anything this empty be so full of stars? They were so small, surrounded by immensity; even the Core had been small, how could he possibly grasp . . .

Ah, that's better, Torres said, sounding relieved.

What? Johnny managed to grasp.

Pick a direction, Torres thought. *You can narrow the focus. Focus on the 'yard first, you'll get it.*

Johnny felt like he'd been vaped and was clutching onto his colours and name. In a panic, he threw his view towards the receding ghostyard—somehow the shock of the stars had made him miss that it was still there. He tried to imagine swinging three eyes, focusing in. Immediately, his vision narrowed, the sides and ceiling and floor closing off, then the front view followed, leaving only the ghostyard, receding.

Relief flooded over him. He still felt nauseous, although he had no body so it was more an impression of a feeling than something real.

The ghostyard continued to fall behind: quickly at first, then seeming to slow. Johnny had accelerated away from enough things to understand that abstraction.

Then again, he hadn't accelerated away from something like this. Johnny had no idea of scale, but he felt like they'd been moving fast despite there being no pressure of acceleration or inertia—how messed up was that?

From the outside, the ghostyard looked remarkably simple: a rectangular cuboid exoskeleton, open-ended, bathed with its own internal light. Despite how small it already looked, Johnny knew it was massive, at least a dozen kilometres in length. Small shapes orbited the structure; what they were for, he had no idea.

Johnny focused on the open end, straining to see a splash of skid colour somewhere in its enclosure. But even if he'd had his eyes to scope, there was no way.

Shabaz was gone.

As the sheer overwhelming panic receded, Johnny became aware that the ghostyard wasn't the only thing in the pin-pricked expanse.

Behind the 'yard, a surface, also receding. It took Johnny a minute to realize he was looking at a globe like the Skidsphere, except on an astounding scale. The ghostyard was a speck against it.

And unlike the Skidsphere, it didn't glow with a million hollas shouting life into the space around it. This sphere was almost completely dark, though here and there a light could be seen, some steady, some blinking in and out with a regular pulse, some with a broken flicker that reminded Johnny of the fractured lines of the Thread.

The face of the planet appeared entirely mechanical in nature—Johnny didn't see anything that wasn't machined. It was clearly damaged, although what was broken and what might be part of the intended contours was hard to tell.

Is that the Thread? Onna whispered.

I don't know, Johnny thought to himself. But he pictured the Skidsphere, his whole world, hanging in space, flickering with thousands of lives, and all of it just one small part of a far grander pattern. What if this sphere was the same? How were they going to fix something so massive?

How could anyone abandon something like this?

As they gained distance, the ghostyard grew smaller and smaller, until it became indiscernible from the mass behind it. Johnny caught sight of other structures above the sphere's surface, some the same shape as the yard, others different, all in orbit around the globe the same way shapes had orbited the yard.

But that can't be a star, Torres said suddenly. *It would have to be glowing, right?*

Johnny had no idea, he was just trying to get a grip on his senses.

Out of nowhere a range popped up in his vision like an eyes-up display, along with a speedometer. *Whoa*, he thought, *I got a range*. Snakes, they were going fast.

How—oh, there we go, Onna said.

If we can get an altimeter, Torres said, *shouldn't we be able to access all our scans? This thing has got to have them, too.*

No sooner had she said the words than Johnny felt his senses expand, as a full set of sensors kicked into gear. They were still accelerating, even faster than Johnny had estimated. The ghostyard was already hundreds of kilometres away, with the surface behind it two hundred kilometres more.

Which meant they'd just done the equivalent of the Rainbow Road in less than five minutes.

I think I found the sun, Onna thought. *That's what*

Krugar said, right? *That all these stars are suns? Using the 'yard as your fix, go right forty degrees and up fifteen. That sucker's a lot brighter than anything else.*

It was easy to spot once you knew where to look. This sun was much dimmer and smaller than the sun that hung above the Skidsphere—even if it was obvious now that the Skidsphere's sun was just a construct of the sim—but it was bright with enough of a vague warmth to allow them to make the connection between sun and stars.

The distance stunned Johnny. Because while all the other stars felt instinctively far, with this one he got a reading. The Rainbow Road was the longest game the skids played, two and a half times the length of the Slope, five hundred kilometres long. The star he was looking at was over twenty billion kilometres away.

Snakes, this place is big, Torres muttered.

Hey, Onna thought, *check this out. Uhh . . . try looking inside.*

Inside what?

The ship. Don't focus out, focus in. This is sweet.

It took Johnny a second. He was used to changing or even splitting his focus, but he didn't tend to look inside his own body much. Then he thought of all the times he'd expunged Vies from his body, pushing from the inside out, and his focus shifted again—another impression of nausea, not nearly so fierce this time—and the infinity of stars was replaced by a jumble of rooms.

It's a little like having a hundred eyes, so pick three or less, Onna said, although he instinctively grasped the concept before she finished speaking. Now that the views were finite—he counted seventy-eight—it wasn't that different from balancing multiple eyes.

The interior of the ship resembled the sim where they'd tried to rescue Albert, although it was much smaller. Two levels, one central corridor in each. The back third of the ship was occupied by what Johnny assumed was the mechanism to move it. Two rooms on each side of the corridors, then one large room towards the front. He cycled through multiple views and angles of each place, settling on the main front room. It had two stations near a front wall that held a giant holla of space—presumably in the direction they faced—then one station in the centre of the room, along with one on each side.

The ship was empty.

Well, this isn't creepy at all, Torres said dryly. *No one flying, no one home. Who's moving this thing?*

Maybe we are, Onna murmured.

No, Johnny said. That didn't feel right. *It must be automated.* The ship had been designed for someone, but it certainly wasn't skids. He could imagine Krugar sitting in one of those banks.

Wonder where we're going? Onna said.

Hold that thought, Johnny replied and swung part of his awareness out. Now that he wasn't dealing with the infinite, he could handle splitting his focus. In his mind, the forward view appeared. He took a second to let the juxtaposition between that and the internal view of the bridge he still saw settle down—he might not actually have three eyes right now, but his brain could still compartmentalize visual information. The front view was the easiest view. Out front there was nothing but stars which didn't seem to move or grow bigger, despite their continued acceleration.

No sign of where they were headed. He checked the rear—it was getting easier—and saw they were traveling away from the planet at a greater rate than they were moving away from the nearby star, moving at an angle adjacent to the star, although at those distances it was tough to judge for certain.

Not a lot else to go on.

We need to see better, he thought at the others. *We obviously can access some cameras. Let's see what else we can find.*

It took some time, but step-by-step they discovered a profound volume of information. The ship was able to read itself and its surroundings in far greater detail than they'd ever been able to read themselves, its scanning methods both greater in number and deeper in depth.

The sphere behind them appeared almost dead. There were odd spots of energy—they were able to locate the ghostyard they'd left, but only with a very focused scan. On the other tread, some of the readings seemed to indicate activity, protected from deeper scans by layers of protection. From a certain perspective, the sphere felt like a fortress.

A shattered fortress. With each new scan they discovered, it became apparent that whether the globe housed the whole Thread or not, this part of it was as physically damaged as its virtual aspect.

I got something, Torres said, and, as Johnny felt her mind touch his in guidance, the scans gained long range definition. The entire system appeared: the star, two billion kilometres distant; a single massive planet much further in, hundreds of times larger than the nearby sphere; then nothing for one and a half billion kilometres. Then the sphere with the ghostyard. Then . . .

What are these, now? Onna said.

Opposite from the direction they were moving—a

few million kilometres on the other side of the nearby globe—multiple small signals moved on their scans, over a hundred, heading towards the globe.

Johnny knew an attack posture when he saw it. The games might pretend to be games, but they were all, with the exception of a few like the Pipe, vessels for violence. Certain patterns carried bigger threats than others, and this one carried plenty.

They're coming. . . .

The phrase had been said, to him and others, multiple times. Wobble had said it, Peg had said it, even Bian back in that first horrible experience with the grey. They'd always thought those words referred to something inside the Thread.

Apparently, they'd been wrong.

We need to turn this thing around, Johnny said. He experienced a ghost-feeling of turning, an action he'd done a thousand times or more, reacting to danger, to himself, to anyone he cared for, reacting without thought because that's how he rolled. But it was only the ghost of a feeling . . . the ship didn't turn.

I don't think we can, Torres said. *There's a lock on the controls.*

I don't care, Johnny said, throwing his consciousness at the place where he felt the controls were. It was like throwing himself at a wall in the Combine. He didn't care. Shabaz was back there. He threw himself at the wall again.

Johnny . . .

Again.

Johnny.

Again.

Johnny! Onna yelled at him in his mind, and he actually

felt her bump him away. *You're not getting anywhere and even if you do, we don't know what to do. We don't know those things are threatening.*

They look threatening, Torres muttered.

Whatever, we're still not in control. Onna said.

Don't care, Johnny snarled. *We have to let them know that something's on the way.*

Then signal them, Onna said.

There's a lot of defensive-screens, Torres countered. *I don't think that's going to be any more successful than turning.*

We have to try, Johnny snapped. Shabaz. He found the communications array, they seemed to work in multiple ways. He tried everything.

ATTENTION THREAD, ATTENTION THREAD . . .

Even as he said it, it sounded stupid in his head. But he didn't know what to say, he just had to warn them, to do something. *YOU HAVE ONE HUNDRED INCOMING SIGNALS, POSSIBLY HOSTILE. REPEAT, ONE HUNDRED INCOMING SIGNALS, POSSIBLY HOSTILE.* He narrowed the beam as tight as possible, trying to keep it from leaking beyond the sphere to whatever lay beyond, then set it to repeat.

We should still look for some way to get back, he said. *If we don't even know where we're going—*

I think we're going here, Torres said.

A single blip on the long range scans, directly in their path, millions of kilometres distant. Johnny had missed it, distracted by the mass of signals in the opposite direction.

We should still try to get back, we can check that out later. Besides, even at the rate we're accelerating, we're still not getting there for over a daaaaayyyyyyyyyy . . .

The word/thought stretched out as, suddenly, the universe folded in on itself. In Johnny's vision, the stars seemed to narrow and then fall through space.

Far behind the now empty void where there had once been a ship, one hundred shapes continued towards a sphere billions of kilometres from the nearest sun.

Not long after, one hundred shapes became many, many more.

ACKNOWLEDGEMENTS

A great deal of what I said in the acknowledgements section of *The Skids* still holds true, so I'll summarize and then mention some new folks who've supported me throughout this past year.

A huge Woot! to the Sunburst Awards and their support for *The Skids*, which was shortlisted for the Sunburst Award for Excellence in Canadian Literature of the Fantastic and won the Copper Cylinder Award from their membership. The Sunburst jury compared *The Skids* to *The Princess Bride*, which might just be the nicest thing anyone has ever said to me about anything.

So many organizations that have supported me over the years. The Second City in Toronto, Mysteriously Yours, Theatresports Toronto, and The Bad Dog Theatre, my thanks. To my friends Simon Donner, David and Reagan White, Al and Laura Smith (and Samara-Tiger!); Cary West and Mimi Whalen; Mary Haynes and all her family, my thanks and great love. I'm not here without you.

To TorKidLit in Toronto and the many people who have supported me there. To Adrienne Kress, Lesley Livingston, Megan Crewe, Derek Molata and all the YA crew in Toronto, you're amazing. Special props to Leah Bobet, who beta-reads for me and gives unwavering support. The Stop Watch Gang: Suzanne Church, Richard Baldwin, Brad Carson, Karen Danylak, Costi Gurgu, Stephen Kotowych, Tony Pi, Mike Rimar, Pippa Wysong. When I need a kick in the pants, they do it; when I need a hug, they say, "Dude, you should shower first." Suzanne and Costi both put out books this year, you should check them out.

Special shout-out to Julie Czerneda who has been supportive of *The Skids* since its existence as a short story and wrote an absolutely lovely blurb for this book. She is such a positive force in the Canadian speculative fiction community. If you're Canadian and write genre, Julie has probably said a kind word to you and I don't think there are enough kind words to say about her.

An ongoing shout-out to the most awesome Chris Szego, manager of Bakka Phoenix Books and patient saviour of loud men who complain about their first drafts. Thanks to all the staff at Bakka for their support and patience.

All the folks at ChiZine: what a great company with whom to work. Sandra and Brett who create these little gems and tirelessly support the Canadian community. Sam who helped to keep Torg from drawling too much. Jared, for his beautiful layout. Erik, whose covers just make us all happy. To the whole ChiZine family, my thanks and love.

To my family: My mother, who, as I said in the dedication, has been my biggest supporter in more ways than I could possibly lay out in a section such as this. I'd need a book. My father, my brother David, my sister-in-law Kat, and my nephew Bruce, who fills us all with delight and will one day rule the world.

Then there's you fine folks . . . my readers. I don't know where to start. So many people have said so many kind things about *The Skids* since it came out last October, it's overwhelming at times. Thank you so much. As always, I hope you liked this book and I hope I write you a better one in the future.

And finally, to Jess, who almost made it into the last book and should have. Somehow, you made my first novel coming out—a struggle that took over thirty years—the second best thing that happened to me last year. You are my trillion suns. Kiss in a book.

ABOUT THE AUTHOR

Ian Donald Keeling is an odd, loud little man who acts a little, writes a little, and occasionally grows a beard. His short fiction and poetry have previously appeared in *Realms of Fantasy*, *On Spec*, and *Grain*. He's on the faculty for sketch and improv at The Second City in Toronto. His first novel, *The Skids*, was released in October 2016 by ChiTeen and won the Copper Cylinder Award. He likes all forms of tag and cheese.